Sexual Misconduct

Legal thrillers by Michael Monhollon

Trial by Ambush (Robin Starling #1)

Juggling Evidence (Robing Starling #2)

Dog Law (Robin Starling #3)

Laughing Heirs (Robin Starling #4)

Devil in the Dock (Robin Starling #5)

Gone Ballistic (Robin Starling #6)

Sexual Misconduct (Robin Starling #7)

Criminal Intent

Guilty Knowledge

A Robin Starling Courtroom Mystery

Book 7

Sexual

Misconduct

Michael Monhollon

Reflection Publishing

Abilene, Texas

For John Insley

Chapter 1

We were being bad, starting the day with pastries and coffee.

"Come on, have another fritter," Paul said to me encouragingly. He was kicked back at a secretary's desk in the small common area shared by three offices—mine, Brooke's, and that of a private detective named Rodney Burns. There was as of yet no secretary that went with the secretary's desk. We were all still getting our businesses started.

I said, "I haven't jogged a mile in two weeks. I haven't earned a second fritter."

"You're still in recovery. You need nourishment." He was on this third donut and no doubt was looking for company in his sin, but I didn't think his teddy-bear physique would look good on me.

"Oatmeal with berries is nourishment. An apple fritter is an indulgence."

Brooke put what was left of her second donut down on the secretarial desk next to Paul's left foot. "Now she tells me," she said, still with donut in her mouth.

Mike leaned close to kiss a bit of maple frosting off the corner of her mouth. "*Apple fritters* are an indulgence, she said. Maple cake donuts are in another category all together."

"You wouldn't like me if I were fat."

"Au contraire. When I'm planting kisses on every square inch of your body, our lovemaking won't be over so soon."

Brooke turned pink, a skin-tone that looked cute against her red hair. "Save the bedroom talk for the honeymoon," I suggested. "Only a month to go."

"Five-and-a-half weeks," Mike said.

Paul patted my fanny, and I took a step away from him. The "five-and-a-half weeks," applied to us, too, at least theoretically. Brooke and I had a double wedding penciled in for June.

Carly, the receptionist for all eighteen offices in the executive suites, was nodding her head at Brooke and Mike and smirking, when she glanced out of our offices toward the main doors. She put a hand on Rodney's arm. "Isn't that you-know?"

Rodney Burns looked, and his Adam's apple bobbed. He cleared his throat. I looked, too. Standing halfway between the executive suites' outer doors and its unmanned receptionist's desk was Aubrey Biggs, Richmond's commonwealth attorney. His eyes met mine, and he raised his eyebrows.

"Uh oh," I said.

"Uh oh what?" Paul said, taking his feet off the desk and leaning forward to peer out the archway of exposed brick.

The sight of all six of us looking out at him seemed to unnerve Aubrey Biggs, which wasn't in character. Though Aubrey was no more than five-six with his shoes on, he had an outsized ego to go with his position of prosecutorial power.

Assuming it was me he was there to see, I went out to meet him. "Aubrey Biggs," I said. I didn't know what this visit was about, but I knew it couldn't be good.

"Can we talk?" Though I was a woman, I had nearly half-a-foot on him, and at handshake distance he had to look up.

"Sure." I gestured him toward the archway and the five people still in the limited space beyond it. "Looks like it's back to work for me," I told the group.

Paul stood, giving Aubrey a dark look as we passed through.

When my office door closed behind us, Aubrey said, "I'm sorry. I didn't mean to kill your party."

"It had about run its course." I walked around my desk and sat down. "Have a seat. What is it today, threats or demands?"

His mouth quirked. "Neither. It doesn't have anything to do with the Woodruff case, if that's what you mean. That's over, and as far as I'm concerned, everything you did there was appropriate and even exemplary."

That sounded suspiciously like a compliment, and I raised an eyebrow, or I tried to. Unfortunately, my eyebrows seem to go up and down together, so I probably just managed to look like a startled fish.

"In my opinion, you're the best criminal defense attorney in the city of Richmond," he said.

I didn't have anything to say to that. I couldn't have been more surprised if he'd started speaking in tongues.

"I want to hire you."

This last was equivalent to him sprouting antennae and demanding that I take him to my leader.

"Have you been charged with a crime?" I said, trying to keep my tone neutral.

He shook his head. "It's my sister Alexa. She's been arrested. Charged with killing a Richmond doctor named Brooks Prescott."

"How is she supposed to have killed him?" I asked.

He took a breath. "By beating his head in with a blunt instrument, probably the base of a table lamp."

I was silent.

"She didn't do it," Aubrey said. "Of course she didn't."

"How do you know?"

He turned his hands over. "She's my sister."

"That's the best you've got?"

"So far. She's got her issues, something of a wild streak, but nothing like this. She'd never bash in a man's head . . ." He swallowed, took a breath.

"With a table lamp?" I suggested.

"I want you to represent her."

"You need to rethink that. You've made it clear on multiple occasions you don't like the way I practice law."

"It's looks bad for her, really bad." His voice coarsened, and his eyes looked suddenly bloodshot. "The evidence against her . . . it seems pretty conclusive."

"You'd be looking over my shoulder, second-guessing me every step of the way," I said.

"I'd micromanage this if I could, believe me, but I can't. I know I can't. Alexa won't confide in me, for one thing. Look, I know it's going to cost money. I've got savings. I can drop by a cashier's check for five thousand dollars tomorrow."

I gave him an apologetic look. "If it goes to trial, it's going to cost ten."

The wince was gone almost before it touched his eyes. "You'll do it then? You'll take the case?"

I took a breath and let it out slowly.

"I'm thinking any lawyer who tries this case straight up the middle is going to lose," he said. "This is going to take someone with your . . ."

I waited, interested in hearing what my competitive advantage was, but he finished the sentence with a hand wave.

"Who's going to prosecute the case?" I asked.

"I don't know yet. No one in my office, obviously. The judge will appoint a commonwealth's attorney from another jurisdiction."

I considered the proposition. Financially, I couldn't afford to turn away work, but the thought of

Aubrey hovering in the background unsettled me. Even if he left me alone as promised, something I doubted, every decision I made was going to be called into question if I lost the case—which, according to him, was all too likely.

"Tell me about this doctor who was killed."

"Brooks Prescott. He's an orthopedist with political connections, a big donor to the Democratic Party. You see him and his wife at functions all the time."

I didn't personally, of course, but my biggest involvement in politics was antagonizing the commonwealth's attorney sitting across the desk from me. "Where was he killed?" I asked.

"My sister's apartment. Don't ask what he was doing there, I don't know. I'm hoping she'll open up to you more than she has me."

"Where is she?"

"Richmond city jail. The magistrate denied bail."

"Who's been representing her?"

"Peter Brawley. He was helping her with a sexual harassment claim, so he was the one she called when the police arrested her."

I didn't know Peter Brawley. I wondered what kind of law he practiced. "Is he still representing your sister? How did she find him?"

"I have no idea on either count. She didn't find him through me."

"I assume the sexual harassment claim doesn't have anything to do with this," I said.

"I wouldn't assume anything in this case. It's something to ask her about."

"Okay."

"If you can leave now, I'm parked against the curb out front. How are you, by the way? You look good. Have you recovered physically from . . ." He waved his hands.

"From my near death experience? Yeah, I'll live."

"So. Shall we?" He stood, but I stayed in my seat, looking up at the small man, if only slightly.

"I'll need to see her alone, you know. There's no point in you acting as my chauffeur. Suppose you just drop me by my garage?" Lawyers always see their criminal clients alone. A third-party isn't covered by attorney-client privilege and can be made to testify as to anything incriminating the defendant might say.

"I can wait for you in the parking lot at the jail," Biggs said. "I've got nothing going on as important to me as this."

After a moment, I nodded. "Okay." I reached for my purse and stood.

Because I was an attorney, I didn't have to speak to my client—in this case, my potential client—on a handset with a thick pane of glass between us. The jail provided a small conference room, one with a table and two chairs.

A corrections officer brought Alexa in, her hands free and uncuffed.

7

"You be all right?" the officer asked me.

"Sure," I said.

"I'll be right outside."

When the door closed, I held out a hand. "I'm Robin Starling, a lawyer. Your brother asked me to come see you."

"Of course."

When she didn't expand on that, I gestured to the chairs. "Shall we sit down?"

"I'll remain standing, if it's all right with you." Alexa was taller than I'd expected, about Aubrey's height. Her long blonde hair had a brassy tone and was beginning to show dark roots.

"Sure." For my part, I pulled a chair away from the table and sat. My pen and legal pad were on the table, for one thing. For another, I wanted to set the expectation that we might be there awhile.

"Do you want to tell me what this is all about?" I said.

"Robin Starling," Alexa said in a louder voice, as if I'd only just told her my name.

"Sure."

"What are you doing here?"

I thought I'd been over that. "Your brother . . ."

"Yes, but why? You're Aubrey's worse nightmare."

I felt the corner of my mouth rise. "Or vice versa. We do seem to get under each other's skin."

"Tell me about it," she said.

"Well . . ."

But the question was evidently rhetorical. She pulled out the chair across the table from me and sat down. "Why you? He must think you're good. Aubrey's an officious little pipsqueak, but he does love me. I think he does."

"He seems very concerned."

"So what has he told you about the case?"

"Next to nothing. He said I should hear it from you."

"So where is he now? He's not here at the jail, is he?"

"In the parking lot. He insisted on playing chauffeur."

She sat back. "So that's how it is. You go out there, and you tell him everything I tell you. Is that it?"

"No."

"You don't tell him anything?"

"I don't tell him anything unless I think telling him will help the case."

She seemed to turn that over in her mind, looking for a downside.

"I guess he's always looked out for you," I said. "He's a bit older than you, isn't he? He's got to be close to forty, and you're . . ."

"Twenty-seven. Is looking out for me the same as being an intrusive, judgmental busybody?"

"Maybe. Ever been married?"

"Briefly. I was nineteen, the guy was twenty-one. It only lasted six months, but I kept the name."

"You're not Alexa Biggs."

9

MICHAEL MONHOLLON

She made a face. "Not any more, thank God. Alexa Demming may not be the most wonderful name in the world, but it's a whole lot better than Biggs."

"Tell me about the sexual harassment claim Peter Brawley was helping you with."

"There's not much to tell. I'm a pharmaceutical rep for TMH. I made sales calls to the Spine and Joint Clinic; Dr. Prescott harassed me. I reported it to my employer, of course, but they did nothing to protect me. So I filed my claim."

"Wait a minute—Dr. Prescott? Dr. Brooks Prescott, the man who was found dead in your apartment?"

Her mouth stretched. "That would be the one. He was always touching me, asking me out. The last time I was there, he cornered me in a supply closet and somehow managed to unfasten my bra through my blouse. By the time I got out of the closet, my breasts had been palpated to the point I felt like I'd had a mammogram."

"So you went to Peter Brawley."

"I mentioned my problem to him. He suggested I file a claim with the Virginia Council on Human Rights."

The claim would have been against her employer, not against Dr. Prescott himself or the Spine and Joint Clinic. She could sue him for assault and battery, but sexual harassment was a form of employment discrimination, so any liability would be imposed on TMH, her employer. "Why not file

10

with the EEOC?" The Equal Employment Opportunity Commission was the federal agency that dealt with employment discrimination.

She raised a shoulder. "You'd have to ask Peter."

I would ask him. "I got the idea your brother wasn't the one who recommended Peter Brawley."

She gave me a raspberry.

"Did somebody else recommend him? Is he a longtime friend?"

"Not longtime. I met him in a bar in Shockoe Bottom a couple of months ago."

"So he's a boyfriend?"

"No, not exactly."

Not exactly covered a lot of real estate, I thought. "I understand he represented you at your arraignment on the murder charge. Is he still representing you?"

"Not really."

That also covered a lot of territory. "It can't be halfway," I said. "I can represent you, or he can. It's your choice, but you do have to choose."

"I choose you. Peter is sweet . . . well, most the time he's sweet. I don't get the idea he's a very good lawyer. The law is not his passion, anyway."

"So you want me to represent you?"

"How much do you charge?"

"A lot, I'm afraid. For me it's a huge time commitment. For you the commitment is financial. It won't be like buying a new refrigerator or a new living room set. It'll be more like remodeling a bathroom."

"Oh, wow."

It took a while to deal with that aspect of our relationship. When we had the details sorted out and she'd signed my standard agreement, I returned to the facts of the case I'd just taken on: "How did Dr. Prescott come to be murdered in your apartment?"

"That's the big question, isn't it?" she said.

"You don't know."

"Haven't a clue."

"Who found the body—you?"

"No, one of my neighbors did. Whoever killed Dr. Prescott was thoughtful enough to leave the door standing open. When I got home, the police were there already."

"Had Prescott been to your apartment before?"

"Not to my knowledge. Not while I was there."

"How long since you filed the harassment claim?"

"Couple, three weeks."

"So maybe he was there to talk you out of it?"

She shrugged. "Or maybe he was taking his harassment to the next level. Who knows?"

"Had you ever encountered him outside of his medical offices?"

"No."

"Tell me about the day of the murder. You say the police were there when you got home."

"They stopped me on the stairs."

"Where had you been?"

"A sales call to West End Pediatrics."

"So the police stopped you on the stairs, and you identified yourself. What happened then?"

"They marched me back downstairs and parked me in a police car. For a long time, nobody would tell me who'd been killed. For a long time, they didn't tell me anyone *had* been killed. When I saw them loading the body bag into the ambulance, I had still no idea who was dead. They told me, and I thought it must be some kind of joke."

"Did they ever take you inside your apartment?"

"Yeah, after they got the body out."

"And? Can you describe things for me?"

"A lot of blood had soaked into the carpet by the coffee table, it looked like. My chrome table lamp was on the floor by the wall, lampshade all twisted up, lightbulb glass scattered around."

"Who was the police officer in charge, do you know?"

She shook her head. "A woman," she said.

It had to be Emma Michaels. I'd heard of her, but never dealt with her, so I didn't know whether her being in charge of the police investigation was good news or bad.

"Did she ask you any questions?"

"Yeah. Where had I been, who'd been with me, what was my relationship with Brooks Prescott."

"What did you tell her?"

"'I want my lawyer.'"

"You didn't answer any questions?"

A corner of her mouth rose. "Aubrey and I don't have much to do with each other these days, but I

13

have picked up a thing or two. Statements by the accused can be a big part of the prosecution's case."

"That's a good thing to have picked up."

"Yeah, well."

I spent another thirty minutes with her without learning much more. If she was being entirely forthcoming with me, she didn't know much more. Somehow the body of a man she knew had appeared in her apartment, and it seemed likely that the murder weapon had been her own table lamp.

"What's next?" she asked me.

"Preliminary hearing, probably next week or the week after."

"Do I have any chance of acquittal there?"

"Not much chance, no."

"But some?"

"We may be able to get you admitted to bail."

"Oh wow," she said.

That summed it up pretty well.

I saw Aubrey Biggs as I came out of the jail. He was pacing near his car.

"Well?" he said as I approached.

"She hired me. I'm in, Peter Brawley's out."

Some of the tension seemed to go out of him. "Good. That's good then." He beeped his car, and we got in.

"You know what turned the trick?" I asked him. "She thinks I'm your worst nightmare. I don't know whether she got that impression from you or the newspaper."

He glanced at me as he turned out of the parking lot. "Are you looking for an apology?"

"No. I'm interested in the relationship between the two of you, is all."

"There's not much of one. We see each other at our parents' house occasionally, mostly for Sunday lunch. I have lunch with them a time or two a month. She makes it less frequently, so our visits only overlap every two or three months or so. Of course, none of that's going to help you. What did she tell you about Brooks Prescott?"

When I didn't respond immediately, he shot me a look. I smiled. "I can't tell you what she told me. You know that."

"I'm on her side, you know. A hundred percent."

I shrugged.

"I know, I know. Attorney-client privilege. I'm an attorney, you know. Anything I learn is for the purpose of advising her and you, her primary attorney."

"I don't think that would work," I said. "You're not in a position to represent her."

For a while, I listened to him breathe. "Just know that if you need anything . . ."

"Thank you," I said.

"Do you have any ideas about developing a defense?"

I didn't, but I said, "I'm not going to be able to talk strategy with you. You need to understand that up front."

"It was a yes or no question. Mom and Dad are worrying themselves to distraction. What do I tell them?"

"Is it just the two of you, no other brothers or sisters?"

"It's just us."

"Tell them you've hired the best criminal defense attorney in the city of Richmond. It's a nice turn of phrase. If I can get you to sign it, I'll blow it up real big and hang it on my wall as a testimonial."

"You're a piece of work, Starling."

"I might put that on my wall, too: *The best criminal defense lawyer in the city and a real piece of work.*"

He shook his head. When he pulled to the curb in front of the Ironfronts, the Reconstruction-era building where I had my office, he said, "I'll get you that first check tomorrow. It'll take me a few days to get the rest of it."

"That'll work," I said.

"Thank you for doing this. It's a major undertaking, and I know you don't like me much."

I got out of the car and leaned down to say, "You're a man who tries to take care of his family. It's a big point in your favor."

His mouth twisted, but I closed the door before he could say anything.

Chapter 2

I managed to get an appointment with Peter Brawley for that afternoon. His office was on Franklin, a block over from Main Street, nine or ten blocks up from my own office. My parking garage was two blocks in the same direction, so I stopped off to get my car, and I drove the rest of the way.

Brawley's office was in a two-story stone house that might have dated from the 1930s. The plaque by the door read "Dewey, Chester, Brawley & Rowe, Individual Practices of Law," so the lawyers weren't partners, despite the name of the firm that suggested they were. I walked up the steps, pushed open the heavy door with its multiple coats of paint, and went in.

The receptionist was a dark-eyed blonde wearing a white blouse with a draped neckline that showed enough cleavage to be distracting even to a straight female like myself.

"May I help you?" She had a throaty voice that didn't jibe with her youthful appearance.

"I'm Robin Starling, here to see Peter Brawley."

"Of course." She picked up her phone to announce me. "Won't you be seated?" She gestured grandly at the four faux-leather chairs lined along one wall, but before I could take advantage of her offer, a man came out.

I don't know what I expected, but Peter Brawley was a surprise. A horseshoe of hair circled his gleaming globe of a head, and he had a mustache and chin beard that looked too disconnected to be called a goatee.

"Peter Brawley." He had a soft hand and a round face beneath the facial hair. He might have looked boyish but for that facial hair and a certain tightness around his mouth. "Come on back, won't you?"

His desk and the credenza behind it were cluttered with papers and books and file folders. The big dry-erase board on one wall was covered with flow charts and what looked to me like unrelated legal terms, mostly in Latin: res ipsa, sub judice, contra legem. It didn't look like useful work in progress; it looked more like something designed to impress clients.

"Have a seat," Brawley said.

The two client chairs were identical to the faux-leather chairs in the waiting room. I sat.

"You're here in the matter of Alexa Demming, I understand," he said, and he tapped his fingertips on a bare spot on the surface of his desk.

"I understand you've been representing her."

"Yes, in a sexual harassment claim and another matter."

"She's hired me in reference to the other matter," I said.

"The murder charge."

"That would be the one."

"And you're here because . . ."

"Well, to let you know she's hired me, for one thing. If you're willing to talk about what you know about the case, I'd be interested in hearing that, too. If you've started a file, I'd like to see it."

He exhaled some of his tension. "You're taking over the case."

"I am."

"And you want me to share my work product. There isn't much."

"What is there, exactly? Have you been talking to witnesses, lining up experts . . ." I trailed off.

"Actually, there isn't anything other than the court papers. It's a hell of a mess, really. I don't think she did it, you understand, but it is a mess."

I nodded.

"Are you thinking we'll work together on this, or am I out?"

"I'm not thinking we'll work together," I said diplomatically. "I'm here to accept the baton for the next leg of the race."

His laugh was hearty enough that I replayed what I'd said in my mind to see if it were funny. "Very metaphoric," he said. He seemed more relaxed now, almost jovial.

"More of a cliché, I'm afraid. I was an English major."

"I was political science, probably not as helpful, but it's what so many of us prelaw types did in college. You haven't done any modeling, have you?"

I blinked. "What?"

"You've got the face for it, and with your height and athletic build you'd be stunning."

This was the man Alexa had come to for help with her sexual harassment problem? "I don't understand. Are you a photographer as well as a lawyer?"

He inclined his head modestly. "Would you like to see some of my work?" He touched his mouse, and the computer monitor facing me came on to show a woman wearing a short plaid skirt, a button-down shirt with an open collar, and a loosely tied tie that extended well past her waist.

"Isn't that your receptionist?" I said.

"Stephanie." He clicked his mouse and the image changed. It was still Stephanie in her school uniform, but now she was looking at the camera over her shoulder, and an inch or so of bare bottom peeked out from beneath the hem of the skirt.

I stood, not wanting to see whatever the next click of the mouse might reveal. "Okay, I guess we're done here."

The screen winked off. "You can sit down. I just wanted to give you an idea of the quality of my work."

"I think I've got a pretty good idea."

He sat back, lacing his fingers together over a broad stomach. "You wanted to talk about Alexa," he said.

"Did she pose for you, too? Do you have pictures of her on there?"

"The sister of the commonwealth's attorney?" He smiled.

"That's not an answer, but I won't press it."

"The answer is no, she didn't, and I don't. I have one snapshot of her, but it's a different sort of thing altogether."

I sat back down. "I'd like to see it."

"Give me a moment." He moved his mouse around on his desk, clicking it, and then the monitor facing me winked on again. It was Alexa standing behind a pyramid of beer cans that were stacked on a table in a downscale bar somewhere. She had her tongue out as if caught in the act in licking the topmost can.

"You've got a way of catching people at their best," I said.

"Don't I? I got that one with my cell phone. I tried to get her to give me a pose without the porn-star affectation, but she was done."

"You met her in a bar, I understand. I assume you propositioned her."

"Well, yes. Wouldn't you?"

I gave him a look.

"Perhaps not. She is an attractive woman, though. We talked awhile, and of course I asked her if she'd like to model for me."

"Did you proposition her for sex as well?"

"I let her know I'd be interested." He gave me a thin smile. "She wasn't."

"But she didn't go screaming into the night, either."

"No."

"So why were Dr. Prescott's advances so offensive to her?"

"The legal standard is 'unwelcome.' There's no accounting for taste, is there? Truthfully, though, I was the one who suggested it, when she told me what was going on at the Spine and Joint Clinic. I said there'd likely be a settlement, and I'd be happy to handle it for her and split the proceeds."

"So you were the complainant, in effect. She was just along for the ride.

He shrugged.

"Were you suing him personally, as well as filing a claim against her employer for the hostile environment?"

"No, not yet. Alexa asked me to hold off on the lawsuit."

"How did he end up dead in her apartment?"

"No idea."

"Were they sleeping together?"

He hesitated. "Not to my knowledge, no."

"It would have messed up your harassment claim if they were, wouldn't it?"

"It would have complicated things."

"You said not to your knowledge. Does that mean you have suspicions?"

He smiled, brilliantly. "I always have suspicions. 'The heart is deceitful above all things. Who can know it?' That's scripture, I think, though I've probably garbled it."

"So are you going to let me have a copy of your Alexa file?"

"As I told you, I just have the court papers."

"I'd be interested in what you have on the sexual harassment claim, too."

"Okay." He pulled his feet under him, but I had my phone out of my purse.

"Before we go, how about if I took *your* picture?"

His eyebrows went up. "I don't know that anyone's ever asked me to pose for them. Do you want a photograph of me sitting at my desk, or are you thinking of something more provocative?"

I gave him a humorless smile. "You choose."

"Okay." He put an elbow on his desk, leaning forward and looking at me intently over the frames of his glasses. "Just a moment. I can do a little better for you than that." He wasn't wearing a tie, and his collar was open. He unbuttoned a second button, exposing thick, dark chest hair. He leaned forward again. "Better?"

"And better," I said. I snapped the picture, then stood, ready to get out of the office.

He stood with me. "Let me know if you change your mind about posing yourself. I pay pretty well, if that means anything to you. I assume you noticed Stephanie's rack as you came in."

"Her . . . breasts?"

"They're mine."

"Stephanie's got your breasts," I said.

"Mine in the sense that I paid for them. Five thousand dollars, but in return she finds a way to flash me every day. On weekends she texts me a photo if we're not getting together for pictures or drinks or anything. It's the best five thousand dollars I ever spent, let me tell you."

I'd have taken a better look at Brawley's investment, but Stephanie wasn't at her desk when we went out. Brawley led the way to a workroom, where he laid the contents of a file folder in the copier's document feeder and pressed a button. As the pages zipped through, he leaned his hips against a counter and crossed his arms over his chest.

"You look like you're still evaluating my modeling potential," I said. "Don't."

"Hard to ignore so much promise. Really, you'd have complete control. Any pictures you don't like, we delete, no questions asked. And, of course, you'd get a digital copy of everything."

"Suppose I wanted the only digital copy?"

He tilted his head to one side, regarding me. "I'd try to talk you into letting me have a few of the pics, but we can play it that way if you want. You can have just as uninhibited a photo shoot as you want, no consequences."

The copier fell silent. He put the originals back in his folder and handed me the copies. "I can't tell you how glad I am to be handing off this Alexa business. She needs someone good in her corner."

"Thank you."

"You'll think about the photo shoot? You'll let me know?"

I stepped back, cocking a finger at him. "You'll be the first." But my expression was more of a grimace than a smile.

Though it was still spring, it was a warm day, and the air had turned muggy. The heat felt good after the air-conditioned office, though. I took a few breaths, debating whether I should go back to my office or could justify heading home to take a shower. The time was just a few minutes before three o'clock.

"I assume you got the question," came a throaty voice behind me. "Did you take him up on it?"

It was Stephanie, standing with a cigarette to one side of the steps.

"I didn't." Whoever her surgeon had been, he'd showed some restraint, in my opinion, giving her a full bust without over-balancing her slender frame. "You did, I take it."

She laughed. "I know he uses my pictures as part of his portfolio. He pays me extra for it."

"And he handles sexual harassment claims. It seems ironic, somehow."

She nodded. "I met him when I was waitressing at Hooters. Several of us posed for him. It's good money, and he's harmless. He'd never think of touching you without your permission."

"I guess Hooters is a good place for him to find his models."

"Not many of us have a strong sense of personal modesty, if that's what you mean." She dropped her cigarette butt and stepped on it with a bright red pump.

"Young, attractive, exhibitionist . . . it's a target-rich environment for him."

"Don't judge us. We're just trying to make a living for ourselves."

I held up a hand.

Stephanie said, "He's a pleasant man, has a good sense of humor. You'll find yourself warming to him over time."

I went home. Even though I'd be taking my dog Deeks for a run, I took a hot shower before I crossed the street to get him. I was toweling off my steam-heated skin when I felt the need for something more. I got back in the shower and stood for a long time in a spray that was just as cold as I could stand it. This time I came out feeling clean.

Deeks stayed with a retired physician named Dr. McDermott when I was at work. I rang Dr. McDermott's doorbell, and the sound of Deeks's toenails on his foyer floor came almost immediately. It took longer for Dr. McDermott to get to the door, and Deeks whined and gave the door a scratch. Bad boy.

At the sight of Dr. McDermott, wild-haired and rheumy-eyed, I took a step back. Deeks came out on the porch with me, but instead of giving me his usually effusive greeting, he stood looking up with an anxious expression.

"I'm afraid I've got the flu," Dr. McDermott said in a stuffy voice. "Don't worry, I've done everything that can be done—dosed myself with Tamiflu at the first symptoms, lots of rest and fluids since. Now I've just got to wait it out."

He'd seemed perfectly fine that morning. "Is there anything I can do for you?" I asked.

"No, I'll be fine."

"Let me make you some tea."

He shook his head. "I'm just going to go back to the couch. You need to take it easy yourself."

I was still convalescing, he meant. Probably the running shoes and gym shorts I was wearing were overly ambitious, especially given the warmth of the late-spring day. Deeks was eager, though, so I trotted down the street after him for half-a-block before dropping back into a walk. Deeks, when he noticed, circled back to check on me. He was a chocolate Labrador retriever, nearly full grown now, although he still had the lean build and sleek coat of youth. Everyone but me called him Deacon, and he really had grown into his full name, but I couldn't stop thinking of him as Deeks, the little fur-ball Paul had dropped on me not quite a year before.

When we got home, I sat at my kitchen table to catch my breath while Deeks lapped up a bowl of water. I refilled it for him and sat back down. He finished that bowl, too. He was partway through a third before he raised his dripping muzzle to look at me.

"You're feeling all right, aren't you, boy? You're not coming down with the flu?"

He didn't say yay or nay.

"I think these runs get you overheated. How would you feel about a wading pool for the backyard?"

He stepped toward me to shove his muzzle between my knees, and I scratched his neck and ears. It seemed we had a deal.

I ate my salad with deli meat, fed Deeks, then opened my laptop. First, the flu. I checked WebMD and a few other websites. At seventy-six Dr. McDermott might have a tough time ahead of him, which meant I needed to keep tabs. I'd been worried that Deeks might catch the flu from him, but it seemed that dogs didn't catch people flu and people didn't catch doggie flu. It wasn't impossible, at least theoretically, but it just didn't happen. I'd never seen Dr. McDermott let Deeks lick his face, and this probably wasn't the time for him to start, but the risk to Deeks of continuing to spend his days at Dr. McDermott's house should be minimal.

I looked up from my laptop at Deeks, who was sprawled on the floor in the kitchen doorway. He raised his head.

"You'll be all right," I told him.

He lowered his head to the floor, as unconcerned as before.

The next item of business was to google Dr. Brooks Prescott. He was an orthopedic surgeon with an athletic face and clear blue eyes. I was staring at a head shot when the doorbell rang.

Deeks was at the door before me. Paul Soldano, my overweight boyfriend—okay, my overweight *fiancé*—was on my doorstep. He smiled when he saw me.

"You never call," I said.

"I come by."

"I mean, you never call first. Suppose I was changing clothes or taking a shower or something?"

He smiled sunnily. "I'd offer to scrub your back."

"How would you get in?"

"I know where the spare key is. Don't worry. If I hear the sound of running water and no one comes to the door, I'll know what to do."

I made a face as I stepped aside to let him in. "I've got something to show you," I said. "A puzzle."

"Anything to do with Richmond's pompous toad of a prosecutor?"

"His sister, who seems to have a wild streak. You'd think she'd drive him crazy—I assume she does—but he obviously loves her. Enough for him to take a long shot on me."

"You're not a long shot, you're one hell of an attorney."

"He'd probably emphasize the hell part."

The doorbell rang again, and Deeks turned in the air as he leapt toward the door. This time it was

Brooke. I leaned out the door to look past her. "No Mike," I said.

"He didn't call, and I felt like doing something. It seems I have an evening of airy freedom."

"That's hard on Mike," Paul said.

"You know what I mean."

"Maybe." He looked at me. "Did I just cheat you out of an evening of airy freedom?"

Brooke said, "What does Robin need with airy freedom? She has Deacon." My dog was leaning hard against her leg, and she was scratching his head.

There was a knock on the door: Mike, wearing jeans and a polo shirt. "There you are," he said to Brooke. "You don't answer your phone."

She got it out of her purse and looked at it. "I was at a customer's all afternoon. I guess I turned it off." Brooke was an IT consultant for small businesses. Although she'd only been on her own a few months, she always seemed to have work.

"Small wonder you didn't hear from Mike," Paul said.

"Since everyone's here, I'd like you to take a look at something," I said.

"Are we everyone?" Mike asked.

"Unless you know someone else who's coming."

Brooke said, "We could ask old Dr. McDermott over, since we're having a party and all."

"He's not so old," I said. "But he does have the flu."

"Uh oh."

"I know. Come on in the kitchen."

Paul said to Mike, "Since this is a party, we can break out the Lowenbrau I've got stashed in the refrigerator."

"Lead me to 'em."

But Deeks was bumping Mike's leg with his head, and Mike gave up and bent to give his sides a good brisk scratching.

"What else do you have in the refrigerator?" Brooke asked me.

"Open bottle of Riesling." I was fairly new to wines, and Riesling was my new favorite.

"Pour me a glass, too, if you're having one."

"And if I'm not?"

She gave me a look.

"One glass of Riesling, coming up." It didn't take long before everyone was provided with his or her libation of choice. Deeks, instead of settling down as he usually did, went from person to person while I transferred the photograph I'd taken of Peter Brawley from my phone to my computer. Soon I had his face and Brooks Prescott's side by side on the screen. "Take a look at this," I said.

"What are we looking at?" Mike asked.

"Pretend you're a woman, and both of these men are coming onto you. Which one's advances do you find unwelcome and creepy, and which one's do you take as a compliment?"

"Is this a trick question?" Brooke asked.

"No, I'm very serious. Both of these men hit on Aubrey's sister Alexa. One of them she went out with

MICHAEL MONHOLLON

a few times, and the other caused her to file a sexual harassment claim."

Paul said, "I'm guessing she went out with the bald, fat man with the goatee and filed against the guy who looks like he could star on a soap opera."

"Is that really a goatee?" I asked. "I was thinking of it as a mustache and a chin beard."

"That's the definition of a goatee, isn't it?"

"Don't they have to be connected somehow? What this man has are two distinct items of facial hair."

Paul shrugged. Brooke said, "So is Paul right? She filed a complaint against the dreamboat?"

"Not only that, she hired the fat bald guy to help her do it."

"Women find us chunky monkeys hard to resist," Paul said.

"What's he doing?" Mike asked, gesturing at the screen. "Leaning forward, shirt unbuttoned, giving us the look over the tops of his glasses—did you take this picture?"

Paul took a closer look. "She couldn't have." To me: "Why would he be giving you a look like that?"

"You know how hard it is for us girls to resist you chunky monkeys." I gave him a swat on his bottom, and he moved out of reach.

"I really meant just me, not chunky monkeys in general."

"What does this have to do with Biggs coming by your office this morning?" Brooke asked me.

"The dreamboat's dead. Beat to death with a table lamp." Over the next couple of hours, I told them about it while we listened to music and took turns rolling a ball across the floor for Deeks to fetch. Paul and Mike each had a second bottle beer, which depleted Paul's stash, and Brooke had a second glass of wine. I alone exercised restraint in the alcohol department, temperately limiting myself to half-a-glass on the second go-round. It emptied the bottle, which makes my self-restraint a little less impressive, but still.

Chapter 3

My first item of business the next morning was to stop by the courthouse to file the papers that would make me counsel of record for Alexa Demming. The office of the court clerk didn't know yet who would be handling the prosecution in lieu of Richmond's Commonwealth Attorney.

I thanked the deputy clerk and headed to police headquarters. I hadn't made an appointment, but if Emma Michaels, the detective in charge of the Prescott investigation, wasn't there, I was hoping I could get one of my buddies in the homicide division to show me the file.

Detective Michaels wasn't there, but neither Ray Hernandez nor James Jordan seemed in the mood to cooperate. I stood in front of Jordan's desk, looking down at him. His partner Hernandez sat at the next desk over, his chair kicked back and his feet up.

"Don't think we're gonna roll over every time you ask us for something just because this is Biggs's little sister," Jordan said. "We can't do it."

"How about our long friendship?"

Jordan's gaze slid to Hernandez, who said, "It's not our case. We're not in a position to do you any favors."

"Any idea when Detective Michaels will be in?" I glanced around. There were a couple of other detectives in the homicide division that morning, all men, but having looked me up and down they seemed inclined to ignore me.

"Nope," Jordan said, shaking his head.

"We tried getting her to keep us posted on her comings and goings, but she wasn't having any," Hernandez said.

"Tell me about her. Is she pleasant, friendly, likely to be helpful?"

Jordan stroked his biker 'stache, and Hernandez laughed. I didn't feel as encouraged as I could have been.

When the elevator arrived to take me back to the ground floor, a woman got off. She was probably around fifty, and short, which I say not just because I'm five-eleven myself, but because she couldn't have been more than five-two. She was wearing a white shirt and blue chinos.

I said, "Detective Michaels?"

She looked up at me. Her hair was in a ponytail that looked like it was pulled too tight, and her ears stuck out.

"I'm Robin Starling. I . . ."

"I know who you are."

"Could we talk?"

"What about?" The elevator door closed, leaving us alone in an empty hallway.

"Alexa Demming," I said.

"I can't help you on that one. That case is gonna be strictly by the book."

"I understand. I was hoping for a look at the file, though."

"If you were on moon, you could hope for air," she said.

"I don't know when the preliminary is, but I guess I can ask the judge for a postponement and cite lack of police cooperation as the reason."

"Threats aren't going to get you anywhere with me."

"Asking nicely doesn't seem to get me anywhere either."

She stood looking up at me, her nose wrinkling as if she smelled something unpleasant, then she brushed by me and headed for the door of the homicide division. When she reached it, she looked back at me. "You coming?"

"Right behind you," I said.

Judging by the photograph of the back and top of Prescott's head, his killer had hit him at least two times with the table lamp, maybe three. Dark blood matted the hair, and the skull was no longer shaped as God intended.

In a photograph that gave a broader view of the crime scene, the body was draped over a coffee table, head touching the taupe-colored carpet on the side of the table opposite a black leather sofa. It looked as if Prescott might have been sitting on the sofa and fallen forward when he was struck. The chrome table lamp was on the floor at the end of the sofa, its shade bent and twisted, just as Alexa had described it, bits of light-bulb glass scattered on the carpet. A close-up of the lamp showed blood and hair sticking to its heavy, square base.

Sounds grisly, I know. The photographs were grisly to look at. Still, it was my job to look, so I spent some time doing it before laying the photographs aside.

Among the paperwork contained in the file was a police report from an Officer Meghan Daniels, who had arrived on the scene at 3:40 Monday afternoon, just three days ago. The door was standing open, as was the door of the apartment across the landing from Alexa's. Officer Daniels noted the body lying across the coffee table, but the paramedics with the fire department had arrived almost immediately after she had, and it was they who verified that the man hanging over the coffee table was dead. The homicide detectives arrived after that, then an ambulance and the medical examiner.

The neighbor's statement was attached to Daniels's report. Taylor Grimes had noticed Alexa's door ajar. He had put his head in to make sure she was all right, had seen the body, had called nine-one-one. Then he'd gone back into his apartment and not come out again until a police officer—Meghan

Daniels—had called to him from the doorway of his apartment.

I made a few notes on a legal pad, being sure to jot down the address of Alexa's apartment, Officer Daniel's name and badge number, and the name and contact information of the neighbor Taylor Grimes. Setting the report aside, I reached for the next one.

"Are you about done?" Emma said. She had her hips propped against the desk in front of the one at which I was sitting, and her arms were crossed over her chest.

"About," I said. The next report was hers. From it I learned that a key to Alexa's apartment had been on the key ring in Prescott's pocket. There were two toothbrushes by the bathroom sink. In the walk-in closet hung a suit, a sports jacket, three pairs of slacks, and eight shirts.

I looked up from the report. "Prescott was living with her," I said.

"Wow," Emma said. "I'd heard you were good."

"The clothing was his, I take it?"

"The pants and the shirts were the same sizes as the pants and the shirt Prescott had on when your client whacked him with the table lamp, yes."

"The suit jacket and the sports jacket?"

"They fit, too. And his wife identified them."

"What about socks and underwear, that sort of thing?"

"Unh unh."

"What does that mean? No underwear? None at all?"

38

"Not a sock. Maybe he'd just taken home a duffle full of dirty clothes for his wife to wash. Who knows?"

I closed the folder and handed it to her with a smile. "Who indeed?"

She went to stand near Jordan and Hernandez, and I got the idea she wanted to talk about me as soon as I was gone. I turned back at the door. "Where was Prescott's car?" I asked.

Emma didn't answer immediately, and Jordan turned his head to look at her. Hernandez kept his gaze on me.

"Parking lot of Demming's apartment complex," Emma said finally.

"Close to Alexa's building?"

"Right in front."

Hernandez gave me a wink.

I drove out to see Brooks Prescott's widow. It wasn't a visit I wanted to make, but, as my father had often told me when I was little, "If you have a frog to swallow today, swallow it first thing. Putting it off is not going to make it any tastier." I had my car and no appointments on my calendar—no excuses for putting it off.

Toni Prescott had lived with her husband in Windsor Farms, a faux-English village built in the middle of Richmond in the 1920s and -30s. The curving streets had names like Dover, Canterbury, and Berkshire.

The Prescott house had three dormers facing the street along with another eleven windows and a columned front porch. I climbed the steps and rang the bell. As the chimes sounded, I turned to look out over the acre lot and think about how the other half lived. There was a lot of time to think, because no one came to the door. I rang again and counted twelve chimes.

"Hi," I called to the doorpost as if it were only hard of hearing and not as deaf as . . . well, a doorpost. "I'm Robin Starling, a lawyer. I'm here to talk about your husband's murder."

After a two-count, the door was yanked open from the inside. "What are you doing? What the hell do you think you're doing?" She was an attractive woman a few years older than I was—middle thirties or so—wearing a towel on her head and a kimono-style bathrobe. One of her blue eyes, framed with mascara, stood out brilliantly; the other seemed faded and pale. "What would bring you to stand on my front stoop shouting about my tragedy to the entire neighborhood? Who are you, anyway? I'm going to complain about this to your superiors."

"My boss will be mortified," I said, though I wasn't particularly.

"So what the hell do you want?" She looked past me to the street where my red Beetle sat against the curb just beyond the brick sidewalk.

"To talk," I said. "I guess this is a bad time? You look like you're getting ready to go out."

"Yes, I am, if it's any business of yours."

"May I come in? I'll just be a few moments."

"No, you may not come in."

I nodded. "I guess we can talk here."

She slammed the door.

"Or I can talk through the door," I said, raising my voice a few decibels. "I understand you identified some clothing for the police, clothing that was found in the apartment of . . ."

The door whooshed back open and the woman I assumed to be Mrs. Prescott glared indignantly at me, one eye blazing.

" . . . the apartment of one Alexa Demming," I finished more quietly.

"Yes, my husband was having an affair. Is that what you want to hear? Is that what you want the whole neighborhood to hear?" The brilliant eye brimmed with tears, but the pale eye remained dry and calculating. "He cheated on me, and now he's dead, and I don't know what I'm going to do." Her voice caught, and a tear broke free of the brimming eye and drew a streak of mascara down her left cheek.

"I'm sorry for your loss," I said.

"You're sorry for my loss. My left butt-cheek you're sorry. My husband's been dead three days, and you're here to offer your condolences. Is that it?"

"How long had you known about the affair?"

Both eyes widened, and her upper lip rose. I thought for a moment she was going to slam the door again, but she swallowed her emotions and stepped back. "Won't you come in?" she said in a tone of saccharine sweetness.

"Thank you." I walked past her into a tiled foyer with a twelve-foot ceiling. There were framed photographs along one wall, and I stepped toward them. "Is that our last governor?" I asked, pointing. He was standing between the Prescotts, his white teeth sparkling in the flash of the camera. In the photograph, Toni was smiling, too, but Brooks looked solemn.

"Yes, it's the governor. What did you say your name was again?"

"Robin Starling."

"And your connection with the death of my husband?"

"I guess I'm representing the woman he was having the affair with."

"You guess. You've got an unbelievable amount of hutzpah, you know that?"

"That's what people tell me. Really, it's more about presumption of innocence, the Constitutional right to adequate counsel, that sort of thing. If you're in a hurry, we can talk while you do your makeup."

I thought she would reject the suggestion, but she swept past me to go deeper into the house. I followed through a vast living room with two sets of furniture that might have just come off a showroom floor, past a side room with more plush furniture and a big-screen TV, and down a long hall lined with more photographs of one or both of the Prescotts posing with various politicians. I recognized the current lieutenant governor and a former attorney general. "It looks like you're a mover and shaker," I observed as Toni Prescott led me through a bedroom with a king-sized bed and, dominating one wall, a painting of a seascape.

"We're politically active," she said.

The bathroom had sinks on both walls. She sat on a stool in front of the built-in vanity and picked up her mascara brush.

"I understand your husband was keeping some clothes at Alexa Demming's apartment."

"Evidently." Her robe had parted to reveal an athletic pair of legs.

"Did that come as a shock to you, or did you and your husband have an open marriage?"

The hand with the mascara brush dropped to the counter, and she looked at me as if I were a previously unknown species of bug. "You are a cesspool of supposition and innuendo, aren't you?"

"It's just that you seem to take his apparent infidelity very calmly."

"I do my best to take everything calmly. What do you want me to do? Break down, throw things, sob my heart out to a complete stranger?" She went back to working on her bland eye.

"Do you have any idea how long it had been going on?"

"No. Weeks maybe, a few months?" She made a dismissive gesture with her free hand. "It hardly matters at this point, does it?"

"Was it his first time to stray?"

"As far as I know, but I guess we wives don't know everything, do we?"

"I wouldn't know."

She glanced at my left hand, which sported the diamond ring Paul had given me. "You're engaged."

"I seem to be. June wedding."

"How romantic."

I gave her a perfunctory smile. There wasn't anything particularly romantic about my engagement, and probably that was my fault. I knew, at least I imagined, that Paul had expectations in the sex department, but I hoped the sex would satisfy him, and he wasn't planning on us spending a lot of time gazing into each other's eyes. I said, "I understand she was a pharmaceutical rep with TMH, and she met your husband on sales calls she made to his medical practice."

"Alexa Demming," Toni said, over-enunciating the name.

"When did you find out about the affair?"

"Three days ago. Of course, I suspected immediately when a police detective came by to ask me to come downtown with her to identify Brooks's body. She told me where the body had been found."

"Had you ever heard the name Alexa Demming before?"

"No. I hadn't." She turned to meet my gaze, her mascara complete, her eyes like star-bursts. "When she showed me the clothes, of course, and I recognized them as belonging to Brooks, then I knew for certain."

It was amazing how the makeup transformed her appearance, transforming her from an attractive woman to one of the most beautiful I'd ever seen. I wasn't a mascara person myself, but maybe I ought to think about it.

"Did you know she had filed a sexual harassment claim against her employer based on your husband's treatment of her?" I asked.

"His treatment before or after she let him move in with her? None of that makes sense to me."

"No. Me either," I agreed. "So you do know about the sexual harassment claim."

"I do now."

"Any theories?"

"No. Maybe he was trying to break it off, and claiming harassment was her way of getting back at him. Or her way of trying to hold onto him." She thought for a moment, her crimson mouth puckering, then stood, took the towel off her head and shook out raven-black hair. "This may interfere with your interrogation, but I'm afraid I'm pressed for time." She slipped a blow dryer from a hook and turned it on.

In the noisy rush of air, I could do nothing but stand and watch as she dried her hair, brushing it out first with her fingers and then with a round brush. "You're a hard one to shake," she said, when she'd turned off the blow dryer and slipped it back on its hook. "Are you never going away?" She continued to shape her thick, glossy hair with fingers and brush.

"What are you getting ready for?" I asked. "A luncheon of some sort?"

The question provoked no more than a glance.

"Did anyone ever tell you you look a bit like Jackie Kennedy?" I asked.

She slipped the robe off her shoulders and handed it to me as I stepped back with an involuntary intake of breath. Her diaphanous bra and panties were emerald green and did for her figure what the makeup did for her face—not that her figure needed much help.

"I'm sorry, but I am in a hurry. If you'll hang that on the hook behind you, I'll go find something to wear." She disappeared into a walk-in closet that opened off the bathroom, and I exhaled. The disrobing had been a deliberate ploy to discombobulate me, but my knowing that didn't necessarily make it less effective.

"When I told Paul I'd marry him," I said, raising my voice. "I also told him that if he ever cheated on me, I'd castrate him with the pruning shears. Possibly you have a similarly vindictive nature?"

She had a sexy laugh. There were things I could learn from this woman. She came out wearing a sleeveless dress of deep maroon that set off her blazing blue eyes and her black hair. "Could you help me with this?" She turned and bent her head, exposing her back and the nape of her neck. I zipped up the dress.

"Unless you'd like to help me with my jewelry, too, I think we'll say good-bye."

"Ta ta for now?" I said.

Her smile was condescending.

"I'll show myself to the door," I said, but she ushered me out and closed the door behind me. I paused, blinking as my eyes adjusted to the sunlight, and the deadbolt shot home behind me.

There was no reason to think that Toni Prescott was going anywhere that held any interest for me. When you're an intrusive busybody, though, you don't really need a reason to spy on people. Because Windsor Farms was an insulated community with limited avenues of ingress or egress, I felt safe crossing Cary Street, doing a U-turn, and parking against the curb where I could watch the exit nearest to her house.

This close to noon, the day was getting hot, and I kept the car running to power the air conditioner. Over the next half-hour, I switched back and forth between Richmond's classic rock station and its oldies station while I waited for her to show. There wasn't a lot of activity. Two Mercedes, a Lexus, and an Audi left Windsor Farms, all of them turning east on Cary. None of the drivers, visible mostly in silhouette, looked to me like Toni Prescott.

My cell phone rang, and I got it out of my purse. "Hey, Brooke," I said.

"Hey. Are you all right? Carly says you haven't been in."

"I haven't. I started at the courthouse, and one thing's led to another."

"Shouldn't you be taking it easy your first week back?"

"You'll be happy to know I'm doing nothing more strenuous than sitting in a car."

"Any particular reason you're sitting in a car?"

I told her. "I thought she was about to head out, but either I was wrong or she's left Windsor Farms the back way."

"Isn't this the kind of work you could hand off to Rodney?" Rodney Burns was the private detective who had the third office in our cluster of three.

"I don't know if I can afford him. Has Aubrey dropped off a check this morning?"

"Do you want me to ask Carly?"

"Not necessary. It's about lunchtime, isn't it? Who's going?"

"I was hoping you and me."

"Sounds good. Toni Prescott ... Hang on." A sporty car the color of milk coffee turned onto Cary Street and drove past me, Toni at the wheel. "I'll call you back."

I hung back far enough that I couldn't be sure, but I thought I was following a Maserati. It took the entrance ramp onto the Downtown Expressway, then exited on Byrd Street. The Maserati, if that's what it was, disappeared, then reappeared far below me as the street dropped away from me and I coasted downhill.

At the bottom of the hill Toni turned left on 9th Street, which was where I began to consider abandoning what had to be a pointless tailing job.

We passed my parking garage at Cary and 9ᵗʰ. My office was two blocks to the right. Brooke was waiting to go to lunch with me, and what was I accomplishing? But I followed as Toni climbed the hill toward Capitol Square, the park that held the state capitol building designed by Thomas Jefferson. She crossed Bank Street on a yellow light and pulled against the curb, leaning forward to look through the wrought-iron fence. There was a man just inside the gate nearest the Bell Tower.

The light changed, and I added enough gas to climb the hill, though probably not enough to make the people behind me happy. The man came through the gate and reached for the handle of the car door. Toni's car was indeed a Maserati. The man, if I was at all current in Virginia politics, was Nick Cantwell, the lieutenant governor, whose picture I'd just seen on a wall inside the Prescott house.

I rolled past them, bullied along by the flow of traffic. When I gave up on Toni catching up to me, I accelerated, intent on circling the block, but, by the time I got back around, the Maserati had gone. Surely Toni and the lieutenant governor were doing nothing more interesting than going to lunch, possibly even a public event of some sort. Now that I thought about it, I wasn't even sure Cantwell had gotten in the car with her. Maybe Toni had been waiting for someone else, and the lieutenant governor had just happened to recognize her walked out to say hello.

No. I couldn't help feeling I had missed out on something juicy. I circled again and parked at a meter in front of the Ironfronts. For a minute or so, I stared unseeing through the windshield, still mentally occupied with my prurient speculations. My cell phone rang. It was Brooke again. "I've got to go to lunch. Are you coming or not?"

"I'm here."

"Oh, I see you." She came out of the Ironfronts, her purse in one hand and her phone in the other.

Chapter 4

"Actually, this is lucky," she said, opening the car door.

"You were ready to eat," I observed. "Lucky how?"

"You can drive us out to Robin Inn. I'm feeling Italian."

Robin Inn was a wonderful little hole-in-the-wall out in the Fan.

"Okay." I put the car in gear and pulled away from the curb. "What are you thinking, chicken marsala, veal parmesan?"

"I was thinking about a small Greek salad . . ."

"I thought you were feeling Italian."

"Don't be a stickler. Greece is right across the Aegean Sea."

I frowned. I would have said Adriatic, but what did I know? "Isn't the Aegean Sea between Greece and Turkey?" I asked.

"What difference does it make?"

"None, I guess, unless you're sailing the Mediterranean."

"And we're not, are we?"

I bobbed my head in silent concession of the point.

We both had a Greek salad, and Brooke insisted on us each having a glass of Chianti to go with it.

"I think this is the first time we've had wine with lunch on a workday," I said.

"Mike has a beer on Fridays lots of times." She sounded defensive.

"This is Thursday."

"Aegean, Adriatic, Friday, Thursday—are you in a mood, or what?"

"No mood. You can't blame a girl for noticing it's Thursday." I sipped my wine. The problem was, this was something I could get used to.

After lunch we went out to my car, which was parked at the curb, and Brooke stopped with a hand on the door handle. "I want to show you something. Do you have time?"

I shrugged. "How much time?"

"It's close, a block or so. We can walk, or you can drive."

"I've got my cross-trainers in the back. What are you wearing?" I craned my neck, but she was on the other side of the car and I couldn't see her feet.

"Pumps with two-and-a-half-inch heels," she said.

"Drive it is." I opened my door and got in.

Following her directions, I turned down an alley and crossed a side street into a small parking lot. "Isn't this a church?"

"First Baptist, the oldest church in Richmond, though it's only been at this location since the 1920s or so."

I raised my eyebrows.

"I talked to one of the associate ministers earlier this week."

The nickel dropped. "You're planning your wedding."

"Our wedding. We're getting married together, remember."

My breathing started to speed up, and it took a conscious effort to control it.

Brooke was saying, "If we're thinking about a June wedding, it's almost too late. All the cool venues are taken. We may have to get married in a church."

My parents had been married in a church. I'd seen the pictures. "People don't get married in churches?" Despite my best efforts to keep from hyperventilating, I sounded a little breathless.

"How many church weddings have you been to recently?" Brooke asked.

"Huh." I took a breath. "The last one . . ." I let the air flow out of my lungs. I couldn't remember the last one.

"This is a historic church with a beautiful sanctuary. Twenty-five years ago everybody wanted to get married here. Now it's got one booked in August, and that's it for the rest of the year. You're not saying much."

"Oh, wow," I managed.

She gave me a sympathetic smile. She'd been engaged longer than I had and had had an extra couple of months to get used to the idea of tying the noose—the knot, I mean. "I know," she said.

Eventually, I felt up to getting out of the car. I was recovering from serious injuries, I told myself by way of justification for my sudden lack of energy. We entered the church through what turned out to be a side door and walked, heels clacking, down a long corridor tiled with black and white squares. Eventually we went through a set of double doors into the sanctuary, where the carpet was red, the pews were dark wood, and colored light filtered through the stain-glass windows. Brooke led me into a pew, and we sat.

"It's beautiful, isn't it?" she murmured.

It was.

"And it has a center aisle," Brooke said. "Not all churches do."

"Do we want a center aisle? If there were two aisles, we could walk down at the same time."

"This isn't a race. We can't walk down at the same time. It has to be sequential. You'll go, then me."

It seemed to me that it was our wedding and we could handle it any way we wanted. "If we do it alphabetically, you'll go first. Brooke comes before Robin. Marshall comes before Starling."

"You're older."

"By three months," I said.

"A year and three months."

54

"Oh."

"Besides, older is older. It doesn't matter by how much. Older sisters get married before the younger ones. The same applies to close friends having a double wedding. I looked it up."

"You young people are always using that newfangled inter-neet," I said in my best old-lady voice.

I thought it was pretty good, but Brooke ignored my dramatic tour de force. She said, "About a block down Monument Avenue, there's an old house that's been converted into an event center that can handle receptions, but if we want to use it, we may be limited to a Friday wedding. Would you be okay with a Friday evening? There's always the fellowship hall here at the church, but . . . What? What is it?"

I was hyperventilating again. "This is getting a little too real," I said.

"You do want to get married, don't you?"

I moved my head equivocally. "Sort of."

"You love Paul."

"Well, yeah, but . . . Maybe we could just live together."

She gave me a look.

"Or better yet, just start having sex. Forget about commitment. Forget about reorganizing our living arrangements. Sex is all we need."

It was hard to see her eyes in the dim light from the stain-glass windows.

I took a breath. "I know," I said. "Been there, done that. Okay, let's book the church."

"There's a catch."

Of course there was. "What is it?"

"You have to be a church member to get married here."

"Then what are we doing here? None of us is even Baptist. Paul was raised Catholic. I'm sort of a Methodist. You're Presbyterian, and I don't know about Mike." My voice was suddenly too loud in the large, shadowed sanctuary.

"Mike's Baptist. In fact, he grew up in this church, though he hasn't been going much, at least until we started coming together."

"So this is no problem for you. Or do you have to join before they'll marry you to one of their own?"

"No."

"Oh. I have to join." I thought a moment, then nodded. "Okay."

"It may not be that simple."

"I join the church. What could be simpler?"

"Have you been baptized by emersion after confessing Jesus as your Lord and Savior?"

A sense of unreality swept over me in the dim sanctuary with its colored light. "I was a baby," I said. Actually, I was only supposing I'd been baptized at some point.

"So, no," Brooke said. She stood.

"Where are we going now?"

"Back to work. You're not done for the day, are you?"

"No, of course not. But what about . . ." I gestured with one hand, waving it around like I was clearing cobwebs. Brooke caught my hand and held it.

"You've got a lot to think about," she said.

"What about Paul? Why can't he have a lot to think about?"

"Do you think he'd go through believer's baptism for you?" She had the lingo down, I'd give her that.

"Well, sure." Paul would go through believer's baptism for me. He'd walk through fire for me—at least I thought he would.

"Okay, then."

I didn't think we'd reached *okay*. "A man can't get baptized for love of a woman," I said.

"No?"

"Baptism's supposed to have something to do with God. Isn't it?"

She tugged my hand, drawing me out of the pew, and we walked down the center aisle toward the front of the sanctuary, hand in hand.

"I don't guess I'd have the proper motivation either," I said, thinking aloud.

"No. In fact, you'll probably have to convince them you're not joining the church just to get baptized."

"I'm a trial lawyer. If I need to convince them . . ."

We stopped at the front of the church, looking up at the baptistery. The stain-glass window behind it was lit: John baptizing Jesus and a dove descending from above. I felt a pressure in my chest, as if God himself had laid a hand on me and was applying just enough pressure to let me know he could crush me like a bug if he felt like it.

When I pulled the car to a stop in front of the Ironfronts, neither of us got out. I found myself looking up at the four-story building, at the four rows of arched windows. Officing there, Brooke and I were a part of history. The Ironfronts had been built in 1866, the year after the retreating Confederate army had set fire to Richmond's tobacco warehouses so the Union soldiers wouldn't get their tobacco. All of downtown Richmond had burned to the ground, and this particular builder had fronted his new building with cast iron, maybe thinking it would protect his investment against future fires.

First Baptist Church was another bit of history, sitting at the corner of Monument and Boulevard where Stonewall Jackson was cast in bronze astride his bronze horse, but I didn't know whether it was a history I could be a part of—or whether there was any reason to be a part of it.

"There are a lot of venues for weddings," I said.

"Well. Not for June at this point."

"A lot of churches should be available. Some of them might be available to nonmembers. One or two."

Brooke nodded. After another minute of watching me think, she said, "Coming up?"

I shook my head.

"You're all right, aren't you?"

I gave her a lopsided smile. "Sure. It just seems strange this question of religion has come up. Even stranger that it feels so pressing."

"So where are you going? Home?"

"No. I've thought of someone else I can annoy the hell out of."

"That's my girl." Brooke gave my hand a pat and got out of the car.

Brooks Prescott had been one of two partners in the Richmond Spine & Joint Clinic. After a thirty-minute wait in the waiting room and another fifteen minutes in a tiny conference room, Tracy Mulligan, the surviving partner, came in and straddled a chair across from me. I'd been expecting a woman, but Tracy turned out to be a short, muscular man with a square head.

"So," he said. "You're with the police."

"No. I'm investigating the murder, but I'm a lawyer."

"Who's your client?"

"Alexa Demming."

"The woman who killed Brooks?"

"Maybe. I'm not willing to concede the point yet." I smiled.

"I guess not."

"I understand the two of them had gotten involved," I said. "Brooks and Alexa."

His head went back. "Had they?" he said. "Had they really? The old dog."

"His clothes were found in her apartment."

"I could tell she was interested, but Brooks . . . You never know about people, do you?"

I said, "You have it backwards, don't you? Brooks was the one who was interested."

"I wouldn't have thought so. Brooks was in love with his wife. Have you seen her? When that woman turns on the charm . . ." He shook his head.

"You haven't known Brooks to be involved with other women?"

"Not since Toni came along. Of course, he's a good-looking guy. Sorry. Was. He had a successful medical practice, family money . . ."

"Women were attracted to him," I said.

"Let's just say he had opportunities."

"And occasionally took advantage of them," I prompted.

"If you say so. I don't have any knowledge of that."

"But it wouldn't surprise you."

"I suppose it would, a little. Like I said, the man was devoted to his wife."

"So what was there about Alexa Demming?"

"I wouldn't have said there was anything about her."

"Why would she name him in a sexual harassment claim?"

"I have no idea. Maybe she was the one opportunity he took advantage of."

"So you don't think she made it all up?"

"I don't think anything. I just don't know anything about it."

"But you did know about the sexual harassment claim."

"Sure. TMH called, asking questions. Had I seen the two of them together, were they ever alone, who else could they talk to?"

"Did you give them any names?"

Mulligan shrugged. "There weren't any to give."

"Were Brooks and Alexa ever alone together?"

"Who knows? Yeah, probably."

"Did you ever talk to Brooks about it? Did he seem upset about being named in a harassment claim?"

"I talked to him. Yeah, he seemed upset, a little."

"Because his wife might find out?"

"I understand he told her about it."

"How do you understand that?"

"He told me he told her."

That contradicted what Toni had said about it. "What was her reaction? Did he say?"

"I . . . think she took it in stride."

"So why was Brooks upset?"

He rolled his palms toward me, his forearms still on the back of the chair.

I tried another tack. "You knew Alexa yourself, didn't you? You've met her."

"Of course. Like I said, she was with TMH."

"The pharmaceutical company. What did of drugs did she sell?"

"No kind, at least not to us. We purchased biomaterials, mostly replacement joints."

"Did you ever see Alexa and Dr. Prescott interact?"

"Sure."

"Tell me about it."

"There's nothing to tell. Everything I saw was professional and above board."

"You said she came on to him."

"I said I could tell she was interested."

"Can you tell me what exactly gave you that impression?"

He shook his head. "It's been awhile. At this point I can't give you any specifics."

"But she was interested, and he wasn't."

"That was my impression."

"How long had Brooks been married, do you know?"

"Not long. Five, six years?" He shrugged.

"And they were happily married."

"They seemed to be."

"How did he and Toni meet?"

"That I couldn't tell you. They both were into politics. Maybe they . . ." He trailed off, and his eyes became distant. "No, that's not it. They met at Hooter's. Funny how I could have forgotten that."

"Hooter's the restaurant?" I said, feeling my skin prickle.

"My wife calls it a breastaurant."

"Hooter's the breastaurant?" I repeated, unwilling to be sidetracked.

"She was a waitress, I think. A waitress or hostess or something."

For a few seconds, I didn't say anything. Peter Brawley photographed Hooter's girls and bought them breast implants. Brooks Prescott had married a Hooter's girl. Was the world that small?

Tracy Mulligan slapped his thighs and stood. "If that's everything," he said, "I've got patients stacked up out there like cord-wood."

I stood, too. "One of Dr. Prescott's unwelcome advances involved him cornering Alexa in a supply closet, according to the complaint. Do you know anything about that incident?"

"Nothing."

"Could it possibly be true?"

"Who knows? I wouldn't have thought he'd have had clothes at her place. Scratch a saint, find a sinner, I guess."

"Is there anyone else I could talk to, a staff member who worked closely with Dr. Prescott, or who might have seen him interact with Alexa?"

"No, not really."

"There has to be someone," I said.

He shook his head. "I'm sorry."

But I collided with a member of the staff on my way out, a plump woman in black scrubs who broadsided me as we passed a side-passage. "Oh, excuse me." She took my hands and looked up into my face. "I'm so sorry. Are you all right?" It was she who didn't look all right. The skin around her eyes was puffy, for one thing.

"I'm fine. Thanks," I said.

I looked after her as she went past me and turned a corner, then shot a glance at Dr. Mulligan.

"That's Leah. Dr. Prescott's death has hit her hard. She's not the only one of course. He was a genuinely nice guy, whatever peccadillos he may have been engaged in there at the end. We're all going to miss him."

"Leah been with you long?"

"Ten years, more or less." He opened the door to the waiting room for me. "It's been a pleasure to meet you." I gave him a thank-you smile and went out.

Only then did I look down at the scrap of paper Leah had left in my hand. It had been torn from a small, spiral notebook, and on it was written a phone number.

I texted it from my car in the parking lot: "This is Robin Starling. Did you want to talk?"

"Break at 3:30."

I looked at my watch. A bit over thirty minutes, but I was supposed to be taking it easy anyway. I eased my seat back a bit and turned up the radio.

I don't think I fell asleep, but I must have zoned out. At any rate, I started when the passenger door opened and Leah got in. After a quick glance at me, she sat staring through the windshield. I put my seat back up.

"You're here about Dr. Prescott," she said. I took it as a question, despite her intonation.

"I'm afraid I am," I said.

She sighed, nodding to herself.

"Did you have something to tell me?"

She turned an apologetic gaze on me. "I don't have anyone to talk to."

"About Dr. Prescott?"

She nodded. "The police have been here, of course, but . . ." She took a big breath and let it out.

"You talked to the police?"

"They were talking to everyone."

"Were you and Dr. Prescott . . ." I made an ambiguous motion with my hand.

"Oh, no. I mean, he took me out for drinks once when we'd been working late, but he was just being nice." She gave a short, self-deprecating laugh. "Look at me: Overweight, frizzy hair . . . and of course he's married."

"But you loved him?"

Tears welled in her eyes and started running down her cheeks. She wiped at them with the heels of her hands. "I'm sorry."

"It's all right. I understand," I said.

"I think about that evening all the time."

"The evening with the drinks? How long ago was it?"

"Years, almost four. Actually, it will be four years June twenty-second."

She'd had it bad.

"I'm sorry," I said.

She nodded, then sniffed. "Me, too," she said in a small voice.

"He hadn't been married long when the two of you had those drinks," I said.

"You know what the funny thing is? He spent most of the evening talking about his new wife." She laughed, shook her head, her eyes on the hands clasped in her lap. "He was crazy about that woman."

"Right to the end, do you think, or did it wear off?"

"Right to the end."

"Huh," I said. "That makes this whole thing with Alexa Demming all but incomprehensible, doesn't it?"

She looked at me. "Oh, I comprehend it."

"You know about it?"

"I know enough."

"Was Dr. Prescott attracted to her, do you think?"

"No, he was not attracted to her."

"Did he ever do or say anything to her that might have been misinterpreted as an advance?"

Her breath came out in an audible puff of air. I took it as a no.

"Did she come onto him?" I asked.

"I'll say she came onto him. She'd gaze at him with those big dark eyes of hers, touch his arm or his hand every time he got within reach of her. She'd stand too close to him, lean into him . . . She was a complete tramp, let me tell you."

I nodded. "There was a story about a supply closet . . ."

She threw up a hand. "That story about the supply closet! She might have tried to drag him into the supply closet, that I'd believe, but he never touched her. You can bet your life on that. He was not one bit interested."

"But she was interested in him."

"Oh, yes, she . . ." She interrupted herself with a short laugh. "The most unbelievable thing . . ." But she broke off again without finishing her thought.

"Do you think she killed him?" I asked.

"If she couldn't have him, then nobody was going to," Leah said.

Chapter 5

I never made it to the office that day. I went home, collected Deeks, and saw that Dr. McDermott was no worse. He didn't look any better, but at least he didn't seem to be dying.

"I'm going back to bed," he told me in a congested voice. This time I followed him in. By bed, he meant his living room sofa. He had a small trashcan at one end of it, filled with Kleenex and crushed water bottles. I picked it up.

"What have you eaten today?" I asked him, and he waved a hand at me as he lay back down.

"I'll bring you some chicken noodle soup, how's that?"

He shook his head. "I'm not hungry."

"Dr. McDermott," I said in my most ominous voice.

He looked up at me, then moved his head fractionally. "Okay. Maybe I can eat something." He had a wheeze I didn't like.

"You know I'll sit here until it's all gone."

Again the tiny movement of the head. Deeks and I went to empty the trash.

"I appreciate you using the trashcan," I said when I came back. "Makes this easier."

"Deacon . . . eats Kleenex."

"I know. And chokes on water bottles." Though he liked chewing on them, he tended to choke on the strips of plastic he tore off—not that that discouraged him any.

Dr. McDermott lay with his eyes closed, unresponsive.

"Deeks and I will be back with the soup," I said.

Still no reaction. I let myself out.

I thought I was going to have to go buy soup, but it turned out I had a can of Campbell's in the cabinet. I heated it in the microwave while Deeks ate his kibble, then carried it across the street and watched Dr. McDermott eat it. When I got back to the house with the empty bowl, I put it in the sink, then went back into the living room, and sat on the couch. Deeks went to the front door, ready for his evening outing, then came back to look at me.

"Just a minute, buddy. Can you give me a minute?" It had been a full day—not a physical day, but evidently I was still convalescing. I was exhausted.

Deeks ran to the front door and back again, his expression anxious.

"I know. I know. It's that time of day."

He barked once. Yes.

"Give me a minute, then we'll go." I pulled a pillow under my head as I stretched out and closed my eyes.

He gave me maybe ten seconds, then a cold nose touched mine. I opened my eyes to meet the inquiring gaze of my dog.

"I know, Deeks. I know." I closed my eyes again. When I opened them, it was morning, and Deeks was sitting by the front door whining to go out.

Surprisingly, after twelve hours on the couch I felt like my old self. I went on a two-mile ramble with Deeks and found it refreshing. For breakfast, I dumped some granola and some Greek yogurt into a bowl and stirred it together. I enjoyed it so much I thought about having seconds—but resisted the temptation. After a quick shower, I went to the closet to pick out my clothes for the day, thinking that, since it was Friday, maybe I could dress a bit more casually than usual. I reached for a pair of slacks, and my eyes cut to the jeans at the end of the bar. Though I worked for myself, jeans at the office would be pushing it.

My T-shirts hung at the other end of the bar. I pulled out a blue shirt with "Keep Calm and Wahoo On" on the front over a pair of crossed swords. My brother, a medical doctor in Charlottesville who had gone through the University of Virginia's medical school a few years before I went through UVA Law, usually gave me a T-shirt or some other bit of UVA paraphernalia for Christmas and birthdays. He said it was because we were such big fans, but I suspected the real reason was that he was cheap: *My brother built a successful medical practice, and all I got was this lousy T-shirt.* I won't tell you what kind of presents I get him. Let's just say that cheap can be contagious.

I'd picked out a pair of shorts to go with the T-shirt, having decided to play hooky and not go into the office at all, when my cell rang. It was Carly.

"Hi, Carly."

"Hi, Robin. Are you all right?"

"Sure. A bit unmotivated maybe."

"Are you coming in today, or are you going to be out again? A man called for you, a Mr. Borger."

"I don't know any Mr. Borgers."

"Mr. Jim Borger? He says he's the commonwealth's attorney for Dinwiddie."

Dinwiddie was a county an hour south of Richmond. "Did he say what he wanted?" I asked.

"Just that you should call him as soon as you came in."

"Give me the number."

Still in bra and panties, my white shorts and blue T-shirt laid out on the bed beside me, I sat and dialed. My guess was that Borger had been appointed to handle the Alexa Demming prosecution. I gave my name to the administrative assistant who answered the phone, and I waited to find out if I was right.

"Robin Starling." Borger had a deep, big voice.

"That would be me," I said.

"Jim Borger. I wanted to introduce myself and let you know I'd be handling the Demming case. I understand you're representing the defendant."

"I am."

"I also understand you're already hard at work, out harassing witnesses, out intimidating them."

"Is that two groups of witnesses, or have I been harassing and intimidating the same ones?"

"It's not a matter for levity."

"I suppose not. I still don't know what you're talking about, though."

"So you're going to play it that way," he said.

"You mean, ask you to explain your accusation? Yeah, that's the way I'm playing it."

"Did you or did you not visit the home of Toni Prescott?"

"I did. She invited me into her home, and we had a nice chat."

"Did you or did you not stand on her doorstep shouting about her husband's death and his affair with your client so that she'd have no choice but to open her door to you?"

"I did have a brief conversation with her through the door. It was the only possible way to have a conversation before she opened it."

"You're on notice, Ms. Starling. That kind of bullying behavior will not be tolerated."

"Said the bully with the power of the state behind him," I said. "Ms. Prescott let me know she was politically connected, but I had no idea."

There was a beat before he responded, and his big voice was almost soft. "I don't think I appreciate your attitude," he said.

"Good to know. I won't be watching my mail for a thank-you note."

He hung up on me. I punched off my phone and looked at Deeks, who was sitting at attention at my feet.

"If you're looking for tips on how to win friends and influence people, you've come to the wrong place," I told him.

His tail thumped the floor.

I sighed. "I guess I'll be going to work after all."

He came to his feet, clearly ready to go with me.

"I'll have to put some clothes on, first."

He barked.

"You said it, Buster."

So I went to the office, drafted my discovery motions to make sure I got the prosecution's witness list along with copies of the medical examiner's report, the police reports, photographs of the crime scene, and whatever other data the police investigation had uncovered. I put my pumps in my shoe bag, put on my sneakers, then walked my motions across downtown to file them with the court clerk.

I had lunch with Mike and Paul and Brooke. It was Friday, and Mike and Paul had beers with their burgers. Virtuously, I had water with my chicken sandwich on whole-grain bread, and mustard on the sandwich instead of mayonnaise. My moral superiority wasn't much comfort as I watched the juice drip from the men's burgers with each bite and the bubbles rise in their beers, but it was what I had—that, and a physique that was leaner than it would be if I indulged myself at every opportunity.

"So," Mike said, sitting back with his beer and sounding expansive. "How are things going with the big case?" He was the other lawyer at the table. Not being a trial lawyer himself, he was sometimes kind enough to critique the way I handled my cases.

"They're not going, really. I do seem to have a knack for irritating the hell out of people." I told them about my call from Jim Borger.

"I don't know him," Mike said. "Sounds like a jerk."

"Heard anything from Aubrey Biggs since he hired you?" Paul asked.

"He's dropped off a check for five thousand dollars. Other than that, not a peep."

"Five thousand bucks is a pretty substantial communication," Mike said.

"I'm hoping for another five thousand sometime next week." Mike often got a five-thousand-dollar check for a routine social-security-disability hearing, I knew, and those checks were issued by the United States Treasury. "Someday I'm going to elbow myself into a place beside you at the government trough."

"Always room for one more," he said, holding up his beer.

"At taxpayer expense," Paul said darkly.

Brooke said, "You work for the Federal Reserve. You get comprehensive health insurance, regular raises, a guaranteed pension . . ."

It was good to see her sticking up for Mike, but the discussion had the potential to turn into an unproductive political debate. I'd learned from previous conversations that our various political positions were complicated and often inconsistent. I said, "Come to think of it, we're each marrying our way to a place at the government trough. A month from now, the Fed will be paying for my health insurance, too."

"Speaking of which," Mike said, "do you and Paul want to go to church with us this Sunday?"

"Speaking of which?" Paul said. "What does going to church have to do with Robin's health insurance?"

"You and Robin may be getting married at First Baptist," Mike said.

Paul looked at me. "Really?"

"Maybe," I said.

"You and Paul haven't talked about it? You know one of you has to join the church," Brooke said.

"Which means getting baptized," I told Paul.

"Huh." Paul's eyes fell to his beer. He took a big swallow and put the mug back on the table. Mike's eyes went from one to the other of us, then he took a slug of his own beer. Brooke looked from me to Mike to Paul. For once, it seemed that none of us usually vocal people had anything to say.

"How did marriage get all mixed up with religion, anyway?" I asked to break the silence.

"Marriage is a sacrament," Paul said, looking up. "A channel of God's grace."

"It's an ordinance," Mike said, and Brooke the Presbyterian nodded. "An institution established by God."

"An ordinance is a law," I said. "Not an institution."

"God's words are law."

"What God has joined together," Paul said in sepulcher tones. He didn't finish the phrase.

"I withdraw the objection," I said, and we descended again into silence. Religion, it seemed, was at least as problematic a topic as politics. Paul picked up his beer and drained it; Mike followed suit. I took a breath and let it out, then took a sip of my water.

"We don't *have* to get married in a church," Brooke said. "It's just that all the wedding forums in town are booked at least to the middle of August."

"Of course we're going to get married in a church," Paul said. "And if First Baptist is the best place to do it, I'll get baptized. No need for Robin to do it, if she doesn't want to. I've done it already, actually, or had it done to me, but I don't guess God's going to mind a double-dipping." He held up a finger, forestalling any objection from Mike. "Don't say I was only sprinkled the first time. It was baptism by emersion. I distinctly remember the priest dropping me in the baptismal font."

"You were a baby," Mike objected.

"It was traumatic," Paul said. "First I was drowning, then a strange man in a robe was holding me by one leg. You don't forget such things."

Mike's eyes cut to the ceiling.

"We're all in agreement about baptism, aren't we?" Paul asked, looking around. "Baptism is a sacrament."

Brooke and I nodded. Mike cleared his throat.

"Another ordinance?" Paul said in incredulity. "Well, there we have it. It's not the same thing at all. One sacrament of baptism, one ordinance of baptism. I'll be the one person who's sure to have done it the right way."

"You don't have to get re-baptized," I said. "I'll do it."

"What makes you so special? I can be re-baptized."

"Look, I know you're Catholic, but you're not a practicing Catholic. You're not religious."

"And you are?"

"I believe in God the father almighty, creator of heaven and earth," I said.

"And in Jesus Christ, his only son our Lord," Brooke said.

"You're just reciting the Apostles Creed," Paul said. "Knowing the Apostles Creed doesn't make you religious."

I shrugged.

"Hey," Mike said. "Hey, it's all right. We can find another place to have our weddings."

"I don't want to mess things up for you and Brooke," I said. "If it gets too hairy, we can let go of the idea of a double wedding."

He glanced at Brooke. "That's one of the conditions," he said.

We all looked at Brooke. *A double wedding or none?* I thought.

"We can do this," she said. "I'll keep looking."

You think of lunch with friends as a relaxing, convivial occasion, but by the time that one was over I felt like I'd been in trial for a week. I got back to my office, dropped into the chair at my desk, and sat. I had to get baptized for us to get married in the church that was Brooke's first choice. "Had to" overstated it, of course. I didn't have to do anything—not even get married, if it came to it. As a boyfriend, Paul was satisfactory. Living with him was going to take some adjustments. A lifetime commitment wasn't even something I could wrap my mind around.

I looked up at a tap on the door. It was Aubrey Biggs.

"May I?" he said, gesturing at the client chairs.

I nodded, and he sat in one of them, leaning forward with his hands clasped between his knees.

"You look deep in thought," he said.

"Looks can be deceiving."

"Anything you'd care to share?"

I shook my head, then shrugged. "Jim Borger's been appointed to prosecute."

"It's one of the reasons I stopped by, to tell you, if you didn't already know."

"Oh, I know. He's been on the phone already to accuse me of harassing witnesses."

An expression of satisfaction touched Aubrey's face, or maybe it was just my imagination. "And have you been? Harassing witnesses?"

"I wasn't going out of my way to pressure or intimidate anyone. On the other hand, I imagine I can be as big a pain in the rumpus as anyone you'd ever hope to meet."

The smile this time was unmistakable. "I imagine you can," he said.

"Were you coming by for something in particular?" I asked.

"You got my check, didn't you? I should have another one for you on Monday. I wanted to know if you need anything else from me."

"I don't. Not that I know of."

He hesitated. "I don't know if you've had trouble with Detective Michaels. Her natural instinct is to be uncooperative, but you put pressure on her, she'll cave every time."

"Good to hear."

"I got it from Ray Hernandez. You've got a pretty good relationship with him and Jordan, don't you? You need something, call them. I think they'll help you if they can."

I raised my eyebrows.

"They like you. And they might want to call in a favor sometime."

"A favor from you?"

He shrugged.

"Maybe this bit of mutual back-scratching would be a good thing to remember the next time you get the itch to try to get me disbarred."

"You might want to call in a favor sometime, too," he said.

"You never know." I gave him a smile. "Maybe my helping your sister will work out better than us being golfing buddies."

"I don't play golf."

He didn't have much of a sense of humor either, evidently.

"It looks like the preliminary will be next week," he said. "Maybe early in the week."

I nodded.

"You'll be ready?"

I shrugged. "I can hope."

"You don't have the most comforting of bedside manners, you know."

"Good thing you're not sick in bed."

He sat looking at me, then got up to leave. At the door he turned back.

I waited. "Yes?"

"My parents may be in to see you," he said.

"You're kidding. Your parents?"

"And Alexa's. They're worried about their daughter. It's killing them to think of her in a jail cell, Dad in particular."

"But why come see me?"

"Take your measure, I think. They're looking for reassurance."

"I have thought of something I need from you," I said.

He stepped back into the office. "Name it."

"Keep your parents off me. I've got a lot on my plate right now. I'm not sure I can pull off impressive and reassuring."

That was it, as far as productive work went that day. On Saturday, it occurred to me to do a little research on Nick Cantwell, Virginia's lieutenant governor. Fortunately, that was something I could do sitting sideways on my sofa with my feet tucked under Deeks's chest. It turned out that, though the current governor was a Democrat and the attorney general was a Democrat, Cantwell was a Republican, an occasion of split governance that could happen because the governor and the lieutenant governor didn't run on the same ticket. Evidently not caring to have Cantwell any closer to him than necessary, the governor had moved him out of the traditional office space in the Capitol building and relegated him to a small office in the Bell Tower.

The Bell Tower. I'd seen Toni Prescott stop within twenty yards of the Bell Tower to pick him up—if she had picked him up, and I thought she had. Though Biggs had told me that the Prescotts were big into Democratic politics, here Toni was consorting with a Republican.

After a while I gave up on research and began browsing for a new summer bathing suit, pausing occasionally to consider what I knew and didn't know about Alexa Demming and Brooks Prescott. My cell phone rang, and Paul's face appeared on the screen. It meant I was likely done with swimsuit shopping, but it was just as well. None of the swimsuit models I was looking at was anywhere close to six feet in height, and I didn't have any idea how I'd look in one of the suits that looked so cute on them.

"Hey, Paul," I said.

"Hey. Doing anything interesting?"

"Shopping for a bathing suit online. Just window-shopping, actually. I don't have any idea what would look good on me."

He didn't say anything.

"Paul?"

"I don't guess you'd let me pick out something for you."

I snorted. "What would you pick out, a thong and a couple of pasties?"

"I can be tasteful." He sounded hurt.

"I'm sorry. Knock yourself out. But no thongs or pasties."

"Of course not. I wouldn't put you on display."

"So you're thinking of a muumuu of some sort, not a bikini?"

"Actually, I was thinking of a dome tent with a hole cut in the top," he said.

I smiled. "Let's say a one-piece. I look scrawny in a bikini."

"You don't look scrawny. You looked ripped."

I gave him a raspberry. When I didn't add anything to that, he said, "I thought maybe I'd come over. Hang out."

I hesitated, though I didn't have any particular objections to him coming over. Paul was usually amenable to whatever I wanted to do. I just wasn't sure what that was at the moment.

"You know, Robin . . . We can do this any way you want. We can get married in a double-ceremony with Mike and Brooke, or we can have our own ceremony. We can use a justice of the peace or elope. Heck, we can go to Vegas and get an Elvis impersonator to marry us."

"We could just move in together," I said. "It would save us about a thousand dollars a year in taxes."

"Really?"

"No, not really. Well, it is true about the taxes—I checked it out—but I think the tax code drives too many decisions already. I'm just letting you know I understand all options are on the table."

There was a brief silence. "I don't know that I like the sound of that," he said.

"Why don't you pick me up at nine tomorrow? We can go to church with Mike and Brooke."

"Tomorrow?" He sounded disappointed. "How about pizza and a movie tonight?"

"How about you come over, we get a pizza delivered, and we watch a movie on Netflix?"

"Just us?" He sounded hopeful.

"Sure, and Deeks."

So that's what we did. Neither of us had seen the most recent Star Trek movie, and Paul was as big a Trekkie as my father had always been. Despite his fanaticism, though, Paul made a game of the movie, pausing it each time the Enterprise appeared on the screen for a make-out session. Deeks was our chaperone. Each time, he'd let the kissing go on for five minutes or so, then get up and come wedge his head between us.

"You know, buddy," Paul said to him on one occasion. "A month from now we'll be married. You're gonna have to give us more space."

"We'll still have to take breaks to watch movies and take walks and go to work and stuff," I said.

"Well, sure. And eat and sleep. I was thinking I might lose weight, though, with all the sexual activity."

"You're going to be so sleep deprived you walk around like a zombie all day," I said.

"Sounds good to me. Zombies are hot right now."

"Paul Soldano in Zombieland." I nipped his earlobe as I took the remote from him and restarted the movie.

The next day we did go to church with Brooke and Mike. First Baptist's preacher had a full head of salt-and-pepper hair, and his sermon gave me something to think about. Though I don't know anything about church music, the choir and orchestra struck me as pretty good, and of course the sanctuary was beautiful. All that said, the experience had a claustrophobic feel to me, as if my choices were narrowing, the walls were closing in on me, and I didn't have enough air.

Chapter 6

On Monday I went back by the jail for another conference with Alexa, wanting a more detailed account of her movements the day of the murder. She'd made sales calls that day, three in the morning and one in the afternoon. In between she'd stopped off for lunch at Pepper's, a bar-and-grill on West Broad. She'd eaten by herself and hadn't talked to anyone except the waitress.

"Did you pay by cash or credit card?"

"Cash. I always pay cash for lunch."

"Would you still have the receipt?"

She shook her head. "TMH doesn't reimburse."

"And you didn't see anyone you knew?"

"No one."

"Do you remember the waitress's name? Think about her name tag. No? Can you tell me what she looked like?"

"She was young, I think."

"Real young? A teenager, early twenties?"

"Younger than me."

Maybe mid-twenties, then. "Blonde, brunette?" I suggested.

"One or the other."

I rolled my eyes.

"I'm pretty sure she wasn't a redhead," Alexa said.

I sighed, then nodded. "Let's talk about after lunch. Your next appointment was three thirty. You didn't swing by your apartment for anything?"

She shook her head.

"You're sure?"

"I went shopping."

"Shopping can work. What did you buy?"

Again, she shook her head.

"Nothing? What were you shopping for?"

"Well, various things. I looked at some boots at Myrna's, then Macy's."

"Did anyone help you at either place?"

"At Myrna's, there was a really cute guy I talked to a little bit."

"A cute guy is good. Do you remember his name, anything about him?"

"His hair was blond or maybe light brown, and he was tall."

"Taller than I am?"

"Maybe not that tall."

If he was shorter than five-eleven, he wasn't tall for a man. We were looking for a man of medium height with hair of indeterminate color.

"Okay. I'll track some of this down, get confirmations where I can. Depending on the time of death, it might be critical."

"You mean I might have an alibi?"

"Maybe. If I can find these people, and they remember you."

I found Rodney Burns in his office, two over from mine. He looked up from his desk, and his mustache twitched.

"Careful," I said. "Your pet caterpillar is getting away."

"What?" He gave me a puzzled smile and squinted through his glasses.

"Sorry. Never mind. Do you think you can find a picture of Alexa Demming on the Internet?"

"Done." He made a few mouse clicks on his computer, then turned his monitor so I could see it. "I looked her up when you got her case. I was hoping there might be some work for me."

The photograph I was looking at was the one of Alexa with her tongue out, pretending to lick the top can in a pyramid of beer cans. Peter Brawley was not as discreet as he made out to be.

"Can you find any other pictures?" I asked.

He clicked his mouse, and Alexa, wearing a white shirt with an open collar and a business jacket, smiled tentatively at us. "This is her LinkedIn picture," Rodney said.

"I like that one, except she has blonde hair now."

He clicked his mouse again. This time she was squinting into the sun, a forearm braced on one knee and her tank top showing cleavage. Eventually we found a couple of photographs I thought would do.

"You might have lunch at Pepper's Bar and Grill today," I suggested. "Chat up the waitresses under twenty-six or so . . . I know, that might be all of them . . . and show them the pictures. Maybe someone will remember Alexa." It didn't seem likely that anyone would remember when, exactly, she had seen Alexa, but I was doing what I could.

"Sounds like I'm on an expense account," Rodney said, and his caterpillar mustache gave a hopeful quiver.

"Sure," I said, magnanimously. "Let me buy you lunch. Then afterwards, you can go by the medical offices of Dr. Robert Jarvis. He's an OB/GYN, I think. Alexa made a sales call there the morning of May 8. See what time Alexa left his office. After that . . ." I told him about the cute guy at Myrna's.

"This is very positive," Rodney said, writing on his legal pad and nodding.

"Really? You think something might come of it?"

"Sure. Billable hours

"Great," I said.

"Don't worry. I'll make them count."

I had taken three of the five steps back to my office when a commanding voice arrested me. "Ms. Starling!"

I turned to look through the archway. A man and woman who might have been in their sixties were at the receptionist desk. Carly turned to look at me.

I went out to meet them. "That would be me," I said, extending a hand.

He didn't take my hand. "Not very grammatical, are we?" he said. He had silver hair and a silver mustache, and his pin-stripe suit seemed well-tailored.

"No. Woe is I," I said, which is grammatical, but not something you ever hear.

The man gave me a look of disapproval. The woman with him had straight blonde hair pulled back into an elegant ponytail—a phrase I never thought I'd use—and she was thin to the point of emaciation.

Carly said, "Robin, this is—"

"She knows who we are," the man said.

I was afraid I did. Aubrey had not managed to keep his parents off me, after all, and our meeting was not beginning well. "Come on back," I said.

Once I'd ushered them through my office door, I indicated the client chairs and moved past them to my desk. The woman took a seat, sitting forward on her chair with her knees together and pointed to one side, but the man remained standing behind his chair. Evidently, the stick up his rump deprived him of the necessary flexibility for sitting.

I stayed on my feet myself, fingertips resting on the edge of my desk, waiting for him to initiate the conversation.

"I've made inquiries about you," he said. "The word is you fancy yourself some kind of legal hotshot."

"I like to think of myself as a legal eagle," I said. "The rhyme appeals to me."

His eyebrows rose, disbelieving. "Pardon?" He put a hand on the woman's shoulder as if to bestow on her a bit of his strength.

"Could I get you something to drink?" I asked her. "We have coffee in the break room, or a bottle of water."

She shook her head fractionally.

"I've also heard you were impudent and rude," the man said.

That seemed uncalled for, considering that I had just offered his wife some refreshment.

"Arrogance and rudeness is no substitute for talent," he said, giving me a pained smile.

"It's too bad, really. It would put us both right at the top of our respective fields."

He gazed at me unblinking, his worst suspicions confirmed.

"Look, let's start over," I said. "Sit down, and let's just visit a bit." I pulled out my own chair and sat by way of illustration. I looked up at him, smiling, but he stayed on his feet.

"We don't have anything to visit about. I think we've seen what we came to. Helen."

She rose to her feet and he touched a hand to the small of her back to guide her through the door. I followed them as far as the archway, stopping to watch him open one of the glass double-doors for her. As she passed through, he turned to fix me with a hard stare. The door closed behind him, he punched the button for the elevator, and the two of them stood with their backs to me.

"That didn't go well," Carly said.

I gave her a shrug. "If it were up to that man, I'd be off the case."

"It's not up to him, though, is it?" Carly said.

I shook my head reflectively. "I have an idea Alexa stopped letting her father dictate to her a long time ago."

"Oh, that wasn't Alexa's father," Carly said.

"What?"

"That was Bruce and Helen Prescott. They're the parents of the man your client's supposed to have killed."

I did met Alexa's parents at the preliminary hearing the next day. I got to the courtroom early and was sorting through documents at the defense table when I heard my name. I turned to see Aubrey Biggs standing with a short man with curly, silver hair who looked like an older version of himself.

"Robin, I'd like you to meet my parents. Mom, Dad, Robin Starling."

I got up. The woman standing with them was an older version of Alexa, except that she had straight brown hair that stopped at her jawline. The face itself was Alexa's, wide-mouth and brown eyes and all, just more deeply lined and with the cheeks beginning to sag. It was she and not her husband who reached out a hand to me.

"Ms. Starling. We're so glad to finally meet you."

"I'm sorry it had to be under these circumstances," I said.

She tilted her head, giving me an uncertain smile. "We are so afraid for our girl," she said.

"We can't stand to think of her caged up like an animal," the man said.

"I'm sorry," Aubrey said. "George and Fran Biggs."

Fran still had my hand, gripping it by the fingers with her own cool, porcelain hand. "If the judge will admit her to bail, we can pay it," she said.

George nodded emphatically, his serious expression seeming unnatural on his fleshy, mobile features. "We've got a condo in Florida, equity of one-point-two million and maybe more."

"I'll do my best," I said.

"We know you will, dear," Fran said.

I glanced at Aubrey, who had to know that bail was a long shot. His mouth twitched, but he didn't say anything.

The presiding judge for the preliminary hearing was District Judge Timothy Cochran, which was a mixed blessing. I'd appeared before him twice before, and, on the plus side, both those hearings had gone very well. On the minus side, I had the impression Judge Cochran really didn't like me. In fact, I was pretty sure he thought I was unscrupulous, unprincipled, and inexcusably insolent—go figure.

Alexa Demming came in through the side door looking paler than she had the day before, her hair a little brassier. It had been only about twenty-four hours since I'd last seen her, so maybe the apparent changes in her were due to the courtroom lighting. As the deputy sheriff uncuffed her, the tattoo of an emerald-green eye peeked out at me over the collar of her jailhouse-orange coveralls, something I hadn't noticed it before.

"Hey," I said softly. "How're you holding up?"

Her mouth stretched.

"That good," I said.

She laid a heavy hand on my shoulder as she sat beside me at the defense table.

Jim Borger entered the courtroom, striding ponderously down the aisle of the mostly empty gallery. He was a big bear of a man in a black suit, and his movement drew the eye as if he exerted tidal forces. He all but eclipsed the much smaller man walking beside him with the trial briefcase.

They came first to my table, Borger looming over me, and I stood.

"Ms. Starling," he rumbled, and his hand engulfed mine.

"Mr. Borger." He was six-three or -four, maybe three hundred pounds, and he had TV-preacher hair with just a touch of gray at the temples. His was a physical presence that was going to have an impact when we got to a jury.

"My associate, Matt Rogers," he said.

Rogers nodded and stuck out his hand.

When they'd gone to their table and begun to lay out folders and pens and yellow pads, arranging them as carefully as if they were preparing for surgery, Alexa leaned close to me. "What do you think?"

"That pomposity is no substitute for talent." I smiled at her encouragingly, but, according to his campaign literature, Borger had never lost a felony trial. Granted, he was commonwealth's attorney for the rural county of Dinwiddie, but he was in his middle fifties and had been in the game awhile. No felony losses was impressive.

Aubrey Biggs reached across the rail to touch Alexa's arm. "Hey, Sis."

"Hey, big brother."

She saw her parents and gave her mother a little-girl smile. They hugged over the rail that separated the gallery from the front of the courtroom, first Alexa and her mother, then Alexa and her father. The bailiff called the court to order, and everyone stood as Judge Timothy Cochran entered the courtroom.

The judge sat. "We're here in the case of Commonwealth versus Alexa Demming," he said, picking up a document that had been lying on the bench. "The defendant is present in the courtroom. Representing the commonwealth is Commonwealth's Attorney Jim Borger. Representing the defendant is Robin Starling. Do you wish to make an opening statement?"

That last was to Borger, who did in fact want to make an opening statement. He went to the lectern and looked about the mostly empty courtroom with a proprietary air. "Your honor. Ms. Starling. Ladies and gentlemen. We are here today in a case involving murder in the first degree. The victim was Dr. Brooks Prescott, a highly successful orthopedic surgeon whose skills and productive energy can never be replaced. The woman accused of committing this atrocity is one Alexa Demming. She is in sales." So disparaging was his tone that she might have been in the business of selling crack to school children. It took Borger ten minutes to get to the facts of the case, another twenty to tell us the facts he expected to prove.

He didn't notice or didn't care about the effect he was having on the judge, and I tried to imagine how he would be in front of a jury. As Borger continued to talk, Judge Cochran propped his head on one hand. Before Borger was done, he was bouncing a pencil off its eraser. Cochran was a young man, only a few years older than I was, and both his hair and his goatee were dark, without a hint of gray.

Borger said, "At the conclusion of this hearing, this court will have no choice but to certify the case to the grand jury for its consideration. I thank you for your courteous attention."

His chin still in his hand, Judge Cochran rolled his eyes toward me. I half-stood. "The defense waives its opening statement at this time, Your Honor."

"Very well." To Borger, Cochran said, "Call your first witness."

The hearing did not speed up. Jim Borger had a tendency to drag every possible detail out of each witness and belabor each one as if it were of critical importance. It was the middle of the afternoon before he called Detective Emma Michaels to the stand.

Emma Michaels had a degree in criminal justice from Virginia Commonwealth University. She had been on the force for sixteen years and had been in the homicide division for seven, during which time she had been responsible for fifty-some homicide investigations. Acting on a call from dispatch, she had arrived at the defendant's apartment shortly after four o'clock on the afternoon of Monday, May 8. Police officer Meghan Daniels was already on the scene, as were two paramedics. Dr. Birdsong from the Office of Chief Medical Examiner got there approximately five minutes after Detective Michaels did. The forensics unit showed up shortly after that, then, finally, the defendant.

"Let's go back to when you first arrived on the scene," Borger said. "You said, I believe, that the door of the apartment was standing open. Was it only partially open, or all the way?"

"All the way."

The neighbor, a Travis Grimes, had testified to finding it open only a few inches. Evidently, after looking in, he had left it open about a foot—at least, that was the way Officer Meghan Daniels had found it, according to her testimony. Perhaps this attention to extraneous detail was part of a grand strategy to bludgeon us into semiconsciousness, but I was beginning to hope it was just the way he operated, that he would be unable to adjust when we got to trial.

Borger asked Michaels to describe the position of the body, then used her to introduce a number of photographs of the crime scene into evidence, presenting each photograph first to me, then to the judge, and finally to the witness.

"It looks as though the top of the defendant's head was touching the floor on the side of the coffee table opposite the couch. Is that correct?"

It was. The police theory was that Prescott had spilled forward over the coffee table when struck from behind. Probably he's been seated on the couch.

"Could you describe for us the position of the forearms and elbows?"

Judge Cochran said, "Can't we see that from the pictures?"

Borger's head swung toward him. "Excuse me?"

"Are you trying to bring out something not obvious from the photographs? Perhaps the victim was trying to push off the floor? Is that what you're getting at?"

"No, Your Honor. We believe death to have been instantaneous, though we'll learn more about that when we hear from Dr. Birdsong, the forensic pathologist in this case."

"I'm sure we will." The judge's tone was dry, and Borger flushed, the color rising from his collar.

"Your Honor—"

"Mr. Borger, this hearing is preliminary, as the name might suggest. Its purpose is to establish whether there is probable cause to certify the case to the grand jury. Let's not make it more than it is."

"Very well." It occurred to me that, with his size, Jim Borger would look more impressive if he'd had a chin. He had one, of course, but it looked more like his adam's apple was set too close to his mouth in his fat neck.

He brought me yet another photograph, this one of the decedent lying on his back inside an open body bag. I nodded and handed it back to him. He took it to the judge and finally presented it to the witness, who identified it as yet another picture of the decedent that had been taken in her presence at the crime scene.

"Detective Michaels, I draw your attention to the smear of color on the front of the decedent's shirt. Could you tell us what that is?"

"Lipstick."

"Objection," I said, a shade too late to forestall the answer.

"Lipstick," Borger said. "Do you know whose lipstick?"

"Objection," I said again. "Hearsay. How does the witness know this was a smear of lipstick or whose lipstick it was? Was she the one who analyzed the substance on Dr. Prescott's shirt?"

"Were you?" Cochran asked.

Michaels hesitated. "No, Your Honor."

"Sustained."

Borger said, "So you can't tell us of your own knowledge whether this substance matched lipstick found in a drawer in the bathroom?"

"Objection," I said again. "The question is leading and constitutes misconduct and contempt of court, given the court's prior ruling."

"Sustained. Mr. Borger, as far as I'm concerned, the substance on the decedent's shirt was a bit of gravy, and I will continue to believe that until such time as you prove otherwise by competent evidence. Is that understood?"

"Yes, your honor."

"If a jury were present, I'd be holding you in contempt and fining you. Do you understand that?"

"I do, your honor."

Cochran held his gaze for maybe a dozen seconds. "Proceed," he said.

In a preliminary hearing, the prosecution generally puts on the minimum number of witnesses necessary to get the defendant bound over for trial. The defense works to expand the number of prosecution witnesses. In this case, I wanted a chance to cross-examine at least one of the technicians from the forensics unit.

Borger shuffled through his papers, finally opening a folder and taking out a document. He carried it to the judge.

"Your Honor, this is a certified copy of a domestic public record. A copy has previously been provided to counsel to afford her the opportunity to investigate its authenticity. I would like now to show it to the witness."

Judge Cochran looked at it, then gave it back to Borger, who took it to Michaels on the witness stand. "Detective Michaels, have you ever seen this document before? What is it?"

"It's a copy of a document filed with the Virginia Council on Human Rights, a claim of sexual harassment filed by the defendant Alexa Demming complaining about the conduct the decedent Brooks Prescott." The document was dated April 25, just under two weeks before Prescott's murder. Borger moved for admission.

The document was self-authenticating, and I didn't want to give Borger the chance to argue about how relevant it was. "No objection," I said.

Borger shuffled his notes. "Detective Michaels, what can you tell us about the keys found in the victim's pocket?"

"In his left pants pocket, we found a key ring with seven keys on it. One of the keys was for Dr. Prescott's car, a Lexus found there in the parking lot. Two of the keys were house keys; they fit door locks at the Prescott residence. One opened the outer door of the Spine & Joint Clinic where Dr. Prescott practiced medicine. One was a master key that opened all the interior doors at the clinic. One smaller key was for his desk."

"I think that's six keys," Borger said. "You said there were seven?"

"The sixth key opened the door of Alexa Demming's apartment."

"Ah," Borger said. It was good theatre, the best he'd managed so far. "I understand that the effects of a person other than the defendant were found in that apartment," he said. "Is that true?"

I stood, forestalling her answer. "I object to counsel's use of the passive voice, your honor."

"You're kidding," the judge said.

"Saying 'the effects were found' leaves out who it was who did the finding. If Detective Michaels isn't the one who found these effects, then this is another question that calls for hearsay."

Cochran's head rolled on his shoulders so that he was looking at Borger. "Rephrase the question, Mr. Borger. Active voice, please."

"Detective Michaels, did you personally find the effects of a person other than the defendant's in her apartment?"

"Yes, I did."

Both Borger and the judge looked at me, and I sat down, aware of Alexa's gaze. I gave her a slight tilt of my head, the hint of a shrug.

"What were these effects?" Borger asked.

Michaels enumerated them: slacks, shirts, a sports jacket, a gray suit.

"Now," Borger said. "There were two toothbrushes on the bathroom counter, were there not?"

"Objection," I said. "Leading." Leading questions—questions that suggested the answer—

were reserved for cross-examination and, occasionally, for witnesses who proved uncooperative.

"Sustained."

Borger asked the witness, "What was found on the bathroom counter?"

"Two toothbrushes," Michaels said, following where she'd been led.

"Are these the toothbrushes?" Borger held them up and, at a nod from the judge, took them to the witness, who turned each over in her hands before laying it on the rail.

"These are the toothbrushes we found," Michael said. "I scored the handle of each with an X-Acto knife. And, of course, I recognize them."

"Your Honor, I move to admit these toothbrushes into evidence."

I stood. "Could I look at the toothbrushes? I may have a couple of questions on voir dire."

Cochran made a face, then nodded, evidently resigned to the likelihood that the preliminary hearing was going to run to a second day. I looked at each of the toothbrushes and laid them back on the rail of the witness stand. Since Borger was still at the lectern and showed no sign of giving way, I just took a step back from the witness box to ask my questions.

"Detective Michaels," I said. "Are you sure both of those toothbrushes were on the counter, that neither was in a drawer?"

"Of course I'm sure."

"You didn't dig one of them out of the trash."

"I did not," she said.

"One shows a lot of wear, doesn't it? Bristles splayed out, dried toothpaste on the handle and at the base of the bristles. Does that describe it pretty well?"

"I suppose so."

"In comparison, the other one looks new. Pick it up and look at it. Can you tell it's ever been used?"

"I think so. There is a spot of toothpaste on the handle."

I'd missed it. "Was the package that toothbrush came in anywhere in the apartment?"

"Not that we found, no."

"Was either toothbrush tested for the presence of DNA?"

"No."

"Fingerprints?"

"Objection," Borger said. "Calls for hearsay."

"Does it?" I asked her. "I'm not asking whether any fingerprints were found, just whether the police tried to find any. You're the detective in charge of the case. That's not something you would know of your own knowledge?"

"We looked for fingerprints. Of course we did."

"Did you find any on either of the toothbrushes?"

"I'll renew my objection," Borger rumbled.

I said to Michaels, "Mr. Borger's objections suggest you had a limited role in this investigation. You didn't supervise the checking for fingerprints?"

"I did."

"I repeat my question. Were prints found on either of the toothbrushes?"

"They were."

"Did you yourself examine the fingerprints and observe points of identification between those prints and the prints of the defendant or some other person?"

"I didn't do the fingerprint analysis," she said. "No."

She'd phrased that carefully, I thought. "You didn't observe it done?" I asked. "You didn't look at the results of the analysis and see the points of comparison that had been marked?"

She looked at Borger.

"I'm asking you, Detective Michaels. The truth is, you've gone over this aspect of your testimony with the prosecution, haven't you?"

"I'm a prosecution witness. Of course we've gone over my testimony."

"Did the prosecution tell you of its intent not to call anyone from the forensics unit to testify about fingerprints found in the apartment?"

"Objection," Borger said. "Relevance."

"The question goes to the bias of the witness, Your Honor," I said.

"Objection overruled."

Michaels's tongue had appeared between her lips. "Yes."

"So if you can avoid testifying about the fingerprints, the defense will be denied the opportunity to cross-examine on that point at this preliminary hearing."

"Objection," Borger said. "Not a question."

"Sustained," Cochran said.

"Tell us about the fingerprints on the toothbrushes, Detective," I said. "Anything you know of your own knowledge."

She took a breath. "The only fingerprints on either toothbrush were the prints of the defendant, Alexa Demming. On the worn toothbrush here was a thumbprint and partials of three of the fingers on her right hand. On the newer toothbrush the only print was from her index finger."

"So what you found were the prints of the woman who lived in the apartment. Wouldn't it be fair to say her fingerprints were all over the apartment?"

Borger interrupted. "As much as I hate to keep interposing my unwelcome objections, at this point in the trial counsel is limited to voir dire on the admissibility of the toothbrushes."

"Sustained."

I gave the judge a short nod and headed back toward the defense table as Borger acknowledged his victory with a facial spasm that might have been intended as a smile. "Once again, I move that the toothbrushes be admitted into evidence," he said.

I turned, just short of my table. "I object on the grounds of relevance," I said. "The defendant had two toothbrushes on her counter showing very different degrees of wear. So what?"

"In combination with the key in the victim's pocket and with other evidence, the toothbrushes suggest someone other than the defendant was living in that apartment—that Dr. Prescott was living there. The evidence is cumulative, your honor. It all adds up to one thing."

"If the defendant had two extra-large T-shirts lying at the foot of her bed, both of them smelling of her deodorant, would you add that to the total? Would you argue that the man who must have used one of the toothbrushes with her fingerprints must also have worn one of the T-shirts with her deodorant? Evidence that doesn't mean anything by itself doesn't mean anything in combination with other meaningless evidence."

The judge took some time to think about it. "I'm going to admit the toothbrushes," he said. "You've convinced me that the probative value is slight, but that goes to the weight of the evidence, not its admissibility."

I'm not sure Borger could have looked any more smug if he'd wrapped his arms around himself for a big bear hug. Alexa bumped my elbow with her head, and I sat down and leaned toward her.

"No one was living with me," she said.

"Where did Dr. Prescott get the key to your apartment?"

"I have no idea. I didn't give it to him."

"The toothbrushes?"

"Both mine. I think I'd just got out a new one a day or two before all this happened."

"Would you have thrown the old toothbrush in the trash?"

"I think so. The silver trashcan there in the bathroom."

Borger was working with the court clerk to get a clothes rack wheeled into the courtroom. Hanging on it were slacks and shirts and a couple of jackets, one of which seemed to match one of the pairs of slacks.

"Have you ever seen these clothes before?" Borger asked the Detective Michaels.

She had. They were the men's clothes found in the defendant's closet.

"Is there any connection between these clothes and the murder victim in this case, Brooks Prescott?"

"The clothes were the same size as the ones he had on."

His using Detective Michaels to identify the clothes told me Borger did not plan to give me a crack at Toni Prescott in the preliminary. "Move for admission," he said.

I stood. "A few questions on voir dire?

The judge inclined his head.

"Detective Michaels. What sizes were these clothes found in the apartment? What size was the suit, for example?"

"Forty-two Long."

"The shirts?"

"Sixteen-inch neck, thirty-four-inch sleeve."

"The slacks?"

"Thirty-four thirty-two."

"Thirty-four-inch waist, thirty-two-inch inseam?"

"That's right."

"Your testimony suggests you relied only on these clothes sizes to connect these items to the decedent, is that right?"

"No. The widow identified them."

I looked at the judge. "That last bit was hearsay. I move to strike it."

Cochran said to the court reporter, "Strike all of the witness's answer after the word *no*."

"Do you plan to call Toni Prescott?" I asked Borger.

"I do not."

To the witness I said, "How many trials have you testified in?"

"Perhaps a dozen, a few more."

"So you knew you were volunteering hearsay evidence."

"I was answering your question."

"Was the form of your answer one you had discussed with Mr. Borger?"

Borger objected. Judge Cochran overruled him.

"Answer the question, Detective," I said.

She asked me to repeat it, and I got the court reporter to read it from his Stenograph: "Was the form of your answer one you had discussed with Mr. Borger?"

"Yes," Michaels said. She didn't look at Borger.

"Were these clothes here on the rack all the men's clothes found in the apartment?"

"Yes."

"No socks, no underwear, no ties to go with the suit and sports jacket, no belt?"

"No. None of those things."

"Just what we see here," I said.

"Yes."

"Did you have the garments tested for the presence of DNA?"

"No. We didn't."

"Was there any dandruff on the shoulders of the suits, any loose hairs anywhere on the clothing?"

"Not that we observed."

"Nothing to tie these clothes specifically to Dr. Brooks Prescott."

"Not that I can testify to of my own knowledge."

I looked to the bench. "Your Honor, I object to the admission of these clothes. No connection has been established between them and the decedent. The clothes would fit thousands of men in this city."

"Thousands of men with a connection to this case?" Cochran asked me.

"They might well fit Your Honor."

The hint of a smile lifted a corner of his mouth.

"Your Honor," Borger said. "That's absurd."

"Is it?" I asked. "If these clothes fit the judge, then the clothes and the toothbrush connect His Honor to that apartment just as strongly as they connect Brooks Prescott."

"His Honor wasn't found murdered in that apartment. Her key isn't in his pocket."

"But if he had been found there, and the murderer had taken the time to slip the key he'd used onto His Honor's key ring, you would use these same items to suggest he'd been having an affair with Alexa Demming," I said.

"That's enough." The judge's face had lost any hint of a smile. "Again, you've made your point about the probative value of the clothes, at least with the present testimony. I am nevertheless going to admit them as part of the res gestae." *Res gestae* refers to the circumstances surrounding the crime. How much of it to let in was entirely up to the discretion of the judge.

I nodded my acceptance of the ruling and sat. Borger continued with his questions. By the time he finished with Detective Michaels, it was late in the afternoon.

"I assume your cross-examination will be extensive?" Judge Cochran said to me as Borger gathered his folders and legal pads at the lectern.

"Maybe not," I said.

"Any chance you can finish with it in the next thirty minutes?" The time was four forty.

"Every chance, Your Honor."

"Very well," he said.

Chapter 7

I went to the lectern empty handed. It was, I thought, good theatre on those occasions when I thought I could do without my notes and my lists of questions. "Detective Michaels. Your theory of the case seems to be that Dr. Prescott let himself into Alexa's apartment. Is that right?" At this point, I was no longer limited to questions about the toothbrushes or the clothes. On cross-examination, I could ask about any topic that was raised on direct, which opened up everything relating to the apartment and the presence there of Brooks Prescott.

"He could have let himself in," she said. "As I've testified, he had the key. Or the defendant could have admitted him herself."

"How did Dr. Prescott get there?" I asked. "You testified that his Lexus was in the parking lot?"

"Yes, an LS 460."

"So you believe he drove himself there to Alexa's apartment?" I said.

"That is our working assumption."

"Was the car locked or unlocked?"

"Locked."

"Were any of Alexa's fingerprints found in the car?"

She glanced at Borger as he got to his feet. Again he objected to the introduction of hearsay evidence.

"I do think you need to establish the source of her knowledge," Cochran told me.

I tried a different tack. "You have no clue whose fingerprints were in the car, do you?" I said to Michaels. "No clue whose fingerprints were in the car, no clue whose fingerprints were in the apartment. People told you this person's were there or that person's, but you didn't look at the prints. Nobody pointed out to you the points of comparison. They didn't bother, because you don't know anything about fingerprint analysis."

"That's not true."

"Come on, Detective. It's evident from your testimony, from what you're able to testify about and what you aren't. The truth is, you wouldn't know a fingerprint from a blueprint. Isn't that right?"

Her lips had all but disappeared. "I've had training in fingerprint analysis," she said, clipping her words.

"Then why the complete lack of interest in the fingerprints found in this case?"

"I never said I wasn't interested."

"You didn't look at the prints," I said.

"I did look at them."

"You didn't compare the fingerprints of anyone connected with this case to the fingerprints found at the crime scene. Isn't that true?"

Her gaze flickered in Borger's direction, then came back to me. "I didn't do the initial analysis."

"And you didn't bother to look at the analysis after it was completed," I said.

"You don't have any basis for that statement. Of course I looked at the analysis."

I looked at the judge. "I think I've established personal knowledge," I said.

He nodded. "I'll overrule the objection."

I looked at Michaels. "Were Alexa's fingerprints found in the decedent's car?"

"No," she said.

"No prints at all? So your theory is that he was living in her apartment, but she had never been in his car?"

"She did not leave fingerprints in his car."

"Did she leave fingerprints anywhere—in her own apartment, for example?"

"She did," Michaels said. "Numerous prints, as you would expect."

"On her bathroom counter?"

"Yes. The bathroom counter, the kitchen counter, pretty much everywhere."

"The nightstand, the clock, the coffee table, the TV remote, various lamps . . ."

"Yes. All those places—as well as the lamp with Dr. Prescott's blood and hair on it."

Touché. "Would it be fair to say that Prescott's fingerprints were all over the apartment as well?"

"His prints were found in multiple locations."

"But you're not willing to say they were all over."

"No."

There'd been an instant's hesitation before her one-word denial. When she didn't elaborate, I said, "Can you tell us where exactly his prints were found?"

She took a breath, then pulled out her notes and began to shuffle through them. I didn't know whether she referred to her notes in an abundance of caution or to give Borger time to think of an objection. He didn't interpose one, wonder of wonders, and she looked up. "There was a handprint on the coffee table, with the prints of the four fingers of his left hand clearly definable," she said. "There were also prints on a glass in the sink and on a pair of sunglasses on the nightstand."

I waited. When she didn't continue, I said, "That's it?"

"That's what we found."

"Not many prints if the man was living there."

"I wouldn't know."

"You told us you'd investigated how many crime scenes? More than fifty?"

"Yes."

"But you can't say that it's unusual for a man who's been a regular visitor to an apartment, who may even have been living there, to have left his fingerprints in only three places?"

"Okay, it's unusual."

"Have you ever seen it before in your experience?"

"No."

Aubrey had been right. When Emma caved, she caved.

"What was orientation of the handprint on the coffee table? Was the heel of the hand toward the couch or away from it?"

"It was toward the couch."

"So it might have been formed when Prescott fell forward over the coffee table," I said. "Is that right?"

"It's a possibility."

"So that's one set of prints that might not have been there before the moment when he was struck with the table lamp," I said. "True?"

"It might be."

"And the glass and the sunglasses were portable. They might have come into the apartment with his fingerprints already on them. Isn't that a possibility?"

"The glass matched five other glasses in the apartment, four of which were still in the cabinet."

"So two of the glasses were not in the cabinet. Where were they?"

"In the sink. One of them had Dr. Prescott's fingerprints, as I said. The other had the defendant's. The second glass also had what looked like lipstick on the rim."

"Earlier you testified that there was a smear of something that looked like lipstick on the decedent's shirt," I said, and she glanced at Borger. "Did you get a lip print off the shirt?" I asked.

"As I've said before, I didn't analyze the substance on the shirt."

"And evidently didn't examine the analysis that was done," I said.

She didn't fall for my needling a second time. "I read the analysis, of course," she said, "but it's not my field. I can't tell you anything of my own knowledge."

"And you don't know of your own knowledge whether anyone tried to discern a lip print."

"Of course we tried."

"But failed? Was the lipstick or whatever it was on the shirt too smeared to discern a print?"

She seemed to be thinking about it.

"Come on, Detective. Surely you yourself looked at a close-up of whatever it was that was on that shirt."

"There was no discernible lip print," she said.

"Thank you." I looked at the judge. "I'm sorry this is taking longer than expected, Your Honor. I didn't know it was going to be like pulling teeth."

Detective Michaels flushed, and Borger came to his feet to object to my badgering the witness, my flagrant misconduct, and my general lack of decorum.

"Confine yourself to questions, Ms. Starling," Judge Cochran told me. "Leave off the commentary."

"Yes, Your Honor. Detective Michaels, this substance on the shirt—could it have been applied to the shirt with a finger?"

"It could have been."

"Could it have been applied directly with something like a lipstick tube?"

"Maybe. I don't know."

"Did you try using your finger to rub a bit of the lipstick you found in the bathroom on the shirt, just to see what it looked like?"

"No, and I didn't kiss the shirt either."

I smiled and let her answer hang in the air for a few seconds. "Did you get a lip print off the glass?" I asked.

"We did get a lip print off the glass."

I didn't ask her whose the lip print was. "Were Dr. Prescott's fingerprints on that glass?"

"Not the glass with the lipstick, no."

"The lipstick or whatever it was," I said.

"Or whatever it was."

"And the only prints found on the glass without the lipstick were Dr. Prescott's."

"That's right."

"Were you able to get his lip prints off the glass?"

"Dr. Prescott wasn't wearing lipstick."

The judge smiled, and someone in the gallery laughed, but my gaze stayed on Detective Michael's face. After several seconds, she added, "We didn't get his lip prints off the glass."

"Did you try? Did you find the smear of a lip print on the rim of the glass? Anything to show he'd been drinking from it?"

"We found his fingerprints, like I said."

"What was in the glass?"

"About a half-inch of water, traces of red wine."

"Were the two glasses all that was in the sink?"

They were.

"Were these water glasses, juice glasses . . ."

"Wine glasses. Stemware."

"Wine in both of glasses?"

"Yes. Traces of it."

"Where was the open bottle? On the counter, in the trash?"

She shifted in her chair. "We didn't find an open bottle."

"Maybe the fridge?" I suggested.

"No."

"Where was the kitchen trash? Under the sink, in the corner . . ."

"There was a trash can in the cabinet under the sink, but there was no trash in it."

"A new trash bag?"

"No trash bag at all."

"So your theory is that Alexa Demming killed Brooks Prescott in her apartment and then took out the trash," I said.

"We don't have a theory on that, unless she was removing evidence."

I didn't either. I asked Michaels, "Were anyone else's fingerprints found in the apartment, anyone other than Brooks Prescott's and Alexa Demming's?"

"There were fingerprints we couldn't identify, yes."

"Did any prints belong to Taylor Grimes, the neighbor who found the body and called the police?"

"We didn't take his prints."

"You didn't take his prints." When she didn't say anything to my non-question—a pretty damning non-question, I thought—I asked, "What size suit does this neighbor wear? Could it be a 42 Long?"

"I don't know."

"We've seen him here in this courtroom. He's about the same size and weight as Brooks Prescott, isn't he?"

"I don't know. Approximately."

"Did you know that Nick Cantwell, the lieutenant governor of this state, wears a 42 Long?" I didn't know that was true, but I'd seen him and thought he might wear a 42 Long.

Michaels's mouth opened, but Borger lurched to his feet, his heavy table sliding several inches on the industrial carpet and several pages falling to the floor. "Objection! That question is irrelevant, Your Honor, irrelevant and inflammatory. It is an attempt to smear the reputation of a public servant who has no connection to this case."

"Sustained. You haven't laid any kind of foundation for that question, Counselor. Do you intend to?"

"One more question, Your Honor." Turning back to Emma Michaels, I said, "Did you compare any of the unidentified fingerprints in that apartment to the fingerprints of Nick Cantwell?"

"Your Honor!" Borger thundered. "There is no way the witness can answer that question, and asking it is flagrant misconduct. If the prints haven't been identified, they haven't been identified. To ask if they could have belonged to this person or that person with no connection to the case is inflammatory and, more than that . . ."

"Sustained," the judge said loudly, speaking over him. "Ms. Starling, that line of questioning is over."

"Those are all the questions I have. Thank you."

Judge Cochran's jaw was clenched. As he picked up his gavel, I started back to my seat. Borger, still on his feet, was breathing heavily. He held up a hand. "Wait." He took several more breaths, his eyes moving jerkily as his brain recalibrated. "If I could ask just a few questions on redirect, we can be through with this witness."

The judge looked at the clock, which showed the time at five twenty-five.

Borger continued, "Detective Michaels has other cases she's working on. If we can avoid calling her back for another day in court . . ."

The judge took a deep breath and let it out. He put down the gavel, and Borger went to the lectern.

"Detective Michaels. You have no reason to connect the lieutenant governor to this case in any way, do you?"

The question was leading, but I let it go.

"I do not," Michaels said.

"His name has not come up during the course of the investigation. No one has mentioned him or his office. There's no more reason to connect him to this case than the President of the United States or the governor of Hawaii. Is that correct?"

"That's correct. I don't know anything about the lieutenant governor."

Borger turned his head toward me. He still hadn't caught his breath. "Your Honor, may I?" He gestured toward his table and, at a nod from the judge, went to retrieve a legal pad.

Back at the lectern, he said, "Having disposed of the complete irrelevancy that has been dragged into the case, let me ask you this: Did you personally take the lip print of the defendant Alexa Demming?"

"No. I was present when the lip print was taken, though."

"Did you yourself compare the defendant's lip print to the lip print found on the glass in the sink?"

"Yes. I did so working with Tara Clausen in the forensics unit."

"So you can testify of your own personal knowledge to the results of the comparison?"

"Yes."

"Did the prints match?"

"They did."

"No further questions."

I stood, and Judge Cochran eyed me.

"Two questions," I said. "Both related to the lip print."

The silence stretched to the count of two before the judge sat back, flipping his hand toward the witness.

"Detective Michaels," I said. "How many points of identification are required to establish a match between two sets of lip prints?"

She hesitated. "I don't know."

"How many points of identification were found between these two sets of lip prints?"

Again she hesitated.

"Go head, refresh your memory from your notes if you need to."

"It's not in my notes."

"So you don't know how many points of comparison there were."

"No," she said.

I deadpanned Borger. It was beneath me to look smug.

Chapter 8

"So. Are you going to win this case at the preliminary?" Paul asked. He hadn't made it to the courthouse that day, nor had Mike or Brooke, who had joined us at Enrique's It was our favorite restaurant, but one we hadn't been to since I got out of the hospital—out of the hospital the last time, I should say. Criminal defense work was occasionally more dangerous than you'd expect, even for someone with my winsome personality.

"No, I'm not going to win at the preliminary," I said. "Criminal defendants always get bound over."

They all eyed me. Twice I'd managed to win at the preliminary, which I guess shows that lightening can strike twice in the same place, but I knew I could go the rest of my career without managing it again.

"So, was Prescott sleeping with Alexa, or wasn't he?" Mike said.

"She says he wasn't."

"She also says Brooks Prescott was harassing her," Mike said.

"Yeah, that bothers me."

"Because you don't think he was harassing her."

"No, I need to press her on that. Still, based on what I've seen so far, I'd swear the day he died was the first time Brooks Prescott had ever been in her apartment." I told them about the limited number of places in the apartment Brooks had left fingerprints, about the absence of anything of his other than some hanging clothes that might have come straight from his home closet. As I talked, I sipped my margarita. As a general rule, I find it annoying to go back over a long day in court. As a general rule, though, I'm not sipping a margarita.

"There weren't plastic bags on the clothes, were there?" Paul asked.

"No, but that's a good point. They might have come from the dry cleaners."

"Overall, it sounds like you did a good job today," Mike said.

"That's Robin Starling you're talking to," Brooke said.

Actually, there was one aspect of my performance I wasn't happy with: dragging Nick Cantwell's name into the case with no more justification than having once seen him speak to Toni Prescott through a car window. I didn't told them about that. Margarita or no, I wasn't in the mood for a critical analysis of what had been an impulsive decision.

Paul said to me, "If you're right, it means somebody wanted it to look like Alexa and Brooks Prescott were having an affair, that they had more of a connection than him dying in her apartment."

"Sure," I said. "It keeps everyone's attention focused on Alexa."

"And this somebody didn't do a particularly good job of it."

"May have done the best he could with what he had to work with," I said.

"He?" Brooke asked.

"Or she. I'm not particular."

"It shows the danger of coming to conclusions too early," Mike said. "At first glance, it looked like Prescott was spending a good deal of time in that apartment, so the police looked for confirming evidence and ignored any incongruities."

"Does it matter though?" Paul asked. "Nothing changes the fact that Prescott was there—unless he was killed somewhere else and then moved."

"It doesn't seem likely," I said, "but I'll learn more about that tomorrow. The M.E. is on the witness list."

The food came. Brooke and I were sharing the fajita special, which included, on the side, four large, barbecued shrimp. Sounds weird, but the combination worked—at least, I thought it did.

We were pretty much finished, and I was savoring the last few nibbles of my second shrimp, when Brooke said, "In a month, my name's going to be Brooke McMillan. How about you, are you going to change your name?"

It was Paul who answered. "Yes," he said. "Yes, I am."

"You're going to change your name from Paul Soldano to Paul Starling," I said.

"Why not? It has a ring to it. I won't even have to change my initials."

"Robin Soldano wouldn't have to change hers either," I said.

"You're Robin Starling. You can't be anything else," Paul said.

"Well, you can't very well be Paul Starling. Everyone would think you were . . ." I hesitated, looking for a diplomatic way to make my point.

"Exactly," Paul said with such evident satisfaction that I wondered how he thought I'd been going to end that sentence.

"You are not going to change your name," I said.

"Okay, you talked me out of it—as long as you don't change yours."

"If we married, we need to have the same name."

"Too late. If you're Robin Soldano, I'm Paul Starling."

"Okay, so we keep our own names," I said.

The matter was resolved, but it only stayed that way for about five seconds.

"What name will your children have?" Brooke asked.

Paul and I looked at her.

"It's something to think about," she said.

It was. I looked morosely into my now-empty margarita glass.

"Also, how many children do you plan to have? Have you even talked about it?"

I had a vision of trying to walk through the house with Johnny Starling-Soldano clinging to one leg and my belly bulging with his little brother. I pushed back from the table. "And so ends another relaxing evening," I said.

The next day, when I walked across the street to drop off Deeks, Dr. McDermott invited me in.

"You look better," I observed.

"I am better. Still low on energy."

"I won't tire you. I've got court at nine-thirty."

He raised a bony forearm to look at his watch, and I felt a pang on seeing it. Had he always been that thin? "It's only eight," he said. "You've got time for breakfast."

"I had a cup of yogurt."

"Yes, but did you have bacon and eggs and whole wheat toast?" He smiled, turning his head and looking at me out of the corner of his eye.

"Well, no," I said.

"It just so happens that I have an extra plate of bacon and eggs and whole wheat toast in the kitchen. Everything's still warm."

He looked so hopeful—and so pitiful with the tuft of hair on the top of his head sticking straight up—that I couldn't bear to disappoint him. "That sounds wonderful," I said.

Deeks, when he realized I was coming in and not just dropping him off, seemed to take on new life. He circled me twice as I went into the kitchen, and I had to watch to keep from stepping on his paws.

Two places were already set, a newspaper folded open next to the nearest plate. Dr. McDermott went to the stove.

"You seem to have timed this perfectly," I said.

"Yes, yes. Take a look at the paper."

I sat, stroking Deeks's head as I glanced at the paper. Nick Cantwell's picture caught my eye. The headline of the accompanying article was "Lawyer Connects Cantwell to Murdered Doctor."

"Uh oh," I said.

Dr. McDermott was watching me obliquely.

In her cross-examination of Richmond Police Detective Emma Michaels late Wednesday, attorney Robin Starling tried to connect Nick Cantwell, Virginia's lieutenant governor, with the scene of a brutal murder earlier this month. The questioning occurred at the preliminary hearing of Alexa Demming, who has been charged with the first-degree murder of Dr. Brooks Prescott, a prominent Richmond physician. Prescott was found dead in Demming's apartment, the victim of blunt force trauma to the head.

After Michaels testified as to the sizes of the clothing found in the defendant's apartment, Starling asked Michaels whether Lieutenant Governor Cantwell wore a 42 Long, the size of the suit and sports jacket found in the apartment.. She went on to ask whether any of the unidentified fingerprints found in the apartment belonged to

Cantwell, but after District Judge Timothy Cochran sustained objections by Commonwealth's Attorney Jim Borger, Michaels was not required to answer either question. Starling has been unavailable for comment.

Dr. McDermott had stopped halfway to the table, a spatula in one hand and a frying pan in the other. "I hope you like scrambled," he said when I looked up.

My gaze went back to the newspaper sitting harmlessly by my plate. "Evidently I do," I said.

He put eggs on my plate. "Your first foray into politics, I believe."

"Such as it is," I said.

"I didn't even know you were a Democrat."

"I'm apolitical."

Dr. McDermott laid two strips of bacon on my plate. Toast popped up in the toaster on the counter. He said, "I'm anti-political myself. I get tired of politicians and bureaucrats calling themselves public servants when they make more money than their private sector counterparts, have better health insurance, have the only defined benefit pension plans in existence, and spend their working lives making rules for the rest of us to live by."

"When you put it that way," I said, reaching for a piece of bacon.

"Of course, I can't say I have anything against Cantwell personally," Dr. McDermott said. When I didn't say anything, he added, "I guess you have evidence the police don't."

I chewed my bacon.

"You do have evidence the police don't, don't you?"

"Really, I was just stirring things with a stick to see if anything floated to the surface."

He put a plate of toast between us and took a seat. "Don't you worry about being sued for slander?"

"That's the least of my worries," I said. "Lawyers can't be sued for false, damaging statements made in a judicial proceeding. It's an absolute privilege."

"I see. Maybe I should add lawyers to my list of people to resent."

"Sure," I said. "More people who make rules that don't apply to them. What's not to resent?" I gave him a big smile, then picked up my fork and speared a chunk of egg.

I parked in the parking lot behind the courthouse. A storm seemed to be coming. The cloud cover was low, and as I was getting my briefcase from behind my seat, a balled-up sandwich wrapper bounced over my foot and went under the car. My hair was in a ponytail, so the wind couldn't do much to it other than flap it in all directions, but the wind was playing heck with my dress. It got away from me completely once, and I didn't notice the two men getting out of the Ford Explorer until police detectives James Jordan and Ray Hernandez fell into step on either side of me.

"Want me to take your briefcase?" Hernandez said. "If you used both hands, you might be able to keep your skirt down."

"I'd hate to cheat my audience."

"Don't worry. We already got our money's worth." He took my briefcase.

"There we have it," Jordan said. "Proof positive that Ray Hernandez is man enough to carry Starling's briefcase."

"How many people can say that?" I said.

"Actually, helping you with your briefcase is only part of why we're here. We're interested in what you have on Nick Cantwell."

"Why? This isn't your case." With one hand pressed to each thigh, I was finding it easier to keep my dress under control.

"We're on our own time here," Hernandez said.

"So what do you have against Cantwell? You on the opposite side of the political fence?"

"You betcha," Hernandez said.

"So you're Democrats," I said.

"Free citizens," Jordan said.

"We hate politicians on both sides of the aisle," Hernandez said.

"I'd expect you to be on their side. Aren't all of you public servants?"

"Now that's just ugly talk," Jordan said.

"Some of us public servants actually work for the public," Hernandez said.

"Police and fire-fighters, for example," I said.

132

"For example," Jordan said. "Politicians, on the other hand . . ."

"Politicians are mostly parasites," Hernandez said. "If a big-time politician has murdered a man and framed a private citizen . . ."

" . . . even if that citizen is the sister of another politician," Jordan said.

" . . . that's something that interests us," Hernandez finished. "Besides, your client is a pretty young woman with really nice legs. We can't blame her for Aubrey Biggs."

We'd slowed our steps as we neared the courthouse, and now I stood facing the two cops, still holding my dress with both hands as the wind whipped my hair. "You men have your own perspective on the world, don't you? I sometimes wonder how you manage to talk without oinking."

Hernandez grinned, unabashed. "We can't always," he said cheerfully.

"You get any leads a couple of experienced police detectives can run down, you let us know," Jordan said.

"Actually," I said. "All I suspect Cantwell of at this point is having an affair with the Dr. Prescott's wife."

"That could lead to something," Hernandez said.

"Three days after the murder, she was picking him up on Ninth Street outside his office."

"And?" Jordan prompted.

"That's it—that and the feeling that something was going on there."

Hernandez and Jordan exchanged a look, and Hernandez nodded. "It's a start," he said.

"Okay. We'll play with it, see if anything develops," Jordan said.

"You never know." Hernandez handed me back my briefcase.

"So what are you going to do?" I asked, holding the briefcase and clutching the dress with my free hand.

"Stand right here and watch you carry that briefcase into the courthouse. Jordan here is a big fan of pink panties."

I rolled my eyes. My panties weren't pink today; they were red-and-white striped. Maybe they looked pink from a distance. "Knock yourselves out," I said.

The gallery was more crowded than it had been the previous day, or maybe I was just running late. Aubrey and his parents were already in position near the defense table. Dr. Prescott's parents were on the other side of the gallery, two rows back from Borger's table. I wondered how many of the other people present were media.

I stopped in the aisle beside the row where Paul was sitting with Brooke and Mike, and Paul gave me a reproachful look.

"You don't tell us anything," he said.

"I thought you had to work today."

"I did, but when I heard about your hatchet job on . . ." He glanced around us, mouthed, *Nick Cantwell,* then finished in normal tones: "I went home sick. Sort of."

I leaned over him. "How did you hear about Cantwell? You don't get the paper."

"When you're engaged to someone, people mention things."

"I heard it from Rodney Burns," Brooke said.

"And Brooke was already on the phone with me when Paul called," Mike said. "I got it from two sources."

I became aware that everybody within a couple of yards seemed to be sitting a bit too casually, no one looking in our direction, but their ears standing out from their heads an extra millimeter or so.

"Talk later," I said.

I pushed through the rail and put my briefcase on my table. Alexa, already seated, gave me a smile that looked more like an expression of distaste. I looked back at Aubrey and his parents. Aubrey was looking at me as if I were a piece of abstract art, which was hardly fair. When court recessed the previous afternoon, he'd asked me what I had on Cantwell. I told him nothing definitive, and he'd seemed to accept that. Possibly, he'd had time to reflect.

I smiled and nodded at him and his parents to let them know everything was under control.

Jim Borger's first witness of the day was the pathologist who had examined Prescott's body at the scene and later performed the autopsy. Borger spent thirty minutes asking questions about Dr. Birdsong's medical training, his residency, his experience working for the Office of Chief Medical Examiner, and his work experience before that. It was important to establish Birdsong's credentials as an expert so he could offer opinion testimony, and Borger's motto seemed to be, "There's nothing worth doing that's not worth overdoing." Finally, he got around to the cause of death—blunt force trauma to the head, in Birdsong's expert opinion—and the time of death, which was sometime between 11:52 a.m. and 1:52 a.m. on Monday, May 8.

That two-hour window was, from my perspective, the worst possible time for Brooks Prescott to have died. The last of the three sales calls Alexa had made that morning had ended a little before noon, no more than fifteen minutes' drive from her apartment. Her only afternoon appointment had been for three-thirty, and she'd been fifteen minutes late for it. Rodney Burns had managed to find no one to confirm what Alexa had been doing between 11:55 and 3:45, not at the restaurant, not at Myrna's Boots 'N' Bits, not at Macy's.

When it was my turn to ask questions, I asked Dr. Birdsong about the two-hour time window he had given for the time of death.

"I first examined the body at 5:22," he said. "At that time, I judged that the decedent had been dead four-and-a-half hours, give or take an hour."

"And you base that judgment primarily on the temperature of the body?"

"I do. The temperature of the body was 92.8 degrees Fahrenheit. The apartment where it was found was 72 degrees. Assuming that the ambient temperature had not changed over the relevant time period, we would expect the body to lose heat at the rate of approximately one-point-five degrees per hour. It sounds like the heat loss is linear, but it's not, quite. In actual practice we use a formula that involves logarithms." His brief smile seemed to apologize for being such a pointy-headed geek. "The formula's proven to be quite accurate if the temperature of the body is taken within eight hours of death, so it's very likely that the decedent had been dead between four and five hours at the time I examined him. I've given a larger window only because we do have the occasional outlier."

"But you really think the time of death was between 12:22 and 1:22," I said.

"Yes."

"What did you assume was the body's baseline temperature?"

"Ninety-nine point-five."

"Not 98.6?"

"That's a normal oral temperature. In this case, I inserted the thermometer into the liver, where the normal temperature is slightly higher."

"And death was instantaneous, you say."

"Virtually instantaneous," he said, nodding.

"Was the decedent standing or sitting when the fatal blow was struck?"

"I can't say."

"Is it possible that he tried to catch himself on the coffee table as he fell forward?"

"That might have been an involuntary response, yes."

"Is it possible that he wasn't killed in that apartment at all, that the body was moved after death?"

"It seems unlikely. A small pool of blood had accumulated beneath the head, so I would say the body was in the position we found it almost from the moment of the blow was struck. The tears in the skin were not large, and, after the first second or so, the heart wasn't pumping to move the blood. The few ounces of blood we found would have taken some time to drain out, and that time would have had to be immediately after death."

"I assume you checked to make sure it was the decedent's blood under the head."

He smiled and gave a small nod. "We did."

"Of course, some of the evidence on where he was killed would be outside your purview: whether the apparent murder weapon belonged there at the apartment, for instance."

He nodded. "Yes."

"Any blood spatter the forensics unit might have documented," I suggested.

"Of course."

"Was there blood spatter?"

"None that was visible to casual inspection."

"Was your inspection casual, Doctor?"

"I didn't use any chemicals to bring out minute droplets or any residue that might have remained if someone had wiped up a patch of visible blood."

"This pool of blood near the head is the primary reason you think the body wasn't moved?" I said.

"Yes, but not the only reason. As I told Mr. Borger, rigor mortis and livor mortis were both well advanced but not complete. Neither gave any evidence of the body having been moved."

Dr. Birdsong was no help at all. "Thank you, Doctor," I said.

Dr. Birdsong turned out to be Borger's last witness. There was no advantage to Borger of showing more of his evidence than necessary to get Alexa bound over for trial, though, given his ponderous presentation of the evidence he had presented, I'd been hoping he would overdo it.

Borger's closing statement began with him patting his chest and abdomen with apparent affection, though perhaps he was just smoothing his jacket. "Your honor. Counsel." He gave a paternalistic nod in my direction. "I think it's pretty clear what happened here. The defendant Alexa Demming was infatuated with Dr. Brooks Prescott. How that developed, just who pursued whom, just when things began to go sour—these are all things that will be developed at trial. For purposes of this hearing, where the prosecution is tasked only with showing probable cause, it is unnecessary.

"First, we must show reasonable grounds to believe a crime has been committed, and we have done that. Dr. Brooks Prescott died as the result of blunt force trauma to the head. The evidence shows that he was struck with the heavy square base of a table lamp, a lamp to which blood and several of the decedent's hairs adhered. It is unlikely, it is virtually inconceivable, that the head trauma occurred by accident.

"Second, we must show reasonable grounds to believe that the defendant, Alexa Demming, committed this crime. We have done that as well. There is perhaps some question about the depth and the significance of the relationship between the defendant and her victim, but that is here unimportant. Dr. Prescott died in her apartment, struck with her table lamp at some point during a two-hour window in which her activities are unaccounted for. Her fingerprints alone are on the murder weapon. There is no indication that any other person was in the apartment on that occasion.

"Moreover, this would not be the first aggressive action of the accused against Dr. Prescott. She filed a claim of sexual harassment against him with the Virginia Council on Human Rights. Whether or not the claim was justified is unimportant, whether the claim was in response to inappropriate behavior on his part, whether it was filed to punish him for some misbehavior in the relationship, or whether it was manufactured out of whole-cloth—none of that matters. What matters is that there was conflict in the relationship between Alexa Demming and Brooks Prescott. The harassment claim is one evidence of that conflict; the dead body of Brooks Prescott is another.

"Since the prosecution has so clearly met its burden of proof in this matter, it is incumbent on this court to certify the case to the grand jury so that it too may consider the matter and decide whether to issue an indictment. We thank you for your thoughtful and courteous attention." He inclined his head, then took his legal pad back to his table. I replaced him at the lectern.

"I guess the victims of sexual harassment should think hard before filing a complaint," I said. "If the harasser turns up dead, the victim becomes a prime suspect for murder. If we are to believe Mr. Borger, filing a claim is not a defensive action. It is aggressive and a likely precursor to violence. What should a woman do if she finds herself the victim of harassment? There is no defense that is not offensive. Recourse to the courts and to the administrative agencies established for that purpose are not options."

I turned to give Borger a long look, and he returned my gaze stonily. "Mr. Borger has just told you that the prosecution has shown reasonable grounds to believe a crime has been committed. Yes, but what crime? Mr. Borger has characterized the cause of death as a non-accidental head trauma, which is a far cry from the charge of murder of the first degree. He has presented no evidence that Dr. Prescott was killed in the commission of arson, rape, burglary, abduction, or any of the serious offenses delineated by statute. Nor has Mr. Borger shown that the defendant was lying in wait for her supposed victim, or that she acted with willful, deliberate premeditation. For this court to find that the defendant acted with deliberation and premeditation, it must find that she formed the intention to kill and acted on that intention only after enough time had passed for a reasonable person to second-guess the decision. There has been no evidence on this point: no evidence that any time at all passed between the formation of an intent to kill and the act of killing. The prosecution's theory of the case, to the extent it has suggested one at all, seems most consistent with a sudden act of rage or passion.

"I am not asking the court to weigh conflicting evidence. That is the job of the trial court. But where there is *no* evidence as to a required element of the offense, it is appropriate for the court to dismiss the charge. It should not certify the case to the grand jury on a charge of murder of the first degree.

"For any lesser charge, there is no possibility of the death penalty, no possibility of life imprisonment. Given that, Alexa Demming should be admitted to bail. The prosecution has offered no reason why she should not. She is not a flight risk: She is a U.S. Citizen and a lifetime resident of

Richmond, Virginia. She does not have ready sums of cash and, as far as we know, does not even hold a passport. She has no history of missing court hearings or failing to show up for court-ordered appointments—there have been none to miss. This is the first time Alexa has been accused of anything more serious than a misdemeanor traffic violation.

"Likewise, there is no evidence that Alexa poses a risk to the public. She has never been arrested for a violent crime before the present case. The reasons the prosecution presents for believing she had a motive to harm Dr. Prescott, as amorphous and vague as they are, are all personal to Dr. Prescott." I paused, groping for a summation of my arguments that were not merely repetitive. Nothing came to mind, so I said, "Thank you, Your Honor," and I returned to my seat.

Judge Cochran looked at me. His gaze moved to Alexa beside me, then he turned his attention to Jim Borger.

"I'm inclined to agree with Counsel," he said. "This isn't a case of first-degree murder."

"Your honor," Borger said, rising to his feet. "The defendant lured Dr. Prescott to her apartment with the clear intent . . ."

"As I understand the evidence, the decedent was living with her. Isn't that the prosecution's position? I don't remember any evidence about luring or intent, clear or otherwise."

"Your Honor."

Judge Cochran waited, but nothing more seemed to be forthcoming. "Would you like to be heard on the issue of bail?" he asked.

Borger cleared his throat, the sound like the low *blat* of a tuba. "I'm not ready to abandon the issue of murder of the first degree."

"I am," the judge said. "If you would care to address the issue of bail, I am willing to listen."

Borger's mouth worked, then he took a breath and began. "Denial of bail is entirely appropriate in this case, Your Honor," he said. "The defendant is charged not with second-degree murder, but with murder of the first degree, punishable by imprisonment for twenty years to life. Even if the court were to certify the case on the charge of murder of the second degree, that crime is subject to punishment by imprisonment for as many as forty years. Such a prospect gives the defendant every incentive not to appear, but to flee the jurisdiction . . ." He continued in that vein for another twenty minutes or so. By the time he was done, Judge Cochran's cheek had come to rest against his palm, and he was clearly no more than half-listening.

When Borger at last sat down, Judge Cochran said, "I will certify this case to the grand jury on the charge of murder of the second degree. The defendant is admitted to bail in the amount of seven hundred and fifty thousand dollars. I'll put my decision in writing and get it out to you later today. The defendant is remanded into the custody of the sheriff." He banged his gavel and left the courtroom. Alexa looked at me, and I gave her an apologetic smile.

"Believe it or not, we did ourselves some good here," I said.

Alexa's smile was tentative. She got up, and her mother leaned across the rail to embrace her. Her father clapped Aubrey on the back, then extended a hand to me. I took it.

"If you want to put up your condo for bail, I'll handle the paperwork for you," I said.

"Aubrey will handle it. You keep doing what you're doing."

Mrs. Biggs said, "Thank you. Thank you for all you've done for our little girl."

I hugged Alexa, gave her arm an encouraging pat. Then the deputy sheriff led her away in handcuffs.

"Ms. Starling," Borger called as I reached the gate in the rail that separated the gallery from the courtroom proper. "You've lived up to your reputation these last two days."

"Thank you."

"It wasn't a compliment," he said.

Chapter 9

It was raining when I came out of the courthouse, raining when I went to pick up Deeks. Judging by the rain-dimpled puddles and the mushy looking lawns, it had been raining most of the day. Despite the rain, the day was warm, and I had a glass of iced tea with Dr. McDermott, who seemed to have his old energy back. I sipped my unsweetened tea and waited for him to sit at the table with me, and at last he had the right combination of sugar and artificial sweeteners. He dropped a wedge of lime into his glass and came to the table with it.

"How was your day?" he asked. "Any new fireworks?"

"No, but we finished the preliminary. It went well."

"No details?"

"Dr. McDermott. You know I'm getting married next month."

He smiled. "I believe I've heard something about it."

"Brooke's done most of the planning, but there are a few things I have to do for myself."

"Sure."

"I wondered. Would you be willing to walk me down the aisle, give me away or whatever they call it?"

He looked at his tea and swirled it, ice clinking against the sides of the glass. He took a sip, and I realized this wasn't going to go the way I had expected.

"Robin . . ."

I waited.

"You have a father. I know your relationship has been a troubled one, but you're still his daughter and always will be."

"You think I ought to ask him?"

"I do. You getting married is a big deal in his life as well as yours."

After a moment, I nodded.

"I'll be there, of course, as proud as if I was your papa. I just wouldn't be comfortable in the lead role." His eyes looked moist.

"You don't cry at weddings, do you?" I asked.

He smiled. "I won't cry at yours. I'll be there with bells on."

"Tell me you mean that figuratively."

"Only figuratively."

"That's good then." I drained my tea and stood, Deeks coming to his feet with me. Dr. McDermott looked up, still smiling, and I realized he hadn't finished his tea. I sat back down, and Deeks pushed his head against my leg.

"I think that boy needs his run," Dr. McDermott said. "Too bad it's raining."

I scratched Deeks's head. "Deeks doesn't care, do you, buddy?"

"You're going to run in this?"

I nodded. "Neither rain nor snow nor gloom of night," I said. "My life is governed by the expectations of others."

"It shouldn't bother you. You created those expectations with your own past behavior. Everyone just expects you to keep being Robin."

"I guess I'll have to, then," I said, standing. "I'll be Robin all over the place."

"Very good." He stood with me.

"I'll be so Robin, everyone will be sick of it."

"There can be too much of a good thing," he said.

I added a baseball cap to my usual running attire to keep the rain off my head and out of my face and left a towel by the door to dry off Deeks. I should have left a towel for me, too. By the time I got back, I was soaked from my soggy cap to my water-logged shoes. I dripped on the floor as I dried Deeks, then took off my shoes and carried them to the washer and dryer, where I stripped out of my clothes.

The doorbell rang as I was getting out of the shower. I pulled on a pair of gym shorts and shrugged into a fresh T-shirt on my way to the door. It was Paul, his hair plastered to his head.

"Do you even own an umbrella?" I said.

"I keep it in my front closet so I won't lose it," he said. "You need to make sure you know who it is before you open the door." He was holding a droplet-speckled plastic bag that looked like it might contain Chinese takeout.

"Is that food?" I asked, ignoring the implied criticism. "I have to say, your timing is well-nigh impeccable," I told him,

"It's my superpower."

"Ah. I wondered."

After we ate, he broke open his fortune cookie and read, "'All your dreams are about to come true.' Hey, it knows I'm getting married to Robin Starling."

"That's sweet." I leaned across the table to kiss his cheek, then cracked open my cookie. "It is a good time to make personal arrangements," I read.

"Let me see that." He took it from me.

"Is that another way of telling me to get my affairs in order?" I asked. "You get promised the woman of your dreams, and I get a death threat?"

He looked troubled.

"Hey, it's just a fortune cookie," I said. I took his hand, and we walked into the living room to sit on the couch. Deeks wedged his head between Paul's leg and mine, and I scratched the top of it.

"You need to make use of that peephole in your front door," Paul said.

We were back to that. "I will. I promise."

"You're a great courtroom lawyer, you know," Paul said. "You could just try your cases in court."

Talk about your non sequitur. "What do you mean? Where else would I try my cases?" I asked.

"You try them on people's emotions. You don't have to, you know. You don't have to go around irritating the hell out of everybody."

"I have to push them. People aren't just going to give up and give me what I want."

"People get nasty when they feel threatened. You scare people."

"Are you saying you're about to marry the scariest woman anyone would ever want to meet?"

"Absolutely." He kissed me, and I kissed him back. Deeks jumped into our laps, planting one paw directly in Paul's groin.

"We're not taking Deeks on our honeymoon," he said in a strangled voice.

"Dr. McDermott will keep him. Why?"

"No reason."

When Paul recovered, we kissed some more, Deeks worming his way between us to add a few kisses of his own. I was going to have to teach the dog some boundaries, I knew, or the greatest dog in the world was going to become the world's greatest nuisance.

Paul gave up on the cuddle session—all too easily, in my opinion. "So," he said, rubbing Deeks's ears. "I gave my notice today."

"You're quitting your job?"

"I won't be renewing the lease on my apartment. Are we going to look for a house together, or will I just be moving in with you and Deeks? We haven't talked about it."

"No."

"It wasn't a yes or no question," Paul said. "Or do you mean we won't be looking for a house together, *and* I won't be moving in with you and Deeks?"

"No, we haven't talked about it," I said.

"Shouldn't we?"

I felt a stab of unease. I liked my house and my neighborhood, and Dr. McDermott's house was Deeks's second home. "Would you be happy moving in here with me and Deeks, or would you always feel like a houseguest?"

"Home is where the Robin is," Paul said. He kissed my cheekbone, and Deeks licked his chin. Paul sat back again.

"You got me the dog, remember?" I said by way of apology.

Paul opened his hands. "I love Deeks. We're talking about where all three of us are going to live."

I pushed Deeks to the floor. "Lie down," I told him. "We've got grown-up business to attend to."

I kissed Paul, raising a hand in front of Deeks's face when he moved to join us on the couch again. He sat back on his haunches, studying us, then went and lay down by the front door.

"Good boy," I said, my voice only slightly muffled, and Paul growled as he went after my neck. We never did get back to the topic of where Paul and I were going to live.

The next day was Thursday. I had no court dates and was expecting an easy day, but when I got to the office, an attractive woman in her early forties was waiting for me. As I came in, she stood, both hands gripping a Kate Spade purse at her waist. "Robin Starling?"

There was a back door to the executive suites, and I wished, suddenly, that I'd used it. "Yes," I said.

"You don't recognize me?"

"I'm afraid I don't." She was a brunette with dark brown eyes, and she wore a sleeveless dress with a single strand of pearls.

"My name is Anita Cantwell."

"Any relation to our lieutenant governor?" I asked, aware of Carly and her wide eyes at the reception desk.

"I'm his wife." She threw the title out like a challenge.

"Ah. Perhaps you'd like to come on back."

"Everything I have to say can be said right here."

"So it's my job to listen. Okay."

"My husband is a good man and a good husband."

She paused, evidently wanting a response. "Good is good," I said.

"You have no business trying to drag his name into a sordid affair like this murder trial of yours. You can be sued for defamation, you know."

"You might want to talk to your lawyer about that."

The skin tightened around her eyes. "I have resources at my disposal that you can't begin to imagine. Do you know what my name was before I married Nick?"

"Anita?" I ventured.

Her face scrunched up, and her head seemed to vibrate. "Jenner," she said.

"Caitlyn?"

"The former governor!"

"Oh, wow. Do you think you could get me his autograph?"

The shiny leather purse shot toward my face, but I'd been waiting for something like that. I caught her arm on my briefcase, and the purse fell to the floor.

"You're a grade-A bitch, you know that?" she said, rubbing her forearm.

"Whatever that means. I will say dogs have a sweeter temperament than a lot of people I meet."

She bent to snatch up her purse, then glared at me. When I did no more than return her gaze with as mild an expression as I could manage, she stamped her pointed-toe pump, stalked to the glass door, and flung it open so hard that it banged against the wall and rattled the glass. Outside the office she stabbed at the button for the elevator, looked up at the lights that showed it on the first floor, then threw up a hand as she turned toward the stairs.

When she was gone, I looked at Carly. "I need to pay more attention to politics," I said. "Know when I'm talking to a governor's daughter."

"A governor's daughter!" Carly breathed. "That woman is pure class." She looked past me, and I turned to see another woman getting off the elevator, this one a younger woman wearing capris, a light jacket, and a baseball cap.

She came through the doors and stopped, unslinging a backpack from her shoulder. "Robin Starling?"

"That would be me," I said with resignation.

"I've got a package for you."

She bent to fish it out, her ponytail, threaded through the closure at the back of her cap, falling forward. She straightened, flipping the ponytail back into place.

The white, Tyvek envelope she handed me felt as if it held a sheaf of papers. "It's from the commonwealth attorney's office," she said.

The envelope was blank: No addressee, no return address. "Dinwiddie or here in Richmond?" I said.

She smiled. "I'm on a bicycle. Dinwiddie's a bit out of my range."

"Who gave this to you?" I asked, hefting the envelope.

"Curly headed little guy." She laughed. "Looked a bit like a Munchkin in a business suit, but I understand he's the commonwealth's attorney."

"Do I need to sign for it or anything?"

"Nope. Put it in your hands, he said. Gave me two twenties."

Carly and I watched her go. "I like that ponytail look," I said. "I may start wearing a baseball cap."

"I can't. Too much hair." She raised a hand to her cascade of permed curls.

"You could wear a bigger cap."

"And to complete the look, all I'd need would be a red ball for a nose," she said.

I was still grinning as I let myself into my office. I set down my briefcase, unslung my purse, and pulled out a drawer in search of my scissors. Once I had the Tyvek envelope open, I set it on my desk and went to get a cup of coffee.

What Aubrey had sent me seemed to be transcripts of email messages taken from Alexa's account. There was no cover letter, though, not even a sticky note to indicate the sender.

An email dated March 20, about seven weeks before the murder, had been sent to brooks@sandjclinic.com. Spine and Joint Clinic?

Hi, Brooks. I bet you didn't expect to hear from me—at least not so soon. If you get off early one day this week, we could meet for a drink. How about it?

On March 23:

Hi, Brooks. Haven't heard from ya. Let me know.

On March 27:

Dear Dr. Prescott (that sounds so formal!):

Pardon my earlier breach of decorum. I will be in your offices on April 8 for an official sales call. It

155

will be good to see you again. Don't worry. I will be a model sales rep.

Her name at the bottom of that one had some creative capitalization: aleXa. At least it wasn't aleXXXa. The hint of a kiss was better than a promise of pornographic delights. Even so, I feared that Borger would be showing these emails to a jury at some point and making the most of them.

I sighed as I flipped through them, glad that at least I was seeing them now and not in the middle of trial. Since they were something Borger should have sent me himself, the print-outs told me something else, too. Borger thought he had a way to get these emails admitted into evidence without having provided an advance copy to the defense, and he wasn't planning to fight fair.

There were no more emails directed to Dr. Prescott, at least that I could find. As near as I could tell, he hadn't responded to any of Alexa's offerings.

There was another sheaf of papers that looked like printouts of text messages—from her phone, I imagined. I set the emails aside to look at them.

"Hey," said a voice from the doorway. It was Alexa herself, looking as modest as a schoolgirl in jeans and a solid-color T-shirt. "My parents made bail for me."

"That's great," I said. I set my print-outs aside. "Come in. Take a seat."

She did, sitting with her elbows were braced on the armrests and her hands clasped at her waist.

"Did you get your phone back when they released you?" I asked. "I assume the police impounded it when they arrested you."

"They took it. And, no, they didn't give it back to me." She gave me a smile. "I am temporarily phoneless."

I found myself liking this new, apparently chastened Alexa. I said, "Unfortunately, the phone hasn't just been sitting in an evidence locker. These are printouts of your texts and email messages."

The skin tightened around her eyes, a hint of the old Alexa.

"I know," I said. "Someone gets killed in your apartment, and your whole life goes under a microscope." I gave her a few moments to digest that. "Can we talk about it?"

The movement of her head was all but imperceptible. I took it as a nod.

"All the communications I see between you and Brooks Prescott are one-way," I said. "You send him a cute little email; he doesn't respond."

She didn't say anything.

"Did he ever respond?" I asked. "Am I just missing it?"

"He never responded."

"Did he ever send you any sort of communication, email or text message?"

She looked down at her hands, then back at me. "Dr. Prescott had no interest in me."

"He never came onto you?"

She shook her head.

"But you were interested in him," I said.

"He was cute. He talked about his wife. It was a challenge, I guess."

"And the sexual harassment claim?"

"Peter's idea."

"Peter Brawley? What was the idea, do you know? Money, something else?"

She wasn't quite looking at me, her chest rising and falling. I've read that silence begins to make people uncomfortable after just a few seconds. I gave her maybe half-a-minute of it.

"I thought he'd feel the need to talk to me about it," she said at last. "Seek me out. I thought we might have a real conversation."

"Is that what was happening on the day of his death? He was at your apartment for a real conversation?"

"I don't know why he was there. I'd like to think it was to see me."

"But you don't know," I said.

She lifted a shoulder and dropped it.

"Tell me about the key he had."

"The key to my apartment?"

"Detective Michaels testified it was on his keyring."

"I don't know what to tell you about that. Like I told you, I didn't give it to him."

"So how did he get it?"

"I don't know."

"I'm on your side, you know."

"What's that supposed to mean?"

158

"That I'm on your side. You can tell me the truth, no matter how damning it seems."

"You think I'm lying to you?"

"Not at all. In fact, I'm going to build your defense on the assumption that everything you tell me is true. If it's not, Borger's going to knock our case down, and he's going to bury us."

Alexa's stood, pink patches on her cheeks. "I don't think I like talking to you," she said.

"Alexa . . ."

But she was on her way out. I watched her through the door until she disappeared through the archway of exposed brick.

I sighed and went back to the print-outs Aubrey had sent me. I found text messages from Alexa to Brooks, none going the other way.

Curled on my love seat with a glass of Chardonnay. Thinking about you.

I would like to see you some time. We can be discreet.

Good night, dear. I'm turning out the light.

There were more than a dozen messages in all, but they didn't build to anything. There was no crescendo, no climax, no shift of tone to anger or bitterness. Alexa was a woman with a schoolgirl crush and no impulse control.

Still, the whole thing was a mess. I continued to flip through the printouts until I came to Alexa's calendar. On May 8, the day of the murder, she had indeed had three appointments in the morning and one in the afternoon. Nothing during the window the doctor had given for time of death.

As I sat staring into space, it occurred to me that there was another phone I needed to be looking at. I called Detective Emma Michaels. I had to wait about fifteen minutes, but eventually she came on the line.

"I see no point in talking to you," she said by way of hello.

"I have a question."

"You have a question," Michaels said. She sounded bitter. "Look, you had your shot at questions when you had me on the stand."

"I don't see a cell phone on the police inventory of the crime scene," I said. "Was there not one?"

"There was not."

"Not one in Prescott's car?"

"No."

"So you never looked at Prescott's phone in an effort to reconstruct his last hours?"

"We haven't been able to find it."

I made another appointment with Dr. Tracey Mulligan and drove out West Broad to the Spine & Joint Clinic. I signed in at the reception desk and for fifty minutes sat looking at broken down old people, middle-aged people who had hurt themselves playing softball or racquetball or training for marathons, and one girl on crutches who looked like she might have been a high school athlete. Leah, the nurse who'd had the crush on Dr. Prescott, appeared at the door. "Robin Starling?" she called.

I got up and followed her through the door. "You seem busy," I said.

"We haven't found anyone to replace Dr. Prescott yet, if that's what you're getting at."

"I was really just making conversation."

She opened a door and I went past her into the small conference room where I'd talked to Dr. Mulligan before. She stood in the doorway, her arms crossed. "I heard on the news you got Miss Fancypants out on bail," she said.

"The trial's still ahead of her. If she's guilty, she'll be convicted."

"You think she's not guilty?"

"Right now, I'm following the evidence where it leads. Whoever killed Brooks Prescott, I wouldn't want him to get away with it. Or her."

Leah made a face. "Well, I wouldn't either," she said. She stepped out of the conference room and closed the door.

While I waited for Dr. Mulligan, I got my phone out and found my earlier exchange of text messages with Leah. I sent her another one: *When is your break?* She hadn't responded when Dr. Mulligan came in. This time he didn't sit down.

"I really don't have time for this," he said.

"I'm sorry. I'm trying to track down Brooks's cell phone. I don't guess he left it here the day he died."

"No. The police have asked that already."

"Did the police search his office?"

"Yeah, they went through it."

"Did they take anything?"

"I don't think so."

"What were they looking for?"

"How would I know? Look, I hardly have time to think about anything but seeing patients these days. I get home about ten o'clock every evening, I have my glass of scotch, and I go to bed."

"Could I look through Dr. Prescott's office?"

He shook his head. "There's nothing look through. We boxed everything up and gave it to Toni."

"Did he have a computer tablet? An iPad or Galaxy or something?"

He shrugged. "Sure, probably. Like I said, we gave everything to Toni."

"A laptop?"

"Don't know. Here he had a desktop, but he would have had very little on there of a personal nature."

"Maybe we could take a look at his calendar, check his emails from early May."

Mulligan shook his head. "I'm going to take the position that patient privacy trumps your need to know—HIPAA and all that. You can, of course, serve us with a subpoena duces tecum, and we'll give you what we have to, but absent a court order we're not going to let you go poking through our data files."

"*Subpoena duces tecum* isn't an expression I'd expect to hear from a doctor," I said.

"My brother's a shyster. Lawyer. Sorry. He's one of those that advertise on TV for people with mesothelioma and IUDs gone bad."

"A class-action lawyer," I said.

"I guess he's no worse than any of you. I do wish he'd stay away from pharmaceuticals and medical devices."

It was all I got out of him. In the parking lot, I checked my phone and learned that Leah's lunch break was at noon, which was just under thirty minutes away. I called Rodney Burns, my in-suite detective.

"Rodney Burns," he said.

"No, this is Robin."

He waited, giving me time to enjoy my witty rejoinder and get over it.

"Brooks Prescott had a phone and maybe a tablet of some sort," I said. "If I can't get hold of either one, can you get me the information that was on them? Isn't everything in the cloud somewhere?"

"Not that we can access, unless you've gotten hold of his passwords. Even if we had physical possession of his devices, we might not be able to get into them without passcodes and answers to security questions and whatnot."

I digested that. "Another topic. Paul had a theory about the men's clothes that were found in Alexa's apartment. Do you know about the clothes found in her apartment?"

"I know there were men's clothes found in her apartment, yes."

"Paul's theory is that they came straight from the cleaners, that he never wore them."

"And you want to know what cleaners, who picked them up, and when."

"Right. There was a suit, a sports jacket, eight shirts, three pairs of slacks. I'd be interested in any pick-up from the week prior to Prescott's death, especially if the number of items matched."

"Gotcha."

I punched off, and the car door opened on the passenger side. Leah slid in and closed the door. "I guess you found out about me talking to the police," she said.

This was the first I'd heard about it. Clearly, running around talking to people was a worthwhile thing to do, despite Paul's misgivings. "What did you tell them?" I asked.

"I told them about the key."

I waited.

"The key to your client's apartment, the one she sent it to Dr. Prescott. She didn't tell you?"

"You tell me."

"It came in the mail, taped to a perfumed piece of paper with just two words on it: *Love, Alexa.*"

"You saw this piece of paper."

"Yes, I saw it." Alexa, evidently, had lied to me, when I'd have sworn she was telling me the truth.

"You don't know where it is now, do you?" I asked.

"The paper?" She shrugged. "Maybe the police found it when they searched his office."

"Dr. Mulligan said they didn't take anything."

"I don't know. I guess Dr. Prescott threw it away, then."

"Why didn't you tell me about this when I talked to you the first time?"

"She told me not to tell anyone, that police woman. Also, I don't like your client much."

"Who told you not to tell anyone? Detective Emma Michaels?"

"I think so. She said the police always try to hold back some details of in a murder investigation. It helps them to sort out who has guilty knowledge."

"Did she talk to you about testifying?"

She nodded. "I don't want to, but she said I'd probably have to."

"When did Dr. Prescott get this key?" I asked. "Was it before or after Alexa filed her sexual harassment claim?"

"I'm not sure. About the same time, I think."

"Were you there when he opened the envelope?"

"He was at his desk looking at it when I came into his office one day."

"The day he got it?"

"I think so."

"He didn't say?"

"I think maybe he did. We were close in some ways, Dr. Prescott and I. Not in any way that was inappropriate. All of us knew how he felt about Toni."

I drove from the Spine and Joint Clinic to Windsor Farms to see Toni Prescott. I parked on the street in front of the house, just as I had the first time. I crossed the brick sidewalk and walked up the flagstone path to the big double doors. I rang the bell and listened to the chimes. It was déjà vu all over again.

The door was jerked open, and Toni stood there, mascara streaking her cheeks, and her eyes red. That was different.

"What?" she said in a thick voice. She cleared her throat. "What do you want? I consider this harassment, you know. Don't think this is going to go unreported."

"May I come in?"

She stared at me in apparent disbelief.

"Grief is sometimes a delayed reaction," I said. "I'm sorry for your loss."

Her expression didn't change, and I wondered if I'd inadvertently slipped into Farsi, the language of Iran, but the fact that I didn't speak Farsi made that seem unlikely.

"May I come in?" I said again.

She left me in the doorway, walking down the hall past the wall of political pictures. I followed to a room off the living room, a room ringed with comfortable chairs. It had a small desk in the corner and a big-screen TV on the wall. I thought she was going to take a seat at the desk, but she whirled on me.

166

"You've got nerve coming here after what you did," she said, her grief gone, apparently burned away by anger. I took a step back.

"What did I do?"

"What didn't you do?"

She turned again and sat at the desk, hunched forward, her clasped hands between her knees. I scanned the desk, hoping for some evidence of why she had been upset, but there was nothing to see other than a stapler, an ink pen, a pad of paper, and a cell phone with a hot pink protective case.

"I'm looking for Brooks's cell phone," I said, eyeing the one on the desk.

"Huh." She opened the drawer and slid the cell phone into it. Given the color, I didn't think it was his, but I would have liked to see what else was in that drawer.

"It wasn't found at Alexa's apartment, and it wasn't in his car," I said. "His partner, Tracey Mulligan, didn't know anything about it either."

"Well, don't come to me. I wouldn't give you a glass of water if you were on fire." A fresh tear-track had appeared on one cheek, but her eyes blazed through the mask of smeared mascara.

"Do you need anything?" I asked. I sat on the arm of a nearby chair, leaning forward. "Can I help?"

"Help me? No, you can't help me. No one can help me. You've screwed up everything good and proper."

"You were having an affair with Cantwell," I said.

167

She was athletic, and the stapler would have caught me in the forehead if I hadn't moved. Even so, it brushed my ear, then hit the wall, popping open and spilling its staples. I took a step back as she jerked to her feet, expecting her to launch herself at me, but she just stood with her arms stiffly at her sides, her fists clenched.

"Get out," she said. "I don't have Brooks's phone, and I wouldn't show it to you if I did." She took a step toward me, and I retreated a step, keeping the distance between us from shrinking.

"I'm going," I said.

"Get out!"

I got.

"So," Brooke said. "Do you think her grief was real, or was she putting on a show?"

"I don't know. It seemed real. It was going on when I got there."

"But evidently it was connected with you somehow," she said.

"I'd like to think it's confirmation of my suspicions about her and Cantwell."

Mike said, "It's hard to believe she doesn't have either her husband's phone or his iPad . . . unless he had them with him when he was killed, and the killer took them?" We were having dinner at the Taphouse, where he and Paul could sample from a couple of hundred kinds of beer.

"I think you're missing the point here," Paul said, banging his mug down hard enough that some of his beer splashed onto the table. "She attacked Robin. Here we have yet another violent looney toon who thinks the answer to her problem is violence. First Anita Cantwell, now Toni Prescott."

"Two candidates for Prescott's murder," Mike said. "Is that what you're saying?"

"Screw the murder," Paul said. "I'm talking about Robin. Sure, she dodged these attacks, but what about the next one? This criminal defense work is a problem."

We looked at him.

"You've never known me when I wasn't doing criminal defense work," I said. "It's part of the package."

"You're a trial lawyer and a damn good one. You could do anything. It doesn't have to be criminal defense."

"Criminal defense is what keeps coming through the door."

"Have you thought about going back to work for someone else? The Fed is looking for an attorney for its legal department."

"I like working for myself."

"Do you also like being folded, stapled, spindled, and mutilated?"

I inclined my head. "Not so much. I do like not having to put up with all the crap that comes with an employer."

"Have you thought about the possibility that Alexa took Prescott's phone?" Mike said. "She sent him a key, lured him to her apartment, and she killed him."

"And hid his phone, but not her own?" I asked. "Why?"

"And where?" Paul said. "It evidently wasn't in her apartment or her car."

"Suppose she gave Prescott's phone to this Peter Brawley?" Mike said. "They were evidently pretty tight right up to the moment she went to jail."

"Alexa can't be guilty," Brooke said. "She's Robin's client."

"She seems more likely than Anita Cantwell," Mike said.

I smiled at Brooke. "May all my clients be innocent," I said.

"The defense lawyer's prayer," Paul said.

"Amen."

Chapter 10

If you're going to get married, preparing for the big day is more fun with a friend. I'm surprised double weddings aren't more popular. Brooke and I took Friday off to try on wedding dresses.

She modeled four dresses and looked like a fairytale princess in all of them. I tried on three.

"That one's the best on you," Brooke said, when I had one of them on for the second time. "You look like Wonder Woman undercover at her own wedding."

"Ha," I said. "Was Wonder Woman a six-foot tall blonde?"

"You're not six feet tall. I think Gal Gadot's only an inch shorter than you."

I took another look at myself in the mirror, turning in an effort to catch every angle. "Wonder Woman, huh?" I said, looking over my shoulder.

"Definitely," Brooke said.

"I can go with that." Why quibble over a couple of inches and blonde hair?

I'd left my car at Brooke's place. On the way back, I said, "We still don't have a place to do the wedding."

She shot a glance at me, but didn't say anything.

"Do we?"

"I've signed us up for First Baptist."

"What about the joining-the-church thing?"

"Time was running out. I had to make some decisions."

That had an ominous sound to it. "What kind of decisions?"

"Don't be mad."

"Brooke Marshall, what have you done?"

"Nothing. Really, nothing. I made an appointment for you to talk to one of the ministers, is all."

"When?"

"Next week. Tuesday afternoon. It's mainly for marriage counseling, but while you're at it, you and Paul can talk to him about joining the church and getting baptized and all that."

"Have you talked to Paul?"

"Yes. It's on his schedule."

"What about my schedule?" I took out my phone and found the schedule request on my calendar. "Oh," I said, accepting the request. "Mine, too."

"You've been preoccupied," Brooke said. "I didn't want to distract you."

"I guess I have been. Thanks."

"Today, though. Today is all about us." She pulled into a parking space in her apartment complex, and my phone rang.

"Maybe not," I said, tapping the screen. "Hi, Carly." I put her on speaker.

"Robin. How's the dress-shopping going?"

"Pretty good. I've decided to go as Wonder Woman."

Carly snickered. "That's a good one. Who's Brooke going as, Batgirl?"

"She was thinking one of the Powerpuff girls."

"Hey!" Brooke said.

"You've had a visitor," Carly said. "Aubrey Biggs says you haven't been returning his phone calls."

"I just saw him yesterday."

"I'm just telling you what he said. On another note, Alexa called. She got a new phone and wanted to give you the number."

"Good. Could you call her back, make an appointment for her to come see me sometime Monday morning?"

"Sure. Ten o'clock?"

"That's fine."

"Already done. Do you want me to schedule something with Mr. Biggs, too?" She giggled. "I love saying that name. Mr. Biggs. Hey, he could be the villain in this comic strip you and Brooke are putting on."

"Batgirl's pretty much a sidekick," Brooke said. "Maybe I could be Black Widow."

173

"Mike may not like the sound of that," I said. His bride already aspiring to be a widow on the eve of their marriage.

But Brooke disagreed. "No, I think he really likes Scarlett Johansson."

I shrugged. "What did Aubrey want?" I asked Carly.

"To know how things were coming on the case. I told him you were out running down a lead."

"I was trying on wedding dresses. You know that."

"I didn't think it would go over as well."

"I'll call him." I punched off, looked at Brooke.

"Do you want to come in? It's cooler, and I've got lemonade," she said.

"You don't mind me making a phone call?"

"Not at all."

So we went inside. Brooke poured lemonade, and I called Aubrey's cell. He picked up on the first ring.

"So what's the lead?" he asked.

"I've been trying to track down Prescott's cell phone, so far with no luck. On Monday morning, Alexa is coming by to go over things."

There was a silence. "That's all you're going to tell me?"

"For now."

"Are you done for the week, or are you working tomorrow?"

"I'm going to let things percolate, I think."

After a short silence, he said, "That doesn't sound productive."

"It's worked pretty well in the past. I run around talking to people and looking at things. I try not to think too hard about who's telling the truth or what it all means. At some point, an idea bubbles up, or I make a connection."

"You let things percolate." His tone was dry.

"It's my word-of-the-day."

"I assume this drives all your clients crazy. Not just me."

"Everything I do drives somebody crazy. It's my special talent."

By the time I hung up, Brooke had bread, chicken salad, and romaine lettuce on the counter. "You don't drive *everybody* crazy," she said. "Look at Paul and Mike and me. Not to mention Carly."

"I assume you're all just nice about it."

Paul's parents lived in Virginia Beach. I had never met them, and we drove over Saturday morning to correct that omission. Mr. and Mrs. Soldano lived in a big Georgian house about a mile-and-a-half from the beach. We parked on the street.

"Don't get out," Paul told me.

"Don't get out?"

His own door was open. "I'm going to come around and open your door. They may be watching."

"And we want them to think I can't get out of a car by myself?"

"We want them to think I'm a gentleman," he said as he opened my door and held out a hand.

"And I take it you've never met." I took his hand and alighted from the car with as ladylike an air as I could manage.

"Let's just say I have credulous parents." We held hands as we walked up the sidewalk to the front door—more showmanship, but it was nice, too.

The doorbell got one bong out before the door opened to reveal a big woman with dark hair and deeply tanned skin. She was only two or three inches shorter than I was, and she filled the doorway. "You must be Robin!" she said in a booming voice. She was holding out her arms, so I stepped into them and was enveloped. If I'd been shorter, she might have smothered me in her ample bosom, but, as it was, she pressed a slightly oily cheek against mine. "Robin, Robin, Robin," she said, swaying from side to side in apparent ecstasy. As I swayed with her, I could see, over her shoulder, a wiry little guy with curly, snow-white hair and skin as dark as his wife's. His hands were in his pockets, and he was grinning at me.

"I'm Tony," he said. "Paul's dad. I hope you're hungry. Don't crush her, Sophie."

"Starved," I said as Sophie released me.

"Good," Tony said. "We've got a couple of baskets of blue crabs and some friends coming over. We'll eat about three. We'll pick crabs and drink beer and have a great time."

I wasn't wearing a watch, but I didn't think it was much past eleven.

"She can't wait until three o'clock," Sophie said. "Not if she's starved. Come on back, dear, and I'll make you a sandwich."

"That's all right," I said. "I'll . . ." But Sophie was moving deeper into the house, and I fell silent as I bobbed along in her wake.

She stopped in the kitchen doorway and screamed, not even noticing when I ran into her broad, meaty back and bounced off. The island counter and the floor were in motion, crabs scuttling in all directions, their feet clicking on the floor and their claws working. "Tony! Tony, we've got trouble." I stepped back to avoid her rump as she doubled over to snag a crab that was trying to get past us into the hall, but I'd caught a glimpse of the basket on the counter with its lid askew.

It only took ten or fifteen minutes to get the crabs back in the basket, at least all of them that were still in the kitchen.

"Robin and I will grab a snack at the beach," Paul told his mother.

"You're going to the beach?" Tony said. "Nice romantic walk along the shore?" He chuckled as if it were as delightful a prospect as anything he could think of.

"Robin has a new swimsuit she's anxious to wear," Paul said.

"Oh, she does, does she?" Tony said.

"I does?" I said.

Paul smiled. "It's in the car. I'll get it." He left, and Tony stood beaming at me.

"She's not going to model the suit for us, you old coot," Sophie said. "She doesn't want you and me looking her over like she was livestock. Next you'll be wanting to check out her teeth." She was transferring the crabs into a big pot billowing steam, pushing and tapping the crabs with a ladle to keep them from clambering out.

"She's got nice teeth," Tony said. "I can see 'em when she smiles."

"You do have a nice smile, dear," Sophie said to me.

Paul came back with a shopping bag—a small bag, I noted with some dismay. "You can change in there," he said, jerking his head toward a door. "I've got to run upstairs to get one of my old suits."

I took the envelope-size bag from him, taking in the beaming faces of both his parents without looking at either of them directly. I took a breath and crossed the hall into what turned out to be a small bedroom.

The first thing I pulled out of the bag was a pale yellow coverup. *Bless you, Paul,* I thought. I dug deeper and found a pair of boy-short bottoms with drawstring sides, yellow with narrow blue horizontal stripes. I shucked out of my pants and put them on. They covered my bottom and most of my hips. The top was two triangles and a bit of string, the stripes diagonal rather than horizontal. It wasn't a lot of cover for my top half, but then, I didn't have all that much to cover. I shrugged into the coverup—short, but it did come to the tops of my thighs—and went back into the kitchen. Paul was back. His dad took one look at me and punched him in the arm.

"You look very nice, dear," Sophie said.

"What made you think of the coverup?" I asked Paul when we were walking back down the sidewalk.

"Girls like coverups. They'll pick out bottoms that are too skimpy, then spend all day with a towel wrapped around themselves. A coverup works better."

"Well, thank you. Who'd have thought you could do a better job of picking out a suit for me than I could myself?" I bent to kiss his cheek, and there was a tapping from the front window of the house—Tony, giving one or both of us a thumbs up. "I have to say they seem happy to meet me," I said.

"Up until this moment they probably half-believed I was making you up."

"Are you in the habit of dating make-believe girlfriends?"

"Not really, no."

That gave me something to think about. *Not really?* We were pulling into a parking space near the boardwalk when Paul said, "I did kind of pretend to have a girlfriend once."

It took me a beat to recover, then I said, "Was she as pretty as me?"

"Not anywhere close. My imagination failed me."

He opened his car door and came around to open mine. "Too warm for you to want the coverup, probably."

That sounded like a line. "So you're going to take off that T-shirt?" I said.

"Are you kidding? This T-shirt is my contribution to beach beautification."

"Well, I'll make a contribution, too." I started to close the door, but he looked so disappointed that I relented and pulled off the coverup. "Happy?" I asked as I tossed it onto the car seat and closed the door.

He wiggled his eyebrows at me and took my hand.

The walk on the beach was nice. The crab feast at his parents' was fun, too. We ate in the backyard at picnic tables covered with newspaper. With a little instruction, I mastered the art of picking crabs fairly quickly, pulling out the meat and washing it down with Pabst Blue Ribbon beer while rock and roll played on an outdoor sound system. Probably a dozen crabs was excessive for a girl with a new bathing suit, but I did limit myself to one beer before switching to bottled water.

People moved around a lot, and I got to talk to maybe a dozen of the Soldanos' friends before the crab feast was over. Sophie made a point of eating a crab across the table from me to talk about our wedding plans, and I realized, with some embarrassment, just how much of the planning I was leaving to Brooke. Sophie turned out to be an easy-going woman, though. She wasn't concerned about her son marrying a girl she was only just meeting, wasn't worried about his changing religions, didn't think it odd that he was doing so largely to have a nice sanctuary to be married in.

"He's doing it for you," she told me, "and that's okay."

"I'm not Baptist either, actually."

"So you're moving that way together. That's a good thing. There's more than one pathway leading deeper into God."

On the way back to Richmond, I drowsed in the passenger seat while Paul drove, and I didn't wake fully until we got to Richmond and he exited off I-64.

"Did you like them?" he said when he saw I was awake.

"Sure. What's not to like?"

"Dad can be a little . . . I don't know. Everything that goes through his mind is right there on the surface for everyone to read."

"He did seem a little enthusiastic about my bathing suit."

Paul moved his head around. "Hard not to be," he said. "But trust me, Dad's harmless. Mom has him well in hand."

It was after eleven when he pulled up in front of my house. He put the car in park and started to turn off the ignition, but I put a hand over his. "Don't get out. It's late. Too late to get Deeks, even."

"I was going to walk you to the door."

"I know. No need." I leaned across the console to kiss him on the mouth, making it one of my better efforts. "Thank you for the swimsuit."

"You're welcome." He sounded out of breath.

"I'll see you in the morning."

I got out and ran lightly up the sidewalk. At the door I turned back. Paul was still in his car, watching me. I took a breath, turned and opened the door and went in. When I had closed it behind me, I stood watching through the side window. Paul continued to sit out front.

He may have been waiting for me to turn on a light, but eventually—five minutes? Fifteen?—he pulled away from the curb. I turned and sank to the floor, my back against the door. My heart, which had been pounding like a trip hammer, gradually slowed.

"Oh, Paul," I said.

Leaving him in the car and going inside to bed alone might be the hardest thing I'd ever done.

Chapter 11

Monday morning. Alexa was late. I sat behind my desk, my head against the headrest, my eyes half-closed. I thought about the preliminary hearing, replaying bits of the testimony in my mind, and I relived my conversations with Dr. Mulligan, with Leah, with Toni. Mentally, I followed Toni's Maserati onto the Downtown Expressway and up Ninth Street past Capitol Square, watched the man I believed to be Nick Cantwell approach the car. I wasn't thinking so much as allowing what I knew or thought I knew to drift in and out of my thoughts.

I'd let Aubrey Biggs think this was some secret technique of mine, something that led to new insights and serendipitous breakthroughs. The truth was that I tended to daydream when I was stumped. Eventually, I sat forward and pulled over my keyboard. "Nick cantwell lieutenant governor va," I typed.

The search engine didn't take me anywhere immediately useful, but eventually, on the ltgov.virginia.gov website, I found a phone number for the Office of the Lieutenant Governor. I picked the receiver off my desk phone and dialed.

"Hi, this is Toni Prescott," I said to the woman who answered the phone. "Is Nick available?"

My request was met with silence.

"Hello?" I said.

"Just a minute."

It was four minutes and forty-two seconds before a man's voice came on. "This is Jacob Chapman," he said. He sounded young, though he had a deeply resonant voice that made it hard to tell.

"I asked for Nick. This is . . ."

"I thought we agreed you weren't going to call here again. You weren't going to call or make any other attempt to contact Mr. Cantwell."

"Did I make that agreement with you or with Nick?" What this man was characterizing as an agreement sounded more like the unilateral severing of a relationship, not something mutual. Nick dumped her because of what I'd done at the preliminary hearing? That would account for how angry Toni had been with me. It might account for her smeared and tear-streaked mascara, too.

"I'm speaking for Nick," Chapman said.

"This isn't who you think it is, Jacob," I said.

He hesitated, then began, "It's not . . ."

"My name is Robin Starling. I'm the lawyer representing Alexa Demming, the woman charged with the murder of Brooks Prescott."

Jacob Chapman hung up on me.

I looked at the receiver in my hand, and the holes in the ends of the receiver looked back at me. In the doorway, Carly cleared her throat. She was leaning against the frame of the door with her arms folded across her chest.

"Are you on the phone?" she asked.

"Evidently not." I put the receiver back in its cradle.

"Alexa Demming is here for her appointment."

I glanced at my watch. She was fifty-five minutes late.

Alexa had had her hair bleached again. It had gone from brassy to bright, almost white, and the dark roots were gone. She was wearing distressed jeans that fit her thin legs like sausage skins. As she took a seat, I closed the door behind her, and she crossed her legs.

"Has my brother been in to see you?"

I shook my head as I walked around my desk. "He did call Friday."

"Lucky you. He calls me every day, Mom does, too. She only puts Dad on a couple of times a week, but he's the worst of all."

"You could be spending the next forty years in prison. They're worried about you."

She shrugged. "Worrying's not going to change anything."

"No. Hard for most people to avoid, though." Alexa's demeanor was nothing like that of the diffident young woman who'd been in my office the week before. Her manner had regained its brassiness even as her hair had lost it.

"It does get me late at night sometimes," she acknowledged, tossing her head to get the bangs out of her face. "It was worse in the city jail though."

"Probably hard for you to be alone right now," I suggested.

"What's that supposed to mean?"

I shrugged. "Nothing."

"I'm not sleeping with anyone, if that's what you're asking."

"I wasn't, but it is the kind of thing you need to tell me."

"Who I'm sleeping with?"

"Everything. You need to think of me as 'dear diary.' Anything I don't know is something I can't prepare for. It's like giving Borger a bunch of IEDs to plant in front of us. Something comes out at trial, and it knocks a hole in the theory of the case I'm trying to sell the jury—or it makes the prosecution's unassailable. Either way, it can put you in prison for forty years."

"You're just being paranoid." But uncertainty had crept into her voice. I pressed the point.

"Am I? One of our theories is that Brooks Prescott was making unwelcome advances. That's why you filed your sexual harassment claim. Now we know the prosecution can produce emails and texts that turns that story on its head. It's the kind of thing that could have blind-sided me at trial."

"But you know about that now."

"I also know how Dr. Prescott came to have a key to your apartment."

"Are we back to that again?"

"He got it in the mail," I said. "It came taped to a piece of scented paper signed *Alexa*."

"Who told you that?"

"Not you, and that's the problem."

"Whoever told you that is a liar. I never sent him a key."

"The witness seemed very credible."

"More credible than me," she said flatly.

I took a breath. "Let's leave it for the moment. Let's just . . . talk."

She waited. "About what?" she said.

"Tell me something I should know about but don't."

"That's ridiculous. How am I supposed to know what you should know?"

"You can't. That's why you need to tell me everything."

She gave a snort of derisive laughter, whether directed at herself or me, I couldn't tell. "I wouldn't know where to start," she said.

"Just tell me something, and we'll go from there."

"Tell you what? I can't just start blabbing about stuff."

"Why not?"

"It would be . . ." Her mouth moved as if she were trying out words to complete the sentence.

"Embarrassing?" I suggested.

"Intolerable."

"More intolerable than 40 years in prison?"

She lowered her gaze to stare introspectively at the edge of my desk. "Okay. I have a drinking problem, okay? That day, the big day, May 9, I had a few hours to kill before my afternoon appointment. I spent some of the time in my car sipping from a bottle of honey bourbon."

"Where did you get it?"

"I bought it."

"That same day? Where?" I picked up a pen.

"H-n-H Liquors."

"The one on Broad?"

"Parham."

"See?" I said. "Now that's promising. I don't guess you have a receipt. One wouldn't have been crumpled in the floor board of your car."

"I don't mess with receipts."

"Even if you paid with a credit card?"

"That's something else. I don't have credit cards. I've had . . . problems in the past."

"Well, someone might remember you. It would be nice to have an alibi that covered any part of the time when Dr. Prescott might have been killed."

"This would have been later than that doctor was talking about."

"We'll check it out anyway. What else can you tell me? Start with something you'd rather not."

After several seconds of silence she said, "I do sometimes sleep with Travis."

"Travis Grimes, the neighbor who discovered the body?"

Her mouth stretched. She nodded.

"That's another good one," I said. "Someone with a possible motive."

"Not Travis."

"We don't have to prove he did it or that anyone in particular did it. We do need to expand the list of possible suspects."

"Still."

"If Travis saw a man letting himself into your apartment, he might have been jealous."

She was shaking her head.

"It's plausible," I said. "Plausibility may be all we need. Did you have sex at your place or his, when you had it?"

"Mine, usually. Look, I don't want you to go after Travis."

"Some of those unidentified fingerprints would be his," I said.

"Yeah, sure. Probably."

Those weren't his clothes in the closet, were they?"

"No. I never saw those clothes before."

"Let's go back to this key that Dr. Prescott had."

"The key that I didn't send."

"How many keys to your apartment are there?"

"Three. That I know of."

"Does Travis have one?"

She rolled her eyes. "Yes, Travis has one. He has one, okay?"

189

"Okay. It means he could have let himself into your apartment the day Dr. Prescott was killed. The door wasn't necessarily standing open."

"He just had it for emergencies. If I got locked out, or I needed him to go in and check on something."

"Who had the third key?"

"Peter Brawley."

"Your lawyer Peter Brawley?"

"I wasn't sleeping with him though."

"But he has been in your apartment."

"No, or I don't think so. He was looking around for a new place to do one of his photo shoots, and he was going to look at my apartment as a possible setting."

"Why not just come by when you were there?"

"He didn't want to be a bother, and of course he might have had someone with him. A woman to photograph. You know."

"But as far as you know he never came by."

"I don't think he got a chance—before all this happened."

I thought about it.

"You don't think Peter had something to do with Brooks's murder," Alexa said.

"You've conceded that Brooks didn't harass you," I said. "That's right, isn't it?"

She moved her head around in a way that wasn't really an answer.

"So tell me how you came to accuse him of sexual harassment," I said.

"I don't know. Peter Brawley suggested it when we were drinking one night, I think."

"And somehow it seemed like a good idea?"

"I guess. I told him to go ahead."

"Is this also when you gave him your key?"

"I think that was another time."

"Before? After?"

She shrugged. "I don't know. A couple days either way."

"He never gave it back to you?"

"Unh unh."

"How long had you known Brawley at the point you gave him your key?"

"Couple weeks, maybe three."

"How did you meet him anyway?"

"It was just one of those things. I was at a bar, sitting there not thinking about much of anything. He slipped onto the stool beside me, and we struck up a conversation."

"So he picked you up," I said.

"If you want to call it that. It's not like we went anywhere and had sex."

I nodded. "You said he's never been to your place. Have you been to his?"

"Once. He has a place up in Mechanicsville. His bedroom is set up like a photographer's studio—nice, you know?"

"But you didn't pose for him."

"Not seriously. He had his camera out, of course, but it's not like I . . . you know."

I nodded, but I was beginning to think I didn't know, that really I had no idea.

I walked her to the elevator. Probably we made some small talk, but I was distracted by thoughts of Peter Brawley, who looked increasingly to me like a puppet master—staging scenes, moving characters about to fit some plot-line of his own.

When I returned to my office, I changed into sneakers for the walk to my parking garage, then turned off my computer and slipped it into my briefcase. I stood just as a man appeared in my doorway—a tall man, the top of his head almost touching the doorframe. Carly was behind him, craning her neck, jabbing a finger at him and mouthing something like, *You have a visitor.*

News flash. I gave her a nod, and she turned away, satisfied that she'd done her duty.

"You wanted to see me?" I asked.

The man had a long neck, rising six inches or more from the unbuttoned collar of his rumpled white shirt and adding several more inches to his height than seemed entirely natural.

"May I come in?" He was young, maybe no older than I was, but his voice was a deep bass. He hadn't shaved that morning and his skin had an oily sheen to it.

"Sure," I said. "Have a seat." I sat myself.

"Thank you." He stepped jerkily to the chair and sat. Once sitting, he crossed one long leg over his knee and used both hands to pull it toward him. His gray suit was as rumpled as his shirt, and his striped tie hung at half-mast.

"What can I do for you?" I asked, wondering if he had just pulled a caffeine-fueled all-nighter.

He was looking at me curiously, the muscles in his face moving as if he were trying out various expressions in search of one that might be appropriate to the circumstances. I was looking at him curiously, too, of course, but doing my best to keep my own face still.

"I'm Jacob Chapman," he said finally.

That's where I'd heard his voice. "Did I just talk to you on the phone?" I asked.

"That's right." He pulled at his crossed leg. "I'm Nick Cantwell's chief of staff."

"You're younger than I'd have expected for a lieutenant governor's chief of staff."

"Thirty-four." His mouth moved, a twitch that affected only one side of his face.

Not quite as young as he looked, then. "It's been, what, thirty minutes since we spoke on the phone?"

He let go of his leg to look at his watch. "Almost forty. You're a five-minute walk from the Capitol."

"Ah. What kept you?" I said.

"Very funny."

I inclined my head modestly.

"You called Nick Cantwell's office claiming to be a Toni Prescott," he said.

"*A* Toni Prescott?" I said. "I didn't claim to be *the* Toni Prescott?"

"Let's not play games, Ms. Starling."

"Okay." I waited.

"So why did you call?"

"To talk to Mr. Cantwell."

"What about?"

"That would be between me and Mr. Cantwell."

"There's nothing between you and Mr. Cantwell."

"Well, that's true. My love so far has been wholly unrequited."

"That's *not* funny."

"No," I said. "I've met Mrs. Cantwell."

He eyed me. "Like I said, I'm his chief of staff. You can talk to me."

"I could," I said.

"Look. You can't expect to reach Mr. Cantwell just by calling the Office of Lieutenant Governor."

"However, I evidently can expect a prompt visit from his chief of staff."

"What are you trying to accomplish? This isn't going to get you anywhere, you know."

"I don't need to get far."

"On the phone you said you wanted to talk about a murder case. Last week you brought Mr. Cantwell's *name* into a murder case."

"I understand Brooks and Toni Prescott were big donors to Mr. Cantwell's campaign," I said.

"You understand wrong."

"You do know that Nick Cantwell's donors are a matter of public record," I said.

"Thousands of people donate money to his campaign. Mr. Cantwell doesn't know a fraction of them."

"Not everyone has a picture of themselves and Mr. Cantwell hanging in their hallway."

"Just what do you want here?" Chapman said. "Do you hope to accomplish something, or are you just playing the part of a human hand grenade?"

"I don't think Alexa Demming killed Brooks Prescott," I said. "I'm hoping to get her acquitted."

"And you somehow imagine Nick Cantwell can help you with that? On what basis?"

"Because of his connection to the Prescotts. To Mrs. Prescott particularly."

"What do you mean by that?"

"I think you know what I mean."

Chapman stood, jerking from his chair to what seemed like an impossible height. "You're playing a dangerous game, Ms. Starling."

I stayed in my seat, looking up. "That sounds vaguely like a threat."

"Aren't you threatening Mr. Cantwell?"

"So there's moral equivalence," I said. "Touché."

His eyes narrowed. I thought maybe he was giving me the hard stare, so I narrowed my eyes, too. I don't know how tough we looked, the two of us squinting across the office at each other, but that's how it ended. Chapman turned abruptly and went out.

I put my head back, thinking. I must have closed my eyes, because Brooke's voice seemed to come out of nowhere. "Are you all right?"

I opened my eyes and saw her standing in the doorway. "Peachy," I said.

"That last conversation sounded unpleasant."

"Not really. Just a little verbal fencing, each of us trying to draw the other out without saying anything ourselves."

"You gonna be here for lunch?"

"I don't know. I need to pay a visit to a pornographer."

"Peter Brawley?"

"Perhaps 'pornographer' is unfair. He likes to take pictures of naked women."

"And you're going to see him why?"

"I don't think he met Alexa in a bar by accident. I think he followed her in, and he cultivated the relationship on purpose."

"How come?"

I shook my head. "Somehow it feels like a set-up."

"For murder? Are you saying he killed Dr. Prescott?"

"Not yet," I said. "But I think he was involved somehow."

"And you aim to find out how?"

"I aim to find out," I said.

Famous last words. Peter Brawley wasn't in the office. There was just Stephanie, wearing a white blouse with enough buttons undone to hint at the richness of Brawley's investment.

"He hasn't come in today?" I asked her.

"He's in court."

I'd heard that one too often to believe it, even when it was true. "Oh, come on. Where is he really?" I said.

She hesitated. "I don't know. He doesn't answer his cell phone."

"Is that unusual?"

"No, not really. He could be doing a photo shoot."

I raised my eyebrows. "The photo shoots I've seen don't seem to be an early morning activity."

"Mr. Brawley prefers the morning, actually. The models are at their best, and the natural lighting is good."

"I'm curious. Does he practice law at all, or has he figured out some way to monetize his hobby of photographing women in various stages of undress?"

"I wouldn't know anything about that."

"Good answer. Very discreet. I would like to talk to him, though. Do you have his home address?"

"Not that I can give out."

"He takes a lot of his pictures at his home, doesn't he? Suppose I told you I was looking to get photographed?"

She smiled. "I wouldn't believe you."

"I'm getting married next month. A nicely bound photo album is something my new husband might really appreciate."

She shook her head.

"I was thinking of titling it *Robin Barebreast*."

She snorted. I didn't seem to be convincing her. I got a business card out of my purse and laid it on her desk.

"Tell him I stopped by," I said. "I'd like to talk to him."

"About getting photographed?"

"That and one or two other things." I gave her a smile, but she just looked at me speculatively. I let myself out and went down the stone steps to my car.

I thought I could find Brawley's address on the internet, but I was wrong. I called Rodney Burns.

"It's me," I said. "You busy?"

"Just waiting for your call."

"I need Peter Brawley's home address."

"Peter Brawley the lawyer?"

"You've heard of him?"

"Just from you."

I rolled my eyes. "Yes, that Peter Brawley then. Not the other one."

"There's another one?"

"Oh, for goodness sake, Rodney, just get me the address."

"Give me a moment." Rodney was about as humorless a man as you'd ever want to meet, but I could swear I heard a smile in his voice.

He came back with the address. I punched it into my phone, then worked my way to I-95 and headed north.

Brawley lived in a ten-year-old development just over the Hanover County line. The house was built of light-colored brick and had a ton of windows. In addition to the usual assortment of casement windows, there were Palladian windows on either side of the front door, a fanlight above it, a muntined hexagon above that. I parked on the street and mounted the steps to the front door.

I could hear the doorbell, but no one came to the door. Brawley wasn't in his office, he didn't answer his phone, and he wasn't answering his door. Where had the man got to? Though there didn't seem to be much point in trying the bell again, I did anyway. No answer.

From the sidewalk, I looked up through the hexagonal window at a catwalk with a railing of light colored wood. A row of casement windows marked the second story, but I couldn't see anything but a bit a ceiling through any of those. Clearly, though, no one was home. I turned back to my car, but stopped when I felt a prickle at the nape of my neck. I spun. Still no one at any of the windows, but I mounted the steps again and rattled the doorknob. Locked.

I started around the house toward the driveway, but my heels sank into the lawn and came out muddy, suggesting the sprinklers had been on that morning. Walking on my toes as much as possible, I made it as far as a window that looked into the garage. There was a light-colored car in the garage, a four-door sedan of some sort, but that was all I could see.

I straightened, considering my options. The driveway was closer than the sidewalk, so I went that way. No privacy fence enclosed the backyard. There seemed to be no privacy fences anywhere in the neighborhood: I could see the back decks of three different houses from where I stood. I fished my phone out of a skirt pocket and found Jordan's number, but changed my mind and didn't tap it. What were the police going to do, put out an APB for Brawley? Send in the SWAT team?

Back at my car, I sat in the front seat with my door open to change into my sneakers—more practical footwear to walk around to the back of the house. When I got to the back deck, I climbed the steps to the double back doors, which were mostly glass. Brawley had a large kitchen, all white tile and chrome and Corian countertops.

I tapped on the glass and, when I didn't get an answer, tried the door. The knob turned. Cue the spooky music. My heart began to hammer as temptation hit me full force. An unlocked door was as hard for me to resist as . . . Well, actually, I didn't know how hard an unlocked door was to resist. I'd never resisted.

Standing there on the deck, my heart in my throat, I turned to look at the other houses across the expansive lawns. Three houses, all with windows facing me. No one was on the decks, no one in the backyards, no one at any of the windows, at least that I could see. Were the houses empty, their occupants at work? There was no way to tell.

Why in the world does a man with Brawley's hobby live in a glass house within eyeshot of so many neighbors? He has to have women coming and going all the time. That might be a good thing, actually. Someone like me at the back door might be nothing to draw attention.

Or so I told myself. Taking a breath, I turned back to the door and, turning the knob, pushed it open.

Whatever I'd been expecting, nothing happened. No alarm sounded, and no one came running to investigate. Taking that as encouragement, I stepped into the house and closed the door behind me.

"Peter? It's Robin Starling."

The house absorbed the sound of my voice, and again there was silence.

"Here for my photo shoot," I added, more weakly. I crossed the kitchen, my sneakers silent on the tile floor.

Through the archway was one big room with a dining area and two clusters of sofas and uphol-stered chairs. A hallway opened off the great room, leading to several open doors, and a staircase led up to a catwalk that connected upstairs rooms on either side of the house.

"Hello?" I said.

The hallway on the main floor took me to a room set up as a library and another room with a half-dozen racks of women's clothes. I lifted out a hanger with a short black dress that wouldn't have come close to fitting me, another hanger with two strips of a polka-dotted fabric that I thought was a swimsuit—it was an itsy bitsy, teenie weenie, yellow polka-dot bikini! I laughed, and my hand went to my mouth to muffle the sound.

I listened, but I didn't seem to have alerted anyone. I took a few deep breaths. Other hangers held short shorts, tank-tops, cut-off T's, women's business attire, a nurse's uniform, a police uniform, miniskirts, feather boas, and belts wide and narrow. There were other props as well, a polished-wood stepladder—I pictured a woman in a short skirt atop it—a long pole—my imagination failed me—and shelves with several styles of eyeglasses, hair scrunchies, high-heeled shoes, a hand mirror, you name it.

I retraced my steps and headed up the staircase. From the top of the stairs I was on a level with the hexagonal window above the front door. I couldn't see into the kitchen from there, but I could look down into the rest of the house. Picking a direction at random, I went to the end of the house with what turned out to be the master bedroom. There was a bathtub in the middle of the room, one of those big ovals with water jets and the tap on one side, but at least the king-sized bed didn't have mirrors above it. I checked out the bathroom with its more prosaic sink, shower, and toilet, then headed back along the catwalk to the other end of the house.

There were two rooms, one with a queen bed and a nightstand and a bureau, so evidently Brawley had guests who didn't share his bed, at least on occasion. I crossed the hall to a room with a big leather chair and a desk holding three computer monitors and the docking station for a laptop. The desk only got a glance before my attention zeroed in on the man lying face down on the floor with what looked like a letter opener sticking out of his back. I think my heart stopped. The man was Brawley, the horseshoe of hair circling his bald head instantly recognizable.

An indeterminate amount of time passed before I recovered enough to kneel beside him and look into his floor-puckered face. His wide eyes stared through me to infinity, and no breath came from his partially open mouth. I touched a finger to his cheek, and it had a cold, rubbery feel.

I'd come across a dead body before, but, despite what may seem a coldly clinical description, nothing prepares you. I stood abruptly, my head swimming, my gaze fixed on the gold-handled letter opener someone had planted just inside Brawley's right shoulder blade. I had to get out of there—but could I?

On entering the house, I'd been careful. I hadn't touched the banister going up the stairs or anything else I could remember. Outside, though, my prints were probably on both the front and back doors. I couldn't leave. I had to call the police. The sooner the police arrived on the scene, the smaller the coroner's window would be for time of death.

I fished my phone out of the pocket of my skirt, my eyes scanning the room. Where was Brawley's camera? He was certain to own a nice one. His killer took it, perhaps, along with his laptop computer . . . unless it was in one of Brawley's desk drawers. Call the police, go through the drawers while you're waiting, I told myself. My gaze fell to the corpse. The fabric of Brawley's pants protruded at an odd angle near his hips: something was in his pocket.

I stared at it. A cell phone? Slipping my phone back into my skirt, I squatted beside the body and felt the hard, rectangular dimensions. Breathing rapidly, I worked my fingers into the pocket and drew out a Samsung Galaxy. My hands were tingling, and my legs felt weak. I stood, swayed, realized I was hyperventilating. I made a conscious effort to slow my breathing.

After a few moments, I tapped Brawley's phone with my thumb. The screen came on to show the time and date over a close-up of a woman's bare chest, possibly one that had been surgically enhanced.

"You sad, sorry . . ." I stopped. My voice seemed to carry and grow in the still silence of the house— and maybe Brawley hadn't been sad or sorry. Maybe he'd been living the dream.

I didn't know the passcode that would unlock the phone, but Brawley was right there, lying with his left arm extended and his right hand caught beneath his body. Was he right-handed or left-handed? I tried to remember whether there'd been any indication on my previous meeting with him. I couldn't. I moved to his left hand and bent to grasp his stiff hand and touch his index finger to the fingerprint scanner. When that didn't work, I tried his thumb, working the phone into his partially closed hand, rigid with rigor mortis. Still no results.

My breathing had quickened again, and I took a couple of slow deep breaths before scrambling around to his right side. His right arm wouldn't move. I had never observed rigor mortis before, but I had cross-examined more than one medical examiner about it. It started in the face and jaw after two to six hours, a large window. For it to have reached his shoulder and arm, it might have taken another four to six hours. So he'd been dead at least six hours and maybe twice that. According to his phone, it was 11:49, which put the time of death prior to six a.m. that morning, maybe prior to midnight.

If I forced his arm out, it would break the rigor mortis in his elbow and shoulder and make it clear to everyone that someone had tampered with the body. I didn't want that. It might not take them long to discover who that someone was.

Setting the phone on the floor, I gripped Brawley's shoulder and his pant leg to push him onto his side. Planning out a course of action, foolish as it may have been, had calmed me, though my breath was probably still coming faster than the exertion warranted. Brawley's right hand was against his stomach, unmoving, the fingers in a loose fist, the thumb protruding. I put my knee against his body to hold it while I got the phone, pushed the button to turn it on, then pressed the screen's fingerprint area against his thumb. I dragged the screen so that his thumb moved toward the home button, and the screen changed. I was in.

I stood, letting Brawley's body roll back onto its stomach, and blackness crowded my vision. I leaned forward, my heart hammering in my ears, my forearms braced on my knees. Dear God, dear God, have mercy on me a sinner. Dear god, dear God, have mercy on me a sinner. That wasn't how it went, but it was the phrase that echoed in my head. I calmed down enough to straighten up.

Stop doing stupid stuff, said a voice in my head. God?

I shook my head. If I was going to keep Brawley's phone, it was time to get out of the house, I thought. I glanced again at the screen in my hand and its columns of icons. I tapped the screen. I was going to have to keep doing that: if the phone went to sleep again, I'd be locked out, and all this would be for nothing.

Drop the phone and leave it, said the internal voice. You don't need to do this. I recognized the voice now. It wasn't God; it was Paul.

"There's stuff on that phone I need," I told him silently. "The prosecution isn't sharing." Standing over the body, looking down, another thought occurred to me. Alexa said she had given Brawley a key to her apartment. Were the police going to find her key on the keyring in the pocket of another dead man? She didn't think he'd been in her apartment, but suppose some of the unidentified fingerprints in her apartment turned out to be Brawley's. Suppose some of the fingerprints in Brawley's house were hers.

On the other hand, suppose Alexa's key wasn't on his keyring. That would raise some interesting possibilities. I acted as I considered them, and I had Brawley's keys in one hand and his phone in the other as I moved catlike down the stairs in my sneakers.

It wasn't going to be that easy. As I reached the bottom of the stairs, the doorbell rang, freezing me where I stood. The silhouette that was visible through the frosted glass looked like a woman's. Surely not Detective Michaels. A neighbor? Stephanie?

The woman tapped on the glass. "Peter?" The doorknob rattled as I began to move again, hotfooting it across the living room floor. There was a roll of paper towels in the kitchen standing upright on a wooden dowel. I tapped the screen of Peter's phone to give me a few more minutes and slid it into the pocket of my skirt with my own phone. I ripped off a few paper towels and used them to turn on the water at the kitchen sink. The front door opened as I turned it off.

"Peter? It's me."

Me. Could she possibly be less informative? As I went through the back door, I wiped the lever handle with the wet paper towels and ran them briefly over the edge of the door where I might have touched it.

I went down the deck steps at a jump, fishing for my keys and beeping my car door unlocked as I rounded the corner of the house. A Kia hatchback was parked behind my car. There was no sign of the woman now: the door of the house was standing open. I yanked open the door of my Beetle and swung in, jamming my key into the ignition, then stopped. I probably had a few seconds to improve the situation. I pushed up out of the car again and ran for the front door.

I had touched the front door's handle set, and I couldn't count on the woman, whoever she was, to have obliterated my prints. I sprinted to the steps and up them, what was now a soggy mass of paper towels still clutched in my left hand. I was running them along the handle set of the open door when a wailing began inside the house, coming from upstairs. I ran back down the steps and banged my head getting into my car. Already, I was fishing in my pocket for Brawley's phone. I couldn't let it go into sleep mode. If it locked me out now, I was lost.

The woman had seen my car, of course. If she'd noticed the license plate, if she had seen me, I was done, but I'd made my choices, and I was going to have to live with them. I shoved the car into gear and stepped on the gas.

Brawley's house was on a long street with a number of cul-de-sacs opening off it; no cross streets. I was near the entrance to the subdivision when I heard a siren, faint in the distance. I slowed. The odds that the siren had nothing to do with me seemed too long to bet on. As the siren grew louder, I turned into the last cul-de-sac and circled so I was facing out. I looked again at the phone in my hand, tapped the screen with my thumb.

That was when I noticed the blood on my leg, just above my right knee. My gorge rose, and I swallowed hard, shifting my feet in an effort to get a look at the soles of my running shoes. If I had blood on my knee, I probably had blood on my shoes, too—and now trace amounts of blood on the carpet of my car. The sound of a second siren joined the first.

Change of plan. I fished out my own phone, giving the screen of Brawley's another tap. I needed to change his password before it locked up on me, but right now I didn't have the time. I punched nine-one-one into my phone as a police car went by on Brawley's street, siren blaring. As it faded with distance, the sound of the second siren grew, then a second police car went by, the sound of its siren diminishing, then cutting off completely. I tapped the green button on my screen and held the phone to my ear.

"Nine-one-one," the dispatcher said. "What is your emergency?"

"This is Robin Starling. A man's been murdered. I found the body."

"Who's been murdered? Where are you?"

I told him who. "He was in his house, lying on the floor with something sticking out of his back. The door was unlocked. I—I went in and found him."

"Are you at the house now? Are you safe?"

"I had to leave. Someone was there, coming in the front door. I ran out the back to get away. I'm in my car now. I'm so scared. I—oh, my gosh—I almost . . . Oh, I can hardly drive."

"Calm down," the dispatcher said. "Are you where you can pull over, get off the road?"

"The address is 745 High Meadows. Mechanicsville," I said, giving him Brawley's address. I made a retching noise. "I think I'm going to be sick." I punched off and dropped my phone in the cup holder. Brawley's phone still showed the rows of icons, but the screen had dimmed. I tapped it, and it brightened.

For the moment, I didn't hear any sirens, so I put my car in gear and pulled out of the cul-de-sac, turning away from Brawley's house. Almost immediately I heard the sound of yet another distant siren, but I kept going. A fire truck rolled into the subdivision as I was turning out of it, and I was free, at least for the moment.

My phone was ringing, nine-one-one calling back, but I ignored it. There was a 7-11 on the corner just before I got to I-95, and I pulled into the parking lot to take a closer look at Brawley's phone. My phone stopped ringing.

I was part of the Apple universe, so the Galaxy wasn't familiar to me. I went into Settings, looking for a way to reset the passcode or to keep the phone from locking when it went to sleep, but either option required me to enter the existing passcode. A Camaro pulled into the parking space next to mine, the bass of its sound system vibrating the fillings in my teeth, but I gave it no more than a glance. It was possible to add a fingerprint to the list of those that would unlock the phone—but that also required me to know the existing passcode. I was going to have to keep tapping the screen.

I put the phone in the empty cup holder, but had another thought. Picking up the phone again, I went back into Settings and found Auto-Lock. It was set to one minute. I changed it to Never. With any luck, that should take care of my problem, one of them. I put the phone back in the cup holder, put my car in gear again, and headed for my office and Brooke Marshall, my resident computer whiz. As I drove, I kept glancing at the screen of Brawley's phone, but it continued to glow brightly, the rows of icons only partially obscuring Stephanie's breasts.

Chapter 12

I went into my office only long enough to put down my briefcase, unsling my purse, and let it drop to the floor behind my desk. Brooke Marshall was at her computer. As I entered her office, she moved her mouse, leaning forward, then gave the enter key on her keyboard a last tap. I closed the door.

"What's up?" she said.

"I've been bad."

"You stopped at Krispy Kreme for an apple fritter?"

I shook my head. I laid Brawley's cell phone next to her computer keyboard, pulled up a chair, and sat.

"That's not your phone," Brooke said.

I shook my head.

"Say something. You're freaking me out."

"It's Peter Brawley's phone."

Brooke looked back at it. "What's that he's got for wallpaper? It looks like . . ."

"Two breasts, I know. I think they belong to a woman named Stephanie."

"And you have Brawley's phone—why?"

"I stole it."

"And managed to unlock it? I'm impressed."

"I had to use Brawley's finger." I took a breath. "He's dead. Somebody killed him. We may not have much time. I may not."

Her eyes had gone wide, but she said, "What do you need me to do?"

"Get everything you can off that phone."

She picked it up, and I felt the lifting of a burden.

I said, "I don't know whether Alexa had anything to do with Brawley's death or not. She . . ."

"What's that on your knee? Is it blood?"

"I think so. Yeah. I haven't had a chance to do anything about it." A shiver started between my shoulder blades and worked its way up.

"Here, I'll fix you." She grabbed a bottle of the stuff she used to clean her computer monitor and gave my knee a squirt, then bent over it with a Kleenex. On the white tissue, the reddish color was obvious.

"I think I'm going to be sick," I said.

"No time for that." But she dragged her trashcan between us. "Besides, I find nausea contagious. If you throw up, I'll throw up."

There was a rap on Brooke's door. "Is Robin in there?" Carly's voice.

"Showtime," I told Brooke. I stood up.

"Brooke?" Carly said.

Brooke opened her desk drawer and slid the phone into it. I waited for her to close the drawer before I opened the door. Behind Carly stood Detective Emma Michaels and a big, beefy guy wearing a short-sleeve shirt and a tie, his police badge on a flap tucked into his shirt pocket.

"We'd like to talk to you," Michaels said.

Michaels's partner was named Matt Jones, a cop I'd seen before but never dealt with. We were in my office, me in my high-backed chair with the desk between us. "I assume you're here about Peter Brawley," I said.

"You admit to being in his house? Today?"

"I found the body. I'm the one who called it in."

Her eyes narrowed.

"Isn't that why you're here?"

"Matt." She jerked her head at the door, and he got up and left, pulling out his phone.

We waited for him in silence, Emma's steely gaze fixed on my face, me maintaining as mild an expression as I could manage under the circumstances.

Matt came back. "She made the call from her cell phone at twelve-eleven."

"Nice of them to tell us." She looked at me. "You left before the police got there. Why?"

"I couldn't call from the house. Someone was there, trying to get in. I called as soon as I was safe."

"Safe from—"

"The intruder, whoever it was. I don't think he saw me."

"He? You don't think *he* saw you?"

"Or she. I didn't wait around to see."

"I understand Alexa Demming was here to see you this morning."

"Among others."

"And immediately you raced out to Peter Brawley's house."

"I'd been meaning to talk to him for days. I went to his office first, but he wasn't there."

"Uh huh."

"Who was it trying to get in? Did you catch him?" I asked.

"Her. *She* waited for the police."

"Who was it? You don't think she was the killer, coming back to clean up after herself, do you?"

Her mouth stretched. "We don't."

I said, "When you're there with a dead body, a man on the floor with a knife or a letter opener or something sticking out of his back, all you can think of is that the murderer's coming back."

"It was Stephanie Pritchard, Brawley's administrative assistant. She saw your car out front, even caught a glimpse of you driving off."

"So that's why you're here," I said.

Matt Jones entered the conversation. "How did you get into the house?" he asked.

"The door was unlocked."

"Stephanie Pritchard says it wasn't."

"The back door," I said.

Jones exchanged a glance with Emma Michaels. "What caused you to go around to the back door?" he said.

"Brawley didn't answer the front. I didn't plan on going in, of course. I thought I'd just look in the windows and make sure everything seemed okay." I lifted my shoulders. "At his office they told me he'd gone incommunicado."

"But you tried the back door, and it was unlocked," Jones said.

I gave a short laugh, mildly gratified at the hint of hysteria. "I don't know what made me try it. It swung open, and I got this creepy feeling. Brawley didn't answer my shouts, and I thought he might have had a stroke or a heart attack or something."

"An unlocked door made you think he'd had a heart attack," Michaels said flatly.

"Just that something might be wrong. I didn't stop to think it out."

Jones said, "Did you touch the body?"

I nodded. "It was cold." As I recalled the rubbery, unnatural feel of his face, the shiver came naturally. "I knew right then there was nothing I could do to help."

"But you saw the letter opener, you knew he'd been murdered. Yet you delayed calling the police," Michaels said.

"Someone was coming in." I managed a small laugh. "I about jumped out of my shoes when the doorknob started rattling, let me tell you. Then there was a scratching at the lock, but I was halfway to the back door by then."

"We'd like to see your shoes," Jones said.

"Sure." I bent over to unlace them and take them off, then set the Asics on the top of my desk. Michaels turned them over to look at the soles. They looked clean to me.

"Think we could get anything off these?" she asked her partner.

"Might get something off her carpet," he said. "Look at that."

Michaels and I both craned our necks. There was a smear of something on the medium brown carpet, visible even against the texture.

"I think I'm going to be sick," I said.

Jones got down on his hands and knees to sniff the carpet. Showing rare impulse control, I resisted the urge to tell him, *Good boy*.

"Is it blood?" Michaels asked.

"Can't tell. I think so. We better take it with us," Jones said.

"My carpet?" I let a note of incredulity enter my voice.

Michaels looked at me, her expression sour. "Of course, she admits she touched the body," she said to Jones.

"Still," he said. "We don't know how this is going to develop."

"I must have stepped in his blood," I said. "Oh my gosh." I leaned forward, bracing my forearms on my knees, but Jones was opening up a knife that looked appropriate for gutting deer. I straightened as he stabbed down into my carpet and angled the blade to cut a long gash in it.

"Hey, what are you doing?" I said. "You can't do that."

"Sure I can," Jones said. "Watch."

"Where's your warrant?"

"We don't need a warrant," Michaels said. "Plain sight."

"What's in plain sight, a spot on my carpet? You don't have any idea what it is. If you want to tear up my carpet and take away a chunk of it to analyze, you need probable cause to believe it's blood—and not just blood, but blood from Brawley's house."

"We find ourselves confronted with an emergency that threatens destruction of the evidence," Michaels said. "We leave to go get a warrant, you get out the paper towels and the spray bottle."

"This isn't an emergency," I said, though Jones had already cut three sides of his rectangle. He lifted the carpet to hold it as he started on the fourth. "There are two of you," I said. "One of you can stay here while the other one goes for the warrant. Heck, you can both sit right there and get a magistrate on the phone."

Michaels's smile was more of a smirk. "What are you worried about?" she said. "You've admitted to touching the body."

"What I'm worried about is your partner's cut a hole in my dad-gum carpet."

"You do righteous indignation really well," Michaels said. "Must be a great asset for a trial lawyer."

"There's not a thing you can do with that strip of carpet, you know. In these circumstances, whatever is on it is inadmissible."

"Then you've really got nothing to worry about."

Jones stood with his bit of carpet.

"Do you have an evidence bag, or are you going to walk around risking contamination? The two of you have been in that house, too. No telling how much blood you brought out of it."

Michaels came to her feet. "I imagine we'll be seeing you in court, Counselor," she said. She picked up my shoes, too.

"What? You're going to take my shoes?"

She only smiled.

When the two of them had left, I sat staring at the carpet pad visible through rectangle of missing carpet. It was badly scored from Jones's knife.

I've admitted to being in Brawley's house, I told myself. *If that's his blood on my carpet, if there are traces of blood on my shoes, it isn't probative of anything.* But my shiver this time was completely involuntary.

"You okay?"

I started. Rodney Burns was leaning into my open doorway. He smiled apologetically. "Sorry. Are you in?"

I sat back. "Sure."

The rest of Rodney's body followed his head into the doorway. He was carrying a legal pad. "I have something to report," he said.

219

"Good news." My voice sounded stressed, even to me, and he hesitated. I extended a hand to one of the client chairs. "Sit," I said.

He sat, but remained forward in the chair.

"What's Brooke doing, did you notice?" I asked.

He shook his head. "She left." He cleared his throat. "I understand Peter Brawley was found dead at his residence this morning."

"Yes. I found him."

Rodney relaxed a bit. "So you were the one who called the police?"

"I was."

He sat back and crossed his ankle over his knee. "That's okay, then," he said.

"We can hope."

He nodded. "So that's okay," he said again.

"It is." My gaze strayed to the hole in my carpet, which Rodney the detective had so far failed to detect.

My gaze came back to Rodney, and he started, as if only just remembering why he had come in. "I found the Prescotts' dry cleaners." He lifted several pages from his legal pad and extracted several sheets of copy paper that had been tucked into it. He laid them on my desk and pushed them toward me.

They were photocopies of five claim checks from Keen Cleaners. I shuffled through them. "What do we have here?" I asked. "A blazer, a blouse . . ."

"Eight shirts, three pants, a two-piece suit, four skirts, and one dress," he read from his legal pad.

"So if you strip out the women's clothes, we're looking at eight shirts, three pairs of slacks, a suit, and a sports jacket." The clothes found in Alexa's apartment.

He nodded. "That's what I thought."

"Those clothes are most of the evidence that Brooks Prescott was staying at Alexa's apartment. Whoever picked them up at the cleaners might have taken them straight out there and hung them in her closet."

"The bill was paid by credit card." He took another sheet of paper out of his legal pad, this one the photocopy of a credit card receipt for $68.80. The signature was almost illegible, but the last name clearly started with a P.

"Toni Prescott?" I said hopefully.

"You think that's a T?"

"You think it's not? It can't be a B, can it?"

"Doctors have notoriously bad handwriting," he said lugubriously.

It wasn't what I wanted to hear. "Can you find out? Go by the Spine and Joint Clinic and see if you can get a copy of his signature."

"You got it." He got up, sweeping his paperwork off my desk.

"And Rodney?"

He turned back in the doorway.

"Thanks."

His mustache spasmed, and he was gone.

"So was that blood on your carpet or not?" Brooke asked.

She had texted me, and I had joined her for a very late lunch at our favorite hamburger place downtown. Though I usually had a chicken sandwich with mustard on a whole wheat bun, today I was eating a hamburger with mayonnaise instead of mustard and all the vegetables. Hamburgers, rather than ice cream or pastries, are my comfort food, and today I felt in need of it.

"I love a hamburger with mayonnaise," I said, talking around the food in my mouth.

"What does that have to do with blood on your carpet?"

I swallowed. "Not much," I conceded. I took another bite.

"Not much?"

"Okay, it doesn't have anything to do with it. Give me a moment." I closed my eyes as I chewed. When I'd swallowed, I opened them again to find Brooke giving me the eye.

I sighed as I reached for my Diet Dr. Pepper. "It might be blood," I said. "Anything's possible."

"Does it make any difference? I don't understand why they cut out the carpet to take with them. You've admitted you were out there. You called nine-one-one and said you were there."

I shook my head. "My thought is they're leaving their options open. If they decide to prosecute me for the murder of Peter Brawley—or maybe as an accessory—they're going to want as many links in their chain of evidence as possible."

She regarded me silently for a moment, then took a bite of her own sandwich.

"What about you?" I said. "You've had nearly an hour with Brawley's phone. You get anything?"

"I did find an interesting file on his Google Drive." Her iPad had been sitting on the corner of the table. She opened the flap as she pushed it between us, then touched the button.

The screen lit up to show Toni Prescott reclining in the bathtub I'd seen in Brawley's bedroom. The thick foam of soap bubbles didn't quite cover the tops of her breasts.

"Whoa!" a man said, stopping beside our table with his tray of food. He was twenty-five or so, blond and good looking in his white shirt and tie.

"Do you mind?" Brooke said, looking up at him as she folded the flap back over her screen. "We're looking at pictures of naked women here."

"I don't mind at all." He pulled out a chair and sat down. "That wasn't either of you, was it? Looked like a brunette to me."

"It was a brunette," I said. "Good eye."

He wiggled his eyebrows at me.

"Okay, that's a bit much. You can go now."

"Do you like men, too, or just women? If you like men, then I just blew it big time."

"We're selective, but yes, you did. Big time."

"Well, crap."

When he was gone, I said, "He turned out to be kind of creepy."

"Of course, we're the ones sitting in a restaurant looking at pictures of naked women," Brooke said.

"Good point. Let's see that picture of Toni Prescott again."

"Is that who it is? I pulled up the photograph of her that was in the paper, but it was a small picture and I couldn't be sure." She uncovered the screen again and touched the home button.

"It's Toni Prescott," I said. "Five years ago, maybe." As strikingly attractive a woman as Toni was now, she didn't have the fresh-faced, girl-next-door look of the girl in the photo.

"So Brawley knew her," Brooke said.

"And pretty well, looks like. Is that the only photograph he had of her?"

"Not even close. Do you want to see the rest of them?"

"I don't see the point. Anyone else we know?"

"Maybe." She didn't elaborate.

"Well? Don't keep me in suspense."

"Brawley had surprisingly few pictures of women who were completely naked," Brooke said. "Most of the photos hide key body parts with bubbles or a strip of fabric—even a strategically placed object or piece of furniture. Of course, very few of the photos show women completely clothed, either."

"Brooke," I said warningly.

"Okay, okay. Here's a folder Brawley put together just a couple of days ago. No nudity involved."

She tapped the screen a few times, then tilted the tablet toward me.

"What," I began as the screen rotated toward me, and stopped. Toni Prescott and a man not her husband were sitting at a small table with a white table cloth, both of them in profile, but both recognizable.

"That's . . ."

"I know," Brooke said.

It was Nick Cantwell, Virginia's lieutenant governor.

There were other photographs of the two of them together, some at obviously public functions, others of the two of them going into and out of restaurants and bars, once going across what looked like a hotel lobby. Individually, none of the pictures was especially damning. Cumulatively, though . . . cumulatively, they seemed to tell a story.

"What do you think Anita's reaction to these would be?" Brooke asked.

"Hard to know."

"We know her father was a governor and she has a temper," Brooke said.

"We do know that."

"And Peter Brawley had photographs that suggest her husband wasn't entirely faithful to her. I wonder what he was doing with them?"

"That's the question, isn't it?" I said.

Chapter 13

Peter Brawley had a bathtub in the middle of his bedroom. Mike McMillan had a hot tub set in the deck behind his house. That evening the four of us were in it, though I don't mean to suggest decadence by association. We were all wearing bathing suits, and Paul even had a T-shirt over his. The drinks we all had near to hand came not from a pitcher of margaritas, but from a pitcher of fruit-infused water with a column of strawberries and limes at its core. Mike had just acquired the specially constructed pitcher courtesy of Brooke, who seemed to have developed a concern that we were all becoming hard-core alcoholics.

"You have beer, don't you, Mike?" Paul had asked when she brought out the pitcher that evening.

Mike looked at Brooke, who said, "We don't have to drink *every* night."

"I know we don't have to," Paul said. "We *get* to—but, actually, we don't. What does it come to, a couple of beers or a glass of wine two or three nights a week?"

"Or three or four," Brooke said. "Actually, pretty much every time we're together."

"When we're together, it's a festive occasion," Paul said.

"Not tonight it's not. We have a lot to talk about. You and Robin have the first of your counseling sessions tomorrow, and Robin's about to be arrested for murder."

"You told me that was going to be okay," Paul said to me. "That you explained."

"Sure," Brooke said. "A man's blood is splattered all over her office, but she explained."

"It was one spot—a few spots—and it wasn't splattered," I said.

"She told them she broke into Brawley's house and played patty-cake with his corpse," Mike said. "You can see why the police would find that explanation deeply satisfying."

Paul had sunk down in the water so that only his nose and eyes were above the bubbling surface.

"I said I touched his corpse," I said. "And those spots on my carpet may turn out not to be blood at all," I said. "They might be a few drops of spilled coffee that've been on that carpet for weeks."

"Wouldn't that be nice?" Brooke said.

"I admitted to being in Brawley's house," I said. "Maybe I shouldn't have been, but when I found his body, I called the police, just as any good citizen would have. I would have waited for them, but someone else was there, trying to get in. I got scared, and I ran."

I didn't think it was a bad story, but a stream of bubbles exploded from Paul's mouth.

Mike said, "It would be nice if you'd been the first one to call the police—not the scary someone trying to get in."

"It would have," I conceded. "I should have been calling as I ran. The scary someone—who turned out to be Stephanie Pritchard, by the way, Brawley's receptionist—had seen my car, even if she hadn't noticed the license plate."

"You had a lot to think through," Brooke said. "Probably only a couple of minutes passed between you leaving the house and your phone call."

"It her usual high-wire act," Mike said. "Any other lawyer would have gone back to her car when no one answered the door. Heck, nine out of ten lawyers wouldn't have been there in the first place."

"Was there a survey?" I asked.

"And once you found the body . . ."

"I got some good stuff out of that house," I said. "A phone, a ring of keys. I still need to go by Alexa's apartment to see if the key she gave him is on that ring."

Paul was still blowing bubbles, his nostrils flaring between bursts as he inhaled.

"What are you doing?" Mike asked him irritably. "You aren't concerned about all this?"

Paul pushed up out of the water enough to speak. "Oh, I'm more than concerned, I'm terrified. What am I going to do, though? I'm marrying a legal Evel Knievel. Somehow I've got to get used to it."

228

"Who is Evel Knievel?" Brooke said.

"Stunt man in the sixties and seventies," Mike said. "Mostly did motorcycle jumps. You can still see some of them on YouTube."

Paul pushed up out of the water enough to say, "And there was a movie starring a very young George Hamilton."

"Who's George Hamilton?" Brooke said. "And don't tell me he's an actor. What's he been in?"

Paul and Mike started naming movies. The conversation had clearly drifted, which suited me fine. I drained my strawberry-and-lime-infused water and reached for the pitcher for a refill. As I settled back into the bubbling water, Paul and Mike averted their gazes.

"Excuse me?" I said.

"Yes, excuse you," Brooke said, and she gave Mike's leg a hard push with her foot.

"I'm sorry," he said. "Your eye just tends to follow movement."

"*Your* eye tends to follow movement," Brooke said.

"Anybody's eye. You looked, too."

"Oh, good grief," I said. "Do we all need to wear T-shirts?"

"How do you like her swimsuit?" Paul asked Mike. "I picked it out."

"So you said."

"You noticed her abs, didn't you? She thinks she looks scrawny."

"This is ridiculous," Brooke said. She stood, dripping water. In the dim light of twilight, you couldn't see that the blue of her simple bikini matched her eyes, or even that her suit was blue, but you could see that she looked good in it.

"You see?" Mike said. "Robin looked."

Brooke snatched our coverups off the nearby chair and tossed mine to me. I stood in the hot tub to put mine on as she was shrugging into hers, and the boys got their show.

"You realize this defeats the purpose of a coverup," Paul said. "They're soaked now. What are you going to put on when you get out?"

"Those big old beach towels," I said, pointing.

"That's no fun."

Brooke said, "We won't have any choice. Wet coverups don't cover up anything."

Paul and Mike exchanged a look, and I got the idea they didn't see a problem.

"Tell me about this counseling session I'm signed up for," I said. "You've had yours, haven't you?"

"The minister wanted us to talk about what we had in common," Brooke said. "The things we liked to do together. Do you know what Mike told him?"

Paul reached for his water.

"I just quoted a bit of scripture," Mike said, sounding defensive.

"You said sex," Brooke said. "You said we couldn't keep our hands off each other, that's what we had in common."

"I amended it. I said we were looking forward to . . ." He moved his head. " . . . to sex."

"Because it is better to marry than to burn with lust, you said."

"Paul said it—different Paul—First Corinthians, I think."

"I say it, too," Paul said. "I'm not in favor of burning with lust."

"So we need to think of things we like to do together," I told him. "Not sex or drinking or eating until we feel sick."

"What else is there?" Paul said.

"There's getting together with friends. There's taking Deeks for a walk."

"There's politics," Mike said. "I understand a scandal involving the lieutenant governor is about to break."

"And that's something we wouldn't know anything about if Robin hadn't taken Brawley's phone," Brooke said.

"Thank you," I said.

"The pictures suggest Prescott had a motive for killing Nick Cantwell," Mike said. "You think he tried, and the wrong one ended up on the floor?"

"I don't know. Can you think of a reason they'd have had their showdown in Alexa's apartment?"

Paul said, "If Prescott went there to kill Cantwell, why would he let Cantwell get behind him with a table lamp?"

"Brawley had photographs," Brooke said. "Cantwell sure had a motive for killing him."

"Maybe Prescott had photographs, too," Mike said. "We don't know what was on his phone."

"No, we don't," I said. "One thing we do know now: Peter Brawley knew Toni Prescott and he's known her for years."

"That is a coincidence," Paul said.

"It's a huge coincidence," I said. "Toni Prescott is having an affair with Nick Cantwell, okay. Alexa Demming has been flirting big time with Toni's husband, still okay. He was a nice looking guy, and any number of women might have been flirting with him. It's when Alexa meets Toni's good friend Peter at a bar that it all becomes too much."

"Six degrees of separation," Mike said. "Every person on the planet is connected to every other person by a chain of no more than five acquaintances."

"*Six Degrees of Separation* was a Will Smith movie," Paul said, as if that gave the theory any credibility.

"That would be fine if they met and had a beer and went their own ways," I said. "They didn't. The two of them cooked up a harebrained scheme that involved filing a sexual harassment claim that named Brooks Prescott, the husband of Peter's good friend Toni."

"Who was having an affair with Nick Cantwell," Brooke said. "An affair that was documented on Brawley's Google Drive.

"An affair that maybe Toni's husband found out about," Mike said. "That maybe he had evidence of."

"Now we're really speculating," Paul said.

"But I'm a lot closer to being able to prove it," I said. "I now have photographic evidence that Toni and Virginia's lieutenant governor were having an affair—and that Toni and Peter Brawley were long-time acquaintances. I just drew a pair of aces."

"People's lives are on their phones," Brooke said. "When she had the chance at Brawley's, Robin had to take it."

"I'd been trying to get hold of Prescott's phone," I said. "Just think what might be on that."

"You're risking prison to win a case," Paul said, darkly. "How is that a good gamble?"

"I'm more worried about her law license," Mike said. "How long can she keep drawing aces?"

"As long as it takes," Brooke told him. She held up her glass of fruit-infused water, and, grateful for the support, I raised my own to clink glasses with her. Then I drained my water as if I were taking a belt of something a good deal stronger. I might have drawn a pair of aces, but for all I knew Jim Borger was holding a royal flush.

As I entered the Executive Suites the next morning, Stephanie Pritchard stood.

"Hi, Stephanie," I said.

"Hi. We need to talk."

"Come on back."

"I'd rather talk here."

My gaze went to Carly, who was doing her best to pretend she had no interest in our conversation.

"I have nothing to hide," Stephanie said. "I want everything to be out in the open."

Sharon Beasley, a woman who handled the business end of a lawn service company, came in behind me and stopped at Carly's desk for her mail.

"I know you were there," Stephanie said. "What I want to know is did you kill him."

Carly and the lawn-service woman were being very still.

"And you think out here in the open is the best place to get a truthful answer to that?" I said.

"Did you?"

"You know I didn't. He was dead long before I came by your office looking for him. If that hasn't come out yet, it will."

"You could have been at his house the night before. Why did you wait until he was dead to start looking for him?"

"A coincidence. If I'd known he was dead, why would I have gone back to his house? Nobody had any reason to connect me to him."

Stephanie was blinking very fast. "A killer always returns to the scene of her crime," she said.

"That's just a saying. A killer returns to the scene of his crime, a dog returns to his vomit. Look, let me get you some coffee. We can sit somewhere and talk about it."

"You'll kill me," she said, just as Dave Johnstone, the other lawyer in the executive suites, came in through the glass doors.

234

"I won't kill you," I said. "I won't even beat you up real bad."

She sucked in a breath.

"I'm kidding," I said. "I have no reason to hurt you."

Sherri and Dave and Carly were all watching us, not even pretending to mind their own business.

"I'm the one who found the body, you know. I told them you were out there," Stephanie said.

"Sure. The police have been here to see me, and I've admitted being there. Now all that's out, and you can't hurt me anymore—so there's no reason for me to hurt you."

It seemed to reassure her. She took a breath, and her shoulders relaxed a bit. "Okay," she said.

"Okay?"

"Okay, I'll take that coffee.

I got her coffee, guided her into my office, and got the door closed behind us.

"I know it was a shock for you, finding the body," I said as she sipped her coffee, holding the styrofoam cup with both hands.

"Peter was such a nice man," she said, her eyes on the surface of her coffee.

"I know you'll miss him."

She nodded, and a tear slid down her cheek.

"It was a shock for me, too," I said. "For my part, I'd like to nail the person who killed him."

She took another sip of her coffee.

"Is there any possibility he was blackmailing someone?" I said.

She looked up. "How can you say that?""

"I'm not saying it. I'm just asking. He had a nice house and enough money to spend on boob-jobs for his models. Where did the money come from?"

"His law practice was very successful, believe it or not."

"What did he do exactly? What was the bulk of his practice?"

"Mostly copyright law." She sniffed.

I frowned. Copyright law fit with his interest in photography, but in Richmond I didn't see much money in it.

"He got a class action certified once a few years ago."

"Ah." A single class action might easily have produced enough money for Brawley to retire on. Mass tort litigation—and law practices like Mike's where your checks came from the government—seemed to be where the big bucks were, so naturally I myself was mired in criminal defense work.

"He never sold a picture back to one of his subjects, as far as you know," I said.

"No. He wouldn't do anything to hurt one of his girls."

"Toni Prescott seems to have been one of his girls," I said. "Did you know her?"

She held my gaze, and for a moment I thought she wasn't going to answer. Then she said, "Her name used to be Rawlings, Toni Rawlings. I knew her at Hooters."

"Is that where Brooks Prescott met her?"

She nodded. "I think so."

"Did Peter and Brooks know each other, too?"

"I don't think so. A far as I know, they never met."

"Not even after Brooks and Toni got married?"

"Not that I know of."

"Did Peter and Toni remain friends?"

"She never came to the office, but I think so, yeah. I think they talked on the phone some."

"Maybe she continued to pose for him," I suggested.

"I wouldn't think so. She had a good thing going, her gig with Dr. Prescott."

"Is that how she thought of it? A gig?"

"That's how I thought of it. I didn't talk to her, so I don't know."

Aubrey Biggs was pacing in front of Carly's desk. I gave him a nod as I walked Stephanie through the reception area to the elevator. He returned the nod, his gaze flicking briefly to Stephanie. There was no reaction to her that I could tell, not even the automatic appraisal that so many men give to women with her face and body. When I came back through the glass doors, he jerked his head and fell into step beside me.

As soon as my office door closed behind us, he said, "Alexa's been rearrested, this time charged with the murder of Peter Brawley."

"What makes them think she killed him?"

His eyes seemed to bore into mine. "You tell me."

"As far as I know, the two of them haven't talked since I took over Alexa's case."

"Then what were you doing at his house this morning?"

"He's the one responsible for Alexa's sexual harassment claim. He also had a key to her apartment. I thought it was time we talked."

"But you didn't get to."

"No."

"I'm not going to ask you if you killed him."

"Thank you."

"I am going to ask if you're covering up for someone."

"Someone like who?"

"Like Alexa."

"Has she seen Brawley since she got out of jail?"

He broke eye contact. "You'll have to ask her. I don't know."

"The answer to your question is no, I'm not covering up for anyone. Until this moment, I had no idea there was anything to tie Alexa to Brawley's murder."

He sagged back into his chair. He seemed very small, no larger than a boy. Of course, in terms of his merely physical attributes, he wasn't much larger than a boy.

"What does tie her to the murder?" I asked him.

He shook his head. "Things are going to get a lot worse before they get better. Search warrants have been issued for your home and office. Emma Michaels is talking to Borger about charging you as an accessory after the fact."

I was silent. Alexa's connection to Borger's murder, whatever it was, raised the stakes for me considerably.

Aubrey said, "They can prove you moved the body."

"They can prove that I moved it?"

"There was blood underneath it and your footprint right in the middle of it."

"That's pretty persuasive," I acknowledged.

"I appreciate all you've done, Starling, all you've tried to do." He fell silent.

"But?" I prompted.

"But I'm afraid I'm going to have to find another lawyer."

"No, you're not," I said.

He raised his eyebrows.

"Only Alexa can fire me."

He made a disgusted noise as he got to his feet. "I'm going to have to talk to her about that."

"Tell her things are beginning to come together, appearances to the contrary notwithstanding."

"Coming together. What are you going to be able to do from a jail cell?"

"Aubrey. Why did you hire me?"

He moved his head, unwilling to concede to anything.

"I didn't get the plaque made, but think about it. You hired me for a reason. The situation looks black right now. They've looked black for me before—haven't they? How many times have you thought you'd strip me of my law license?"

"I can give you 'til—"

I got to my feet, and he stopped.

"You can give me through trial. That's where lawyers earn their fee."

"When you say things are coming together . . ."

"It's nothing I can talk about right now."

He made a face.

"Once I'm in trial, I can call people to the stand and force them to answer questions. Until then—"

"Until then, Alexa's back in jail, and Mom and Dad are going crazy. I'm going crazy."

"So it's your job to hold yourself together. Them, too. Give me some space, and let me do my thing."

His breathing was audible.

"Okay?" I said.

He held his breath for several seconds, then let it out. "Okay," he said.

"Good."

"You can't let us down here," he said. "We're counting on you."

"I won't let you down."

I watched him exit through the reception area, then I headed down the hall toward the back stairs, fishing out my phone as I walked. The police would be showing up with their search warrant at any moment, and they might or might not have an arrest warrant with them.

"Paul," I said when he answered. "Where are you?"

"I'm on my way to get you. We've got our marriage counseling this morning, remember?"

I'd forgotten. "I remember," I said.

"You can still go, can't you? Nothing's come up?"

"I can't still go." Marriage counseling was ideal, actually. No one would think to look for me in a church, yet it wouldn't look like I'd taken to cover.

"Robin, what's going on?"

"Going on? I'm going to church with my fiancé. By the way, don't pick me up out front. I'll be waiting for you in the alley behind my building."

Chapter 14

Neither Paul nor I was very focused on the marriage counseling and perhaps told the preacher more than we would have if we'd been paying attention. Paul didn't talk about burning with lust, for which I was grateful, not wanting to call a minister-of-the-gospel's attention to myself as an object thereof. Paul did discuss being worried about me and about my job and about the terrific risks I took.

"Do you think you could scale it back a bit?" the minister, a man named Ralph Seekins, asked me. He had a full head of wavy, graying hair and an earnest demeanor.

"I'm a trial lawyer," I said. "A certain amount of stress goes with the job."

"I don't think Paul is talking about stress. He's talking about taking chances. If you feel you have to take them and he regards them as unnecessary, it's bound to put pressure on your relationship." Ralph turned over his hands and gave me an apologetic smile. "I'd heard of you, so I googled you in preparation for this meeting today. I found more than I expected."

"If I didn't take risks, I'd never have met Paul," I said. I looked at Paul. "You remember. We found a body together."

Paul looked at the minister, who sat silently a few moments before saying, "Young love," in wistful tones. I suspected sarcasm.

"We are going into this with a bit of baggage," Paul said.

"Baggage is what we don't have," I objected. "No prior marriages, no children by different people, no history of cheating, not even any serious arguments . . ."

Seekins was sitting back in his chair, his fingers steepled.

"Unless we're having one now," Paul said.

"What do you want me to do, be like Mike and take up Social Security Disability? I'd be bored out of my skull."

"I don't want you to do that. I just want you to, I don't know, be careful. Stay in your office, maybe. Let your cases come to you."

"If I do that, I won't know what's going on. I'll be going into the courtroom blind."

"You'd still be one of the best trial attorneys in the city of Richmond." He looked at Seekins. "The problem is, she lacks confidence in herself. She overcompensates."

I looked at Paul incredulously, sensing a gulf of unexpected dimensions between us. I held out my hand. "Allow me to introduce myself. Robin Starling,

243

the most cocky, overbearing female you'll ever hope to meet."

Paul just looked at my hand, but Seekins laughed, bless him. I dropped my hand to my lap. "We haven't talked about baptism yet," I said to Seekins, ready to move to another subject.

"You want to be baptized?"

"Isn't that a requirement for joining the church?"

"Not anymore. We dropped the requirement a few years ago for people who have been previously baptized, even if they were baptized as infants."

"Really?" I said. "How did that happen? I understood that what you call believer's baptism was the denominational distinctive."

"Denominational distinctives aren't as important as they used to be, I don't think. Our senior pastor comes out of the Presbyterian tradition."

Paul said, "I always thought it was a bit odd to say, Baptism is only a symbol, but when and how you do it is critically important."

"You come out of the Catholic tradition, don't you?" Seekins said. "How big a transition is this for you?"

He and Paul talked about that awhile. My phone buzzed, and I turned it over in my hand for a discreet look at the screen.

"Problem?" Seekins said.

Okay, maybe it wasn't such a discreet look. The text was from Carly: *Alexa called from Richmond City Jail. Wants to see you.*

"I've got a client in jail," I said.

"And you can't go to the jail to see your client, because, if you do, you'll be arrested," Seekins said. "True?"

"How do you know about that?"

"*Times-Dispatch* web site. The Richmond police issued some kind of press release about an hour ago."

My gaze slid to Paul, then went back to Seekins's face. "Have you called them? Are they on their way?"

Seekins shook his head. "My job is to bring you deeper into the body of Christ. Calling the police on you would seem to be antithetical to that."

"Where shall I take you?" Paul said as we left the church's parking lot.

"City jail," I said.

"You can't go there. They'll arrest you."

"They're going to catch up with me sooner or later."

"What will you do when they do?"

I shook my head. "It depends on how high they set bail."

"What do you want me to do?"

"For now, go back to work. You've got a job to do."

"I'm at work. For me, Robin Starling is job one."

I felt the corner of my mouth rise. "You may be taking on a lot there."

"A lot or a little, I've taken it on. I'll call in, tell them I came down with some kind of stomach virus over lunch."

"We haven't had lunch."

"I'm glad you pointed that out." He made the block and pulled up against the curb in front of Robin Inn.

"I'm not sure my stomach can handle something as heavy as Italian right now."

"You know better than that. They serve everything here. You can at least have an appetizer and a glass of Chianti."

"I'm working, and it's not even Friday."

"You get a special dispensation on days you're about to get arrested. Pastor Seekins told me."

"I don't think Baptists do dispensations."

"This one does." I wasn't sure whether he was talking about himself or Ralph Seekins, but I got out of the car and followed him inside the restaurant.

When we had ordered, Paul nodded at my briefcase, which I had brought in and set in the seat beside mine. "Is this going to be a working lunch?"

"There is something you could do for me before you go back to work," I said.

"Okay."

My briefcase was more of a computer case with pockets for my iPad and assorted file folders and legal pads in addition to my laptop. I reached deep into it and came out with a set of keys, which I laid on the table between us.

"Let me guess," he said. "Stolen property."

I nodded.

"A dead man's stolen property," Paul said.

"You are good."

"And you want me to take them."

"And go out to Alexa's place and see if any of them will open the door to her apartment."

"Do you think one will?"

"I don't know. Alexa said she gave Brawley a key. On the other hand, Brooks Prescott had a key on his key ring, and we don't know where that one came from."

"I thought Prescott got that one in the mail," Paul said.

"Brawley could have sent it."

"Why would he do that?"

"Don't know. He'd have been playing a deep game."

"But if the Alexa's key is still on his ring—"

"Brawley still could have sent a copy to Prescott," I said. "Of course he could have. Made a copy and kept the original."

Paul nodded. "If none of these keys open her door, that's not definitive either. Alexa's key could be in a drawer in his house. He doesn't have to have sent it to Prescott."

"You're right," I said. "We won't know anything for sure. I'm just trying to get a better sense of the probabilities. In any case, I don't want the keys on me when I get arrested. I'm going to leave my computer with you, too."

He closed his hand over the keys and put them in his pocket. "Do you think anyone's watching her apartment?" he asked.

"I'd be surprised."

"That's comforting," he said. "As the police snap the cuffs on me, I'll say, 'Boy, will Robin be surprised.'"

"Look around a bit before you go in. Pay attention to your surroundings."

Our food came, and we ate for a while in silence. Paul had been right about one thing. I did feel better after a glass of wine and a basket of flash-fried calamari.

We were back in the car and heading downtown on Monument, when Paul said, "You don't want to drop by the parking garage to get your car?"

"I don't think so."

"And you don't want me to wait for you at the jail."

"If the police show up, you need to be long gone with those keys."

"Okay."

"You gonna be all right? I guess this is just the sort of thing you were complaining to Seekins about."

"It's you I'm worried about."

"I don't get it. Since when did you develop all these concerns about my work?"

"Since I got to know you, I guess."

"I don't have concerns about your work."

"How many times has my work put me in the hospital? How many times has a warrant been issued for my arrest?"

"What would I do if I didn't practice law?"

"I don't think practicing law is the issue. How many times has a warrant been issued for Mike's arrest?"

"I misspoke. I meant, who would I be if I wasn't me?"

He shot me a glance, and a crooked smile lifted one corner of his mouth.

"No matter how safe I try to be, I'm still going to grow old and die," I said.

"That doesn't mean you want to grow old in a prison cell."

"Borger's just trying to intimidate me."

"Why isn't it working? He's intimidating the hell out of me."

"I'm making too much progress. I've now got evidence of a lovers' triangle, evidence that Brawley sought Alexa out deliberately, evidence that he was using her."

"You suspected those already."

"Suspecting and knowing are two different things."

"You'd have found a way to bridge the gap."

"A safer, more traditional way?"

"I don't know." He shot me another glance, then took a breath. "Probably this isn't the time to mention this . . ."

My phone dinged. It was a message from Carly: *Police searching office. Brooke's too.*

"Problem?" Paul's said.

I nodded. *Warrant?* I texted Carly, but all I got in answer was a frowny-face.

"What is it?" Paul asked.

I told him.

"Maybe this is the time to mention this," Paul said.

"Mention what?"

"The Richmond Fed is looking for a lawyer in its legal department."

"Oh, I'd go insane. Besides—isn't there a rule against nepotism at the Fed?"

"We're not married yet."

"And we're not going to be?"

"Not if it would keep you safe." He gave me a moment to think about that before adding, "But it doesn't have to come to that. SunTrust is looking for a compliance officer. I could apply for that. We're young, we have skills. We can do all sorts of things, either of us or both."

"Paul."

He stopped at the light where Franklin Street ran into Capitol Square. The Bell Tower was almost dead ahead. He turned his head to look at me, and I returned his gaze. He sighed, then nodded.

"I understand," he said. The light changed, and he turned left to skirt the Square.

"Do you really?" I asked him.

"I actually do. You're not trying to change me; I won't try to change you either."

"Actually, we could both benefit from a few changes," I said.

"Uh oh."

"For instance, you could start exercising with me."

"Whoa!" We went under I-95, and Paul turned left. "Now you're getting personal," he said.

"Well, you can't just sit on the couch drinking beer while I do my exercise videos."

"It's one of my greatest pleasures. Actually, I've already picked up a new outfit for you to workout in. You know. When it's just you and me and Deacon."

I rolled my eyes. "Exercise is not a spectator sport," I pointed out.

"I know, I know. Look, we'll exercise. I'll walk Deacon with you. We can go to the Y. And sometimes I'll spectate."

I heaved a sigh. "Okay," I said.

"Okay, you'll wear the outfit?"

"That I'm not promising. I'll have to see it first."

Alexa didn't look good. The skin under her eyes looked bruised, and, without makeup, her face had an unhealthy pallor. If her hair had been washed since the day before, it didn't look it.

"How are you?" I asked.

"How do you think I am?"

You ask a stupid question, you get a belligerent question in return. "More charges to deal with," I said neutrally.

She looked up at me through her bangs.

"How did the police come to connect you to Peter Brawley's murder?" I asked.

"How should I know?"

Another question. "Have you ever been to his house?" I asked.

No answer.

"Let me be more specific. Were you at his house the night before last, the night he was killed?"

"I didn't kill him."

"But you were there," I said.

"Yes, I was there. And yes, he took a few pictures, all right?" After a few seconds she added, more quietly, "I was feeling down. There's nothing like a man who thinks you're beautiful to give you a lift."

I thought of Paul and nodded. "Peter Brawley seemed to have a knack for making women feel special," I acknowledged.

"Yes, he did."

"Did you go upstairs?"

She nodded.

"Just in his bedroom, or were you in his office, too? Did you notice a letter opener?"

"No."

The problem with asking two questions at once. I ought to know better. "Which?" I said.

"I didn't notice a letter opener."

"So you wouldn't have handled it. It wouldn't have your fingerprints on it."

She shook her head. "It shouldn't. I don't see how it could."

That was something.

"My fingerprints would be in his office, though. And his bedroom."

It occurred to me that I hadn't seen photographs of Alexa among those Brooke had retrieved from Brawley's cloud drive. "What camera did Peter use that night?" I asked.

"I don't know. A black one."

"I don't think there was a camera there when the body was found," I said. "Or a computer of any kind."

"He had a MacBook in his office."

"It was there night before last? You saw it?"

She had. "What kind of car do you drive?" I asked.

"370Z."

"That's something people would remember, if they'd seen it."

She made a face.

"You don't think there's any chance of the camera or the laptop turning up in the trunk of your car, do you?"

She sucked in her breath with a hiss, but after a moment, she shook her head. "I don't see how. You know what stinks about this? I didn't do anything wrong. I'm just living my life . . . okay, I got a crush on a guy, so what? Then, blammo, he turns up dead in my apartment. And now this. Peter's dead, and I'm back in a jail cell. I'm being punished, and I didn't do anything wrong."

I gave her a sympathetic smile and nodded.

"It's like God's trying to get my attention or something," she said.

"You've been thinking about God?"

"I don't have a whole lot else to do, do I? Except worry. Aubrey tells me Mom and Dad may lose their condo, the one they put up for bail."

It meant that a motion had already been filed for forfeiture of bond. "I can at least slow that down," I said. "And if you didn't kill Brawley, you didn't violate the terms of your release. They won't lose their house."

"Well, I didn't kill him."

"Good. They shouldn't be able to prove it, then." I hoped it was true. Surely the prosecution couldn't come up with *two* open-and-shut cases against an innocent woman.

"Aubrey says you're in trouble, too, on this one."

"I'll be okay."

"How can you be so sure?"

"I'm not sure." I gave her a smile. "Not entirely."

"So how can you be so calm about everything?"

I thought about it. "I guess I believe in justice, justice with a capital J."

"And people always get justice in the end? You believe that?"

"Well, no." That would make me naïve and not just idealistic. I tried to articulate an explanation that would make sense to both of us. I said, "If justice exists, if there is such a thing as capital-J justice, then maybe it's like balance. There's a tendency toward balance, you know. If something disturbs it, objects don't stop shifting and sliding until balance is reestablished. Maybe there's a tendency toward Justice that way. We just have to have faith enough to let things shift and slide until we get there."

She chewed her lip. Finally, she said, "I don't know if you're bonkers or you've hit on some kind of secret of the universe."

I didn't either, unfortunately. "I hope I'm not bonkers," I said.

Chapter 15

The sun hit my eyes as I exited the courthouse, but squinting I could make out Emma Michaels and Matt Jones approaching across the parking lot. They separated as they approached, but at least they didn't have their guns out.

Michaels said, "Robin Starling, I'm placing you under arrest as accessory to the murder of Peter Brawley."

"Really? Stepping in some blood constitutes accessory to murder?"

"Not my call. Turn around, please."

I turned. "Borger?" I asked. I turned as Jones circled me. "Is he going to be handling the Brawley case, too?"

"Looks like it." She frisked me as Jones stood with his hand on his holstered pistol. "She's clean," she told Jones.

I was clean, not even a cell phone on me. "Showered just this morning," I said, trying to sound cheerful.

"One thing you're going to learn," Jones said. "Richmond City is not your playground."

"At least I'm learning my playmates don't play nice."

"You have the right to remain silent," Michaels told me, reading from a card. "If you give up that right, anything you say can and will be used against you in a court of law. You have the right to an attorney . . ." She finished the required spiel, and Jones gripped me by the arm.

"Perhaps you could call my attorney so he could meet us at the courthouse," I said as they walked me toward a dark blue Chevrolet Impala.

"Perhaps we couldn't," Michaels said.

"So all that about my right to an attorney was so much hot air?"

"You'll get your phone call," Jones said.

"Okay. I've asked for my attorney. You've denied my request and are continuing to talk to me." We reached the Impala. Michaels opened the door. Jones kept his hand on my arm and put his other hand on top of my head as I got in.

"We're not asking questions," Jones said.

"I would argue that you're making statements designed to elicit information from me," I said. "But play it your way. You're the legal experts."

Michaels got in at shotgun and turned to look at me through the grill that separated us. "Who you gonna call?" she asked.

I didn't say *Ghostbusters*. "Mike McMillan."

"I don't remember hearing his name before. He do criminal law?"

"We lawyers do everything," I said.

"That seems to be your problem," Jones said, turning his head to back out of the parking space.

They took me to the police station behind the John Marshall Courthouse. We went through a steel door into an antechamber so small that we had to crowd together as the door closed behind us. A flap opened in the door in front of us, and a cop looked out through a small window of reinforced glass. Jones nodded at him, and he opened the door.

I'd never been arrested before. I'd walked a client through the process before, but somehow it's different when it's you. A heavy-set, black officer took my fingerprints: "Just relax your hand, young lady. Let me do it." They stood me in front of a wall with height-markings on it, and a heavy-set white woman took my photograph. A skinny white woman took me into a small room to do a much more thorough frisk of me than Emma Michaels had done in the jail parking lot.

"You must not like donuts," I said to her.

"Spread your legs a little more," she told me.

"I've never been felt up by another woman," I said. "It's not as much fun as you'd think."

Despite my bravado, I was feeling shaky by the time they put me in a cell and closed the massive door on me. I sat on the bench that ran along the wall and waited, wondering when they were going to let me call Mike.

They never did. Eventually, though, the door swung open on silent hinges—I'd have expected them to squeal like a maniac—and there he was.

"Hey, Mike," I said, looking up. "How'd you get here?"

"Bang on the door when you want out," the police officer told him. The door shut on us with a muted clang, and the lock thunked into place.

"Paul called me," Mike said. "How are you holding up?"

"Can't complain. How did Paul know I needed a lawyer?"

"An unmarked police car pulled into the parking lot at the city jail as he was leaving. He recognized Emma Michaels, so he hung around."

"I didn't see him."

"He parked his car where he could see who left the parking lot. When the police car pulled out again, you were in the back seat."

Paul was a smart man. "What's he doing now?"

"Arranging some kind of loan against his retirement account so he can make bail."

I felt a pang of guilt.

"He called your mother," Mike said.

"My mother? What did he do that for?"

"He thought she ought to know. They've never met, you know. He was thinking if he didn't reach out to your family at a time like this, let them know what's going on, he was never going to have any kind of relationship with them."

"So everybody's on the way to Richmond," I said.

"Not everybody. Your mother, your father, your brother . . . Is that everybody?"

"It is," I said.

"Then yes, everybody's on his way to Richmond."

"Circus at my house, tune in tonight."

"So what do you want me to do?" Mike said.

"I don't know. Maybe you could advise me to assert my Fifth Amendment rights and decline to answer questions."

"Done," he said.

"When the time comes, you could point out to the magistrate that I'm a homeowner, I'm in the middle of a trial, and I'm not a flight risk."

"I can do that."

"And, depending on how things go, you could call up WTVR or one of the other TV stations in Richmond and see if they'd like to talk to you on camera."

"Hold a press conference?" For the first time he sounded dismayed.

"If you can arrange it. When I found a body and called it in, the visiting prosecutor had me arrested on trumped up charges in a desperate attempt to bolster his case of purely circumstantial evidence against Alexa Demming. You could mention that she's the sister of Richmond Commonwealth Attorney Aubrey Biggs, that he and Borger are members of different political parties and so on. Play it up as best you can. Abuse of discretion, abuse of process, political grudge match . . . those would all be good phrases to use."

He was silent as he processed all that. "I'll see what I can do."

"Good. Bang on the door, and let's go see the magistrate. I'm ready to hear the worst."

The magistrate had an office there in the police station. A police officer ushered us in, and she looked up from her desk.

"Good to see you again," she said. The sign on her desk said her name was Elizabeth Allen. We'd met before under better circumstances, which is to say when I was there as an attorney and not as a criminal defendant.

"I'd like to say the same," I said.

She smiled. "This is your attorney?"

"Mike McMillan," he said. He extended a hand across the desk, and she took it.

"Have you seen a copy of the warrant and affidavit?" She held up some papers that were stapled at the corner. Mike took them and handed them to me. I flipped back the warrant for my arrest—accessory after the fact, nothing new there— to the affidavit. Detective Emma Michaels had signed it. She claimed to have probable cause to believe that, in addition to disturbing Brawley's body, I had made off with his computer, Galaxy tablet, cell phone, and camera, all of which had been in his possession the day before. I had fled the house and not called to report the body until 12:11 p.m., when the police were already arriving on the scene.

"This is where you tell me why she's not a flight risk," the magistrate told Mike.

"She's in the middle of trial," he said. "She's got her teeth into this thing, and she's not going to let go."

She laughed. "I believe you, Counselor. I believe you." She wrote something on the form in front of her, checked a couple of boxes, and signed her name. "I'm going to release her on her own recognizance," she said. Tearing off the form's pink bottom sheet, she held it out to Mike.

"Is it always that easy?" he asked as we were walking to our cars.

"It's never that easy."

"What do you think accounts for it?"

I shook my head. "Your good looks?"

"Come on," Mike said.

"Professional courtesy?"

"You think maybe she cut you some slack because you're a fellow lawyer?"

"Okay, maybe not."

"I think of us more like vultures," Mike said. "When the weak one goes down, the others descend on it, and the feeding frenzy begins." He beeped his car unlocked and opened the passenger door for me.

I waited as he walked around the car.

"So what's your theory?" I asked, as he got in beside me. "Why was it so easy?"

"Politics? Jim Borger's an outsider brought in to prosecute Aubrey's sister. Maybe he's getting more aggressive than some people think is appropriate."

"When you said politics, my first thought was Nick Cantwell," I said.

"That one's harder to see." A few minutes later, he pulled against the curb outside my parking garage. "You still want me to try to set up a press conference?"

I shook my head. "I'll look for a chance at trial to expose Borger for the big, overbearing bully he is."

Mike nodded.

"Of course, I did do pretty much everything Michaels accused me of in her affidavit. The only reason I didn't take the laptop and camera, too, is because somebody beat me to it."

"You must have ice water in your veins," Mike said. "If I was in your situation, I'd be in the hospital now suffering chest pains and shortness of breath."

"What good would that do?"

"I'm not suggesting a heart attack as part of a strategic plan," he said.

"Well, trust me. If I thought chest pains and shortness of breath would get me somewhere, I'd be having chest pains and shortness of breath."

His smile gave his face a puzzled look. "You're one of a kind, Robin."

I patted his hand, which was resting on the console. "That's what Paul tells me. Thanks, Mike. Thanks for being there."

"I hope I never need you to return the favor."

MICHAEL MONHOLLON

"Me, too," I said, and got out of the car.

I headed home through the rush hour traffic. My work day, as full as it had been, had ended right at five o'clock.

My phone rang, interrupting Bob Seger. I pushed the button on my steering wheel.

"Hey, Brooke."

"Hey, how are you?"

"Free."

"I know. What a relief, huh? I just talked to Mike."

"He was a champ."

"He told me he was a placeholder. He signed his name as your attorney and after that just stood where you told him to."

I laughed. "He's too modest. He did what was necessary. Really."

"The police searched our offices, but they didn't take anything."

A discreet way of telling me they hadn't found Brawley's phone, I thought. "Didn't cut any more squares out of my carpet?"

"And didn't take apart your desk chair. They did push up through one of your ceiling tiles to take a look around."

"How about your office? Did they mess it up too bad?"

"They were thorough."

"Sorry about that."

"It's okay. I'm just glad you won't be spending the night in a cell."

"It wouldn't be so bad if they'd let me have Deeks," I said. "Then it would be just another night at home."

"Home is where the dog is," Brooke said.

It occurred to me that I ought to be thinking the same thing about Paul.

"Speaking of home," Brooke said.

"Uh oh. Speaking of home . . ."

"You'll see."

"Brooke!"

But the impudent thing hung upon me.

I knew there was trouble when I turned onto my street. There were four cars parked in front of my house and along the street, among them Brooke's and Paul's. I didn't park on the street. I turned the corner to get to my garage, which opened off the alley.

The door rumbled up, revealing an empty garage. I'd been holding my breath, I realized. I let it out. I got out of my car, then paused with my hand on the knob of the door into the house.

There was a whine and a single scratch on the other side of the door.

I pushed open the door, and Deeks rose on his hind legs, then dropped to all fours again and spun around. He licked my knee. He disappeared back into the house, which was silent but for the sound of his toenails.

"I'm armed, and I don't like surprises," I called.

Deeks met me in the kitchen, barked, and disappeared back into the house again. If I were inclined to chest pains and shortness of breath, this would do it to me.

They were all in the living room, standing and sitting silently.

"You're not armed," my brother Steve said, his tone accusing. He was a physician in Charlottesville. Between his busy practice and mine, I didn't often get to see him.

"But she is dangerous," Paul said. He was standing with Mike and Brooke.

"How did you beat me here?" I asked Mike.

"I just got here. You had to walk up to your car, so I had a head start."

My mother, who had been sitting on the couch with my brother and Dr. McDermott, stood to give me a hug. My father got up from the easy chair and hugged me, too.

"Paul called us," Mom said. "He said you needed help."

"We all brought our checkbooks," Steve said. "It's good to find out we won't be needing them." He kissed me full on the mouth, and I rolled my eyes at Paul as I wiped my mouth with my forearm.

"Steve isn't enjoying himself if he's not irritating the hell out of someone," I said.

Deeks jumped up and put his paws on my ribs, something he almost never did anymore. "You're as bad as my brother," I told Deeks as I dealt with another slobbery kiss.

"I'm just glad I got mine in first," Steve said.

Deeks dropped down and went to Brooke as Mom guided me to the chair Dad had been occupying. "You'll have to tell us all about it. Is everything going to be all right now?"

Paul stepped closer to hand me a glass of red wine.

I nodded in answer to my mother's question, but what I was thinking was that the most exhausting part of my day was still ahead of me.

Chapter 16

Over the next two weeks, I prepped for trial and helped Brooke with wedding preparations. She was getting increasingly nervous as the wedding loomed closer and the to-do list got longer. I don't know whether I myself was more nervous about the wedding or the life-changing marriage that came with it, but I at least had the distraction of a looming murder trial—though that was itself hardly devoid of stress. I developed a generalized anxiety that began to affect my appetite for the first time I could remember. Working on the wedding plans with Brooke didn't help, and being with Paul only made it worse.

The only thing that calmed me and emptied my mind was running with Deeks, and with him I ran harder and farther than had been our custom. Deeks, if he noticed at all, was content with the change. Deeks was always content. Was Paul going to be equally content, year in and year out? I thought he might, but first we had to get the wedding behind us and I had to get over being such an irritable harridan.

The trial of Alexa Demming for the murder of Brooks Prescott began on a Tuesday, ten days before my Friday wedding. When I say the trial began on Tuesday, I mean we got the jury selected, and Commonwealth's Attorney Jim Borger got through his opening statement.

Borger's questioning of the potential jurors was exhaustive. He tried to get four prospective jurors excused for cause, arguing that the suspicions they acknowledged about the honesty of the police and the impartiality of the justice system were disqualifying.

"Your Honor," I said, when he tried to have the first excused. "If we are going to excuse prospective jurors based on their suspicions of police, we will be disqualifying half the Richmond population. It is right that jurors be skeptical of charges brought by the state. Too many assume that because the police arrest someone, that person is guilty. Such an assumption is contrary to law. If at least some of the jurors force the Commonwealth to prove its case, if at least some of them are willing to entertain doubts when the evidence gives reasonable grounds for them, then the defendant will benefit from the presumption of innocence to which she is constitutionally entitled."

Borger stayed on his feet as I voiced my objection. When he began his rebuttal, his opening "Your Honor" was full of disgust. "What the defendant is entitled to is the even application of justice, to a fair hearing of the evidence, not to an anti-police and anti-prosecution bias. If counsel were to have her way, the Commonwealth would never be able to convict anyone. The streets would become unsafe. Lawlessness would prevail."

Judge Cheatham looked back at me.

"I'm sorry that the prosecution feels that constitutional protections are a threat to the fabric of society," I said. "You know and I know that almost everyone assumes that when the police make an arrest, when the prosecution decides to prosecute, the accused is almost certainly guilty. If we can leaven the jury with the occasional person who actually believes in the presumption of innocence deep down, then so much the better. We might actually get a fair trial."

The judge nodded, and Emmett Johnson, a forty-five-year-old African-American, survived the motion to strike for cause, as did the next three Borger tried to get rid of. Borger later used one of his peremptory challenges to get rid of Emmett Johnson, and again I objected, but this time I lost. Borger wasn't striking him because of his race, which would have been a violation of his Constitutional rights under Batson v. Kentucky, but because of his attitude toward police. It was the kind of thing peremptory challenges were designed for, though we only got four of those apiece.

Emmett Johnson didn't seem to be upset at his removal from the jury. To the contrary, he was smiling faintly to himself as he left the courtroom. He was a self-employed electrician who probably cared more about not missing a week's work than he did about any Constitutional rights he had to sit on the jury.

Though I'd made an effort to keep him, Emmett wasn't what I had in mind as the ideal juror when the day began. I'd been thinking I wanted women who might empathize with another woman whose efforts to defend herself from workplace harassment—from alleged workplace harassment—made her a prime suspect for murder. And I wanted men in their twenties and thirties who might find Alexa more cute than threatening. What I got were three African-Americans who fit neither profile, all of them being middle-aged men; four African-American women of various ages; a Hispanic woman in her twenties; and four middle-aged white men, one of them a banker. For some jury pools, four peremptory challenges just aren't enough.

The jury was sworn in at a little after two. Borger made a three hour opening statement that took us past five o'clock. When he had finished, had shuffled together his papers and returned to his table, Judge Cheatham looked at the clock, then over the frames of his glasses at me. "Ms. Starling?"

I jerked in my seat. "I'm sorry, Your Honor. I must have zoned out." I'd been watching the jury out of the corner of my eye, and I was pretty sure most of them had zoned out, too. "I had planned a three-hour opening statement myself, but Mr. Borger, I'm afraid, has stolen my thunder."

Borger surged to his feet amid a scattering of laughter. In the jury box, a couple of the black men were grinning broadly, and I smiled back at them. "Your Honor," Borger said, his jowls quivering with indignation. "Such a statement is entirely inappropriate. It makes a mockery of the dignity of this court, and it constitutes misconduct on the part of the defense."

Judge Cheatham looked at me, and Borger's gaze followed his.

I ignored Borger's evident outrage and said, "I'll reserve my opening statement until after the prosecution has concluded its case, Your Honor."

"Very well." The judge picked up his gavel.

"Your Honor!" Borger protested, but the fall of the gavel cut him off. He glared at me, and I smiled back.

"The courtroom is no place for levity," Borger said as the judge left the courtroom.

"Evidently not." The judge was gone, and the jury was filing out.

"And you're not nearly as funny and clever as you think you are."

"Few people are," I said.

I heard a laugh from somewhere in the gallery, but I tried not to let it go to my head.

The commonwealth's first witness the next day was Taylor Grimes, a carpenter who had only worked a half-day on May 8, the day of Prescott's murder. He lived in the apartment across from Alexa on the second floor of the Copper Creek Apartments. I sat frowning at him as Borger took him through the preliminaries. I'd seen him before court with a young woman in police uniform. Now I wondered: Had they been talking, or just standing near each other?

"Did you have occasion to enter the apartment of Alexa Demming that day, Mr. Grimes?" Borger asked Grimes.

"No, there wasn't any occasion. The door was standing open, and I went in."

"Yes. Very well."

"It wasn't standing open when I got home, actually, but it was a couple hours later when I went out for cigarettes."

"And you looked in."

"No, not then, I didn't."

"But you did look in at some point."

"Sure. That's why I'm here, isn't it?"

"Yes," Borger said. "Tell us about looking in."

"Well, like I said, the door's open when I go out for cigarettes, and it's still standing open when I get back. It makes me wonder. I stick my head in, like you do, and I say, 'Alexa, is everything all right?' At least that's what I start to say, but then I seen this man lying face down over the coffee table, and I could see everything wasn't all right, not all right at all."

"What did you do?"

"I don't remember exactly. I probably took another step or two, calling out to Alexa, seeing if she was home, but she didn't say nothing, and that man on the coffee table, he's just lyin' there not moving a muscle. It's plenty spooky, let me tell you. I feel the hair rising up on the back of my neck, and I get out of there."

"What did you do then?"

"I get out my phone, and I dial nine-one-one, tell them there's a man dead in my neighbor's apartment."

"How did you know he was dead?"

Grimes gave him a look. "Do you like to sleep sprawled on a coffee table? Do you lie there not twitchin' or movin' one little bit?"

Borger took a breath. "My point is, you didn't touch the body."

"Objection," I said. "Leading." This was Borger's witness, and he was supposed to ask questions, not make statements and invite Grimes to agree or disagree.

"Sustained," Judge Cheatham said.

Borger took another breath. "What time did you get home from work that day?" he asked.

"One, one-thirty. Two o'clock, maybe."

"So between one and two o'clock," Borger said.

"Sure. In there somewhere."

"And you went out for cigarettes about two hours after that, say between three and four o'clock."

"It probably wasn't that late."

"You said you were home a couple of hours before going out."

274

"Well, maybe. I don't think it was later than three, three-thirty when I went out for cigarettes though."

"And how long were you gone?"

"Twenty minutes max. It's just a couple blocks up to 7-11."

"Your witness," Borger said to me.

I went to the lectern. "Mr. Grimes, my name is Robin Starling."

He grinned at me.

"I'm representing your neighbor Alexa, who is accused of killing the man you saw in her apartment that day."

He nodded.

"Had you ever seen him before?"

"No."

"Are you sure?"

He nodded.

"You have to answer in words, Mr. Grimes, so the court reporter can get them down."

"Sure I'm sure."

"When you saw him, he was lying over a coffee table with the top of his head resting on the floor—and you only came a few steps into the room."

"That's right."

"So you never saw his face."

"I seen it in the papers after that."

"So that would have been sometime later. Do you subscribe to the newspaper?"

"Naw. I was interested, though, you know? After this went down, I picked up a paper once or twice."

"And you saw his photograph. Was it in the obituaries, or was this a news story?"

"News story, I guess, front page near the bottom, one of those inside sections. I didn't think to check the obits. I never read 'em."

I said, "You'd never seen Brooks Prescott in Alexa's apartment before you found his body, but you weren't sure of that before you saw his picture in the paper, is that right?"

He nodded. "That's right."

"So there were other men you'd seen in her apartment. Until you saw the picture in the paper, you didn't know for sure the dead man hadn't been one of them."

"I seen men coming and going. I never seen 'em what you'd call in her apartment, if you know what I mean."

"How many men have you seen coming and going?" I asked.

"Oh, I don't know." He shrugged. "Three or four. Four or five. Probably not that many."

"More than two."

"Sure. I'd say more than two."

"Can you describe any of them?"

"Mostly they were pretty ordinary. There was a short fat man with a beard."

"Would you know any of them if you saw them again?"

"I'd know the little fat man. The others, I don't know."

It sounded like Peter Brawley. If so, Taylor Grimes was going to be a witness at Alexa's next trial, too. I said, "When you say he had a beard . . ."

"Like mine," Grimes said, stroking his goatee, "except that his cheeks were clean-shaven, and mine have gotten kinda bristly."

"Could this have been one of the other men?" I held up an eight-by-ten. At the prosecutor's table, Borger craned his neck and then surged to his feet.

"Naw, I don't think so," Grimes said.

"Let me see that photograph," Borger said, coming toward me. "Your Honor, this isn't proper courtroom etiquette. It isn't common courtesy. Counsel should have given me the opportunity to inspect . . ." He snatched the photograph from my outstretched hand. "Your honor, this photograph is of Nick Cantwell, the lieutenant governor of the state of Virginia."

There was a murmur in the courtroom. "This is the same stunt Ms. Starling pulled at the preliminary hearing," Borger said, his barrel-shaped body heaving as if he had just finished a long sprint. "It isn't proper cross-examination; it's misconduct, pure and simple. Ms. Starling should be admonished. She should be found in contempt of court. The jury should be instructed to ignore this entire line of questioning about who the witness did or did not see entering or exiting that apartment."

The judge looked at me. With his full head of silver hair, he looked distinguished and benevolent—or he would look benevolent, but for the expression on his face. "Ms. Starling, do you have any basis for believing our lieutenant governor paid a visit to the defendant in her apartment?"

"I was trying to explore what the witness meant by the word *ordinary*, which is how the witness said most of the visitors looked," I said. "Our lieutenant governor is pretty ordinary-looking—even features, average height, and all that.

The judge continued to study me over the black frames of his glasses. When he spoke, his tone was milder than I expected. "Let's have no more of that, shall we?" he said.

"Yes, Your Honor," I said, trying to sound contrite.

"That's it?" Borger said. "That's all the admonishment she's going to get for this outrageous, this uncalled-for conduct?"

"Is that an objection?" Judge Cheatham asked him.

"It certainly is."

"Ms. Starling, do you have a response?"

"Nothing can be more relevant to this case than the people who went in and out of the apartment where the murder victim was found," I said.

"Objection overruled."

"I take exception to that ruling," Borger said.

"Exception noted. Let's move on." Judge Cheatham gave me a nod.

"Thank you, Your Honor." I had come out of that exchange much better than I'd expected, and I made a mental note not to push my luck. Unfortunately, I was notoriously poor at following cautionary mental notes.

"Have you ever seen a woman entering or exiting the apartment of Alexa Demming?" I asked the witness.

"You mean, besides Alexa?" He shook his head. "No. I haven't."

Perhaps he hadn't. I had an eight-by-ten photograph of Toni Prescott in my folder, but, glancing at the judge with his pursed lips, then at Borger, sitting forward in his chair with his fingers white on the edge of his table, I decided that showing the photograph to Grimes was not the best way to attempt to jog his memory.

"How about you?" I asked Grimes. "Was this the first time you'd ever been in Alexa's apartment?"

For an instant he hesitated. "We're neighbors. Sure I been in there."

"Neighbors with benefits?"

"What? No. Did she tell you that?" His laugh was short and not very convincing.

Borger was back on his feet. "Your Honor," he began. "Must every witness face a groundless slur upon his character? Again, this is not proper cross-examination. The question and any answer to it is irrelevant to the issues of the case."

I opened my mouth to defend my question, but the judge spoke first. "Overruled," he said.

My mouth snapped shut. I looked at the witness. "Have you ever had sex with the defendant?"

"No."

"Ever had drinks with her in her apartment?"

Again, the instant's hesitation. "Sure."

"How recently?"

He shrugged. "Not since the murder."

"The murder was Monday, May 8, so you haven't been in her apartment for the past month," I said.

"No, I haven't."

"How about Sunday the seventh? Is it possible you were in her apartment the day before the murder? According to your testimony, you walked into the apartment, saw the body, and backed out. How many of the fingerprints the police haven't been able to identify belong to you?"

"I don't know. Maybe some."

"But none of the fingerprints in her bedroom."

His gaze shifted in Alexa's direction, just a flicker. "I don't think so."

"Were you in her apartment on May the seventh, the day before the murder?"

"No."

"Ever felt jealous about the other men who came to her apartment?"

"It wasn't that kind of relationship," Grimes said. "She had her friends. I had mine."

As I headed back to my seat, I noticed Alexa's tight-mouthed expression, and my gaze rose to Aubrey Biggs and his parents sitting behind her. None of them met my gaze.

I sat down, and Alexa leaned toward me. "I am not a slut," she said.

I gave a short nod. "Sorry."

"Don't do that again without talking to me first."

I took a breath and tilted my head toward her, but I didn't say anything. Police officer Meghan Daniels was being sworn in. She was the police officer I'd seen standing in Grimes's general vicinity before court that morning.

"Okay?" Alexa said.

I touched my head to hers. "How many times have the two of you had drinks in your apartment?" I murmured.

"Taylor and me? I don't know."

"When you've had sex, has it always been in his apartment?"

She pulled back.

"I'm sorry," I whispered. "I just need . . ."

The courtroom had fallen silent. The judge, Borger, the witness, the members of the jury—pretty much everyone was watching us.

"Are you ready to proceed, Ms. Starling?" Judge Cheatham asked.

"Yes, Your Honor," I said.

He gave Borger a nod, and Borger cleared his throat.

"Officer Daniels, how long have you been with the Richmond Police Department?"

He went through her qualifications in as much detail as if he were going to be asking her for opinion testimony, but his direct examination was brief. She had arrived on the scene, had met Taylor Grimes on the landing outside Alexa's apartment. The door to the apartment had been standing open. She'd gone in and found the body. She'd called it in.

"Your witness," Borger said.

I took a breath, then went to the lectern. "Hi, Officer Daniels. I'm Robin Starling." I gave her a smile, but her answering smile was perfunctory. "How long have you known Taylor Grimes?"

She flinched. She was a young woman, probably no more than twenty-three or twenty-four, with dark hair cut short. "Taylor Grimes?" she said.

I waited.

"I . . . not very long."

"What's the nature of your relationship?"

"We're friends."

I abandoned the Puritan Patrol and refrained from asking about benefits. "You don't seem to have had a partner on May eighth. Do you usually work alone?"

"No, I have a partner. Matt Wallaby. He called in sick May eighth."

"So you responded to this call alone."

"Yes."

"Must have been quite a surprise to you, arriving at the scene and finding your friend Taylor on the landing."

She nodded.

"You have to answer orally," I said.

"Yes," she said.

"Yes, it was a surprise?"

"It was a surprise."

"So Mr. Grimes didn't call you when he found the body?"

It was only a few seconds before she answered, but they were long seconds.

"I understand he called nine-one-one," she said.

I'd been doing this long enough to recognize a nonresponsive answer when I heard one. "That's not what I asked you. Did he make a direct call to you, his friend, Meghan Daniels?"

Her answer was a sibilant sigh. "Yes," she said.

"Was it you who told him to call nine-one-one?"

"Yes."

"How did it happen that you got the call from dispatch?"

"I was in the area."

"Was that coincidence? How long did you tell Mr. Grimes to wait before placing his nine-one-one call?"

She took a moment to think about it. "Ten minutes," she said.

"Ten minutes to give you the chance to get close enough to have a reasonable chance of getting the call from dispatch?"

"Yes."

"Why?"

"He was worried about being accused of killing a man he didn't even know."

"How do you know what he was worried about?"

"He . . . I guess he told me."

"I understand from his testimony that Mr. Grimes never saw the dead man's face."

She didn't say anything.

"What was Taylor's connection to Alexa Demming?"

"They used to be, I don't know, boyfriend and girlfriend. Something like that."

"What did he take out of that apartment?"

"Nothing."

"Come on, Officer Daniels. What did he take out of the apartment?"

"Nothing! Just the trash."

"He took a bag of trash out of Alexa's apartment," I said.

"Yes. He did." She sounded defeated.

"What was in the trash, do you know?"

She shook her head. "Nothing, really. Some beer bottles that might have had his fingerprints."

"Did you examine the trash yourself?"

"Yes. There were bottles and yogurt cups . . . you know. Just trash."

"A wine bottle?" At the preliminary, we'd learned that there was wine in the glasses in the sink, but no open wine bottle anywhere in the apartment.

"I think there was one wine bottle," Daniels said.

"Did you wipe any surfaces to remove fingerprints? Did Taylor Grimes, in your presence?"

"Of course not."

"Of course not?"

"That would be altering a crime scene."

Chapter 17

"Boy, when you rip someone a new one, you rip them a new one," Paul said. He'd taken vacation to watch the trial, and now the two of us were sitting on the steps of an old church, eating the sandwiches we'd gotten at one of the food carts along Marshall Street.

I thought about it while I chewed. When I'd swallowed, I said, "I feel bad about that. Meghan Daniels is probably a good cop and a nice person, and very likely I just destroyed her career."

"What choice did you have? What she did was inexcusable."

I took another bite of my sandwich, nodding glumly with my eyes on the passing traffic. "I know."

"On the other hand . . ." He paused to drink some tea. " . . . after watching you go after those first two witnesses, I'm thinking there's a reason people try to hurt you."

"You can add my client to that list. She wasn't happy with what I did to Taylor Grimes."

"And you dragged in the lieutenant governor again."

"Sort of."

"Because you needed an average looking guy."

My mouth quirked. "It didn't sound very convincing, did it?"

"You're still thinking Nick Cantwell is involved in this somehow."

I shrugged. "There was a love triangle, Brooks and Toni and Nick. One of them is dead. Another man had photographic evidence of the affair, and now he's dead."

"It's a long way from proving Cantwell murdered either one of them."

"Sure. It would be nice if I could get Brawley's photographs admitted into evidence?"

"You can't?"

"Probably not. There's a problem with authentication. Where did the pictures come from? Who took them and when?"

"Brawley took them. They were on his phone."

"In the cloud, actually, though Brooke accessed them through his phone. How did she know the phone was his?"

"Because . . ."

She'd known it was his because I'd told her when I gave it to her—after taking it off Brawley's dead body.

"I see the problem," Paul said.

"And *I* wasn't there when Nick and Toni had their little tête-à-têtes. *I* can't say the people in the photographs are who they seem to be."

"So what are you going to do with the whole love-triangle thing?"

"I don't know. I'm playing it by ear."

When court reconvened, Borger called Police Detective Emma Michaels to the stand. She gave us her name and her qualifications, then answered questions about a score of photographs showing the layout of the apartment, the wine glasses in the sink, the position of the body, the back of the victim's head in close-up, the toothbrushes on the bathroom counter, the men's clothes hanging in the closet. Borger got all the photographs admitted into evidence and continued his questioning.

According to Detective Michaels, Brooks Prescott's fingerprints had been on the coffee table, on one of the wine glasses in the sink, and on a pair of sunglasses on the nightstand. The door to the apartment was in good repair; its lock was functioning and had not been tampered with. Alexa Demming had returned to her apartment shortly before six, but they had not allowed her to go in.

It was after five o'clock when Borger finished with Michaels's testimony. Judge Cheatham picked up his gavel.

"I just have one question, your honor," I said, standing.

"Really?" He gave his head a shake. "I'm sorry. Go ahead."

"Detective Michaels. All this time you spent in the defendant's apartment and on the landing, the time you spent coming and going and checking the lock and the door jamb—did you see the defendant's neighbor, Taylor Grimes?"

"Yes, I saw him."

"What was he doing?"

She shrugged. "Hanging around."

"Thank you." Technically, it had been two questions, but possibly since the second was a follow-up it didn't count.

Borger stood as I walked to my table. "Officer Michaels, didn't you take a statement from Taylor Grimes later that evening?"

"I did."

"Had you told him you were going to take his statement?"

"Yes."

"So he was hanging around to make himself available."

I turned to object. "Your Honor, she can't know what his motives were unless he told her. The question calls for hearsay."

"Sustained." The judge's gavel fell, and court was recessed for the day.

"We need to talk," Alexa said.

I looked up at the deputy sheriff, standing by to take her into custody. "Can you give us a minute?"

He stepped back to give us space.

"Why are you going after Taylor like that?" Alexa said. "He's a nice guy who has the misfortune to be my neighbor. He didn't kill anyone."

"Did he come over for drinks the night before the murder?"

"What difference does it make?" she whispered fiercely. "If he came over for drinks, if we had sex at my place or his? We were friends."

"The prosecution's theory seems to be that Prescott came to your place for a nooner, and you bashed him on the head. If that's all the jury hears, it's going to convict you. The jurors need to hear that there were other things going on, other people with an interest in you or him or your apartment. That's how we get to reasonable doubt."

"You can't hang this on Taylor. It isn't fair."

"I'm not hanging it on him. The police aren't going to arrest him or charge him with murder. They don't have that kind of evidence. All I'm doing is raising doubt."

"And is your grand scheme working? You think the jury's listening to all this and beginning to think maybe I didn't do it?"

My gaze shifted. "No. Not yet."

"So you're hurting people—Taylor, this Officer Daniels—and it's all to no purpose."

"So far. Yes."

We were already sitting close, but she leaned closer until our heads were actually touching. "Your job stinks," she whispered. She drew back and jabbed me in the breastbone with her index finger. In a louder voice, she said, "You stink. I'm sick of this whole thing." She got up and strode jerkily to the deputy sheriff, where she held out her hands to be cuffed.

I continued to sit, watching as she disappeared through the door at the side of the courtroom.

"You all right?"

I looked over my shoulder, not at Paul—he was waiting in the aisle for me—but at Aubrey Biggs. "I'm hanging in there," I said.

"Alexa can be emotional."

"She's a passionate woman."

"I'm sorry anyway. You're doing the right thing."

The reassurance rang hollow, somehow, and I felt my lip curl. "Thanks." I stood and began to pack folders and papers back into my briefcase.

Mr. and Mrs. Biggs were standing, too, watching me with anxious expressions.

"Thank you for what you're doing for our daughter," Mrs. Biggs said.

I looked at her, and the muscles in my face relaxed a bit. "You're welcome."

"Will it work, all this, you think?" Mr. Biggs said.

"I hope so." I shrugged, tried a smile. "Not very comforting, I know."

"We're praying for you," Mrs. Biggs said. It's the kind of thing people say all the time, but somehow, looking into her earnest face, I found it comforting.

"Thank you," I said.

Her words stayed with me. "Here's what I've been thinking," I said over dinner. "There is a force in the world moving us toward order and justice and unity.

How else can you explain why humanity hasn't long since descended into chaos? If entropy were the only force at work, surely we would have."

Silence greeted my statement. Finally, Mike asked me what I was getting at. "Does this have something to do with the trial you're in?" he said.

"Maybe the order-force, the justice-force— maybe it has personality," I said, expanding on my theme. "Maybe, when Mr. and Mrs. Biggs say they're praying for me, they're in communication with it."

Paul leaned forward to move the pitcher of margaritas away from me, toward the far end of the table.

"What?" I said.

"You're waxing philosophical. It may be a sign you've had enough."

"Is that your explanation for Plato, for Aristotle? Too many margaritas?"

Brooke started to laugh, but was interrupted by a stream of margarita spraying from her nose. "Ow, that burns," she said.

"Okay, maybe the second pitcher was overdoing it," I acknowledged.

"But the pitcher's here now and only half empty," Mike said. "What can we do?"

We had finished eating, mostly, and were talking over what was left of the second pitcher. "We could stop drinking it," I said.

Paul helped himself to a little more. "I think it's like the mountain," he said. "We climb it because it's there."

"I like your order-force," Mike said, "but don't discount the force moving us toward chaos. Yin and yang."

"Is that what yin and yang are all about?" Brooke asked.

"Who knows?" Paul said. "We're strictly Western philosophers around this table."

It was still daylight when I got home. I picked up Deeks, and we went for a three-mile run, Deeks running off leash through people's front yards and disappearing into the occasional backyard. I continued to mull over that brief philosophical discussion we'd had over dinner. An active force that sustained human efforts toward order and justice. An opposing force that promoted chaos. God and the devil.

I had defended clients in six murder trials, and I had yet to lose one. I tended to trust my ability to exploit developing facts—that, and a good dose of luck. Was there such a thing as luck, though? Or was it my hypothetical order-force weaving its vast tapestry of human effort and virtue?

"Dear God," I murmured as I ran. It seemed pointlessly cumbersome to pray *Dear Hypothetical Order-Force*, so I was using the usual shorthand. "Dear God, if Alexa's isn't guilty, help me to prove it." I tried to think of something to add to that, but found I didn't have anything more to say about Alexa and her problems. I changed the subject to Paul and me and the looming marriage about which I still had lingering reservations. I quickly ran out of things to say to God about that, too, though. I was out of practice. I wasn't religious, never had been, really. I just had a childlike faith in the tendency of things to work out—a startling degree of naivety in a thirty-one-year-old lawyer, but there it was.

When we were less than a half-mile from home, I stretched out my stride, and Deeks appeared out of the gathering twilight to run beside me. I dropped into a walk as we passed my sidewalk, Deeks still with me, his tongue lolling. I myself was breathing hard, my jaws creaking wide to relieve the pressure in my ears.

"You make it look easy," I told Deeks, speaking between breaths, and his gaze shifted to my face. A block past my house, I stopped, bracing my hands on my knees, and Deeks gave me a lick that went from chin to eyebrows. I don't know how much salt dogs need in their diet, but I think that one lick should have satisfied this dog's minimum daily requirement for days to come.

Dr. Birdsong, the pathologist with the Office of Chief Medical Examiner, was the next day's first witness. As he had at the preliminary hearing, he testified as to cause of death—blunt force trauma to the head—and time of death, the two-hour window between 11:52 and 1:52 in the middle of the day on May eighth. When it got to my turn to cross-examine, I had planned to work on him in an effort to expand that two-hour window. I'd spent some time with the autopsy report that morning, though, going over body temperature and the findings regarding rigor mortis, livor mortis, and the contents of the stomach. I just didn't see anything to work with.

"Dr. Birdsong, there was evidently no trace of alcohol in the decedent's blood. Can you account for that?"

His front lip rose, exposing narrow teeth. "I would say the decedent was not drinking alcohol," he said.

"There was no trace of wine inside the decedent's mouth? No discoloration of the tongue, for example?"

"There wasn't."

"But there were two wine glasses in the kitchen sink there in the apartment where the body was found, wine in both of them. One of the glasses bore his fingerprints."

"Is that a question?"

"Dr. Prescott didn't drink any wine out of the glass that bore his fingerprints, did he?"

"Not immediately before his death."

"Did he drink anything? Did you find anything in his stomach?"

"He might have had a small amount of water."

"Or he might have had nothing at all," I said.

"That's possible, too."

I nodded thoughtfully, giving the jury time to process the idea that perhaps everything was not as it seemed.

"Dr. Birdsong, I don't believe you've mentioned any trace evidence found in the wound. Was there any?"

Borger hadn't brought it out on direct, but I knew it was there from the autopsy report.

"A few flecks of silver paint," Dr. Birdsong said.

"The base of the lamp found by the body was a silvery chrome, wasn't it?"

"Yes, it was. The paint in the wound was consistent with the paint on the lamp."

"But there was something else, some iron filings? Was this an iron lamp beneath the paint?"

Birdsong shifted in his seat. "No," he said. "It wasn't."

I gave him time to expand on that answer, but he waited me out.

"Any ideas about the source of these iron flecks? Have you ever come across anything like them before?"

"In a case or two where the fatal blow was struck with something like a tire iron."

"Is it possible that the murder victim in this case was struck twice, once with something like a tire iron and once with the lamp?"

"Yes, it's possible."

"Which was the first blow struck?"

"I can't tell."

"Thank you, Doctor."

Borger came to the lectern. "There was no tire iron found in the apartment, was there, Dr. Birdsong?"

"Not to my knowledge, no."

"You said it was possible that Dr. Brooks Prescott, the victim in this case was struck twice. Is it certain he was struck more than once?"

"No. The base of the lamp was a pyramid sort of structure. It could have accounted for wound inflicted."

"Thank you, Dr. Birdsong."

I stood, but remained at my table. "The lamp could not have accounted for the iron flecks, could it have?"

"No, I don't believe so."

"And you don't have any other explanation for their presence in the wound?"

"No."

I smiled at Jim Borger, blatantly enough to be sure the jury noticed it. He looked only momentarily discomfited. "Call Toni Prescott," he said, pushing to his feet.

She came to the stand wearing a silk dress belted at the waist, modest pumps with two-inch heels, and a necklace of elongated pearls that I assumed were real. With her clothes, her raven hair, and her flawless makeup, she'd have turned heads anywhere, but the most striking thing about her were her eyes, stars in a night sky.

"Ms. Prescott," Borger said gravely. "I want you to know how deeply sorry we are for your loss."

"Thank you." By rights, a woman with her looks ought to have a high-pitched, nasal voice by way of

297

offset, but hers was rich in timbre and well-modulated.

"Could you give us your name and address for the record?"

She could, evidently. She could also tell us she had been married to the decedent Brooks Prescott for four years. At the time of his death they were just six weeks short of their fifth anniversary.

"When did you find out about your husband's death?" Borger asked her.

"On Monday, May 8. Two police detectives showed up at my house, one of them a woman. They gave me a ride downtown to . . . to identify the body." The little gasp in the middle of the last sentence was done perfectly.

"And the body they showed you was that of your husband?" Borger said.

"It was." A tear broke free of her right eye and began to track down her cheek. Call me a cynic, but, boy, she was good.

"Did the police detectives ask you to identify anything else?"

"Yes. They showed me some clothes."

"These clothes?" Borger went to the clothes rack that stood against the wall of the courtroom and wheeled it out.

"Yes. It looks like them."

He took the gray suit off the rack and brought it to the witness. "I show you specifically this suit that has been marked as Prosecution Exhibit 46 and ask if you have ever seen it before."

"Yes, it's one of my husband's suits."

"When was the last time you saw him wear it?"

She shook her head. "I don't know. A week before his death?"

"But you have seen him wear it."

"Yes, or at least a suit just like it. Is it a 42 Long?"

"You tell me." He carried the suit to the witness stand and held it out to her, still on the hanger. She leaned forward to open the jacket and look at the tag in the inside pocket.

"Forty-two long," she said, sitting back. There was now a single tear track down each of her cheeks, both glinting in the artificial light.

"I now show you a pair of blue slacks," Borger said, walking back to the clothes rack to retrieve them, then returning to the witness stand with the hanger.

She identified the blue slacks and, after them, a black pair, and a pair of khakis. The dress shirts, she was less certain about, as, perhaps, she had to be. "He had dress shirts. I suppose these could be his."

"What size shirt did your husband wear?"

"Sixteen neck, 33 sleeve."

He had her look at each of the shirts. All of them had a 16-inch neck and a 33-inch sleeve.

"What cleaners did you and your husband use, Ms. Prescott?" Borger asked her.

"Keen Cleaners on Broad."

"Are you aware that Keen Cleaners puts a small barcode inside the front of each shirt near the hem?"

She shook her head solemnly. This time Borger paraded the shirt to my table, to the judge's bench, and finally to the witness, showing each of us the barcode. "I hand you a powder-blue button-down dress shirt," he said. "Could you look inside the shirtfront to see if a small barcode is pasted there?"

She took the shirt, laid it across the rail, and flipped back the side of the shirt with buttons on it.

"Is there such a barcode?" Borger asked.

"There is. A barcode with some numbers."

"Is there a word beside the numbers? Could you read it for us?"

"K-E-E-N," she read, and looked up. "Keen."

It would have been a nicely dramatic moment to end his direct examination of her, but Borger, with his usual overkill, lead her through the same rigamarole with each of the shirts. It was after lunch before I got to start my cross-examination.

Chapter 18

I began with the toothbrushes that the prosecution had admitted into evidence in the course of Emma Michaels's testimony, retrieving them from the exhibit table and holding them up. "Do you recognize either of these toothbrushes?"

She shrugged, shook her head. "I don't know."

"You can't say that either toothbrush belonged to your husband?"

"No."

"But you very definitely recognized all of the clothes the prosecutor showed you."

"Well. I'm not completely certain about the shirts."

"Did your husband drink wine, Mrs. Prescott?"

"Yes." Her eyebrows furrowed.

"And beer and mixed drinks?" I asked her.

"On occasion."

"But not on this occasion.""

"I don't know what you mean."

"Your husband went to Alexa's apartment, ostensibly to have a romantic encounter with the defendant. There were two wine glasses, a bit of wine left in each. Your husband drank wine, you say, and his fingerprints were on the glass—yet no wine was found in his stomach and no alcohol was found in his bloodstream. Can you explain that?"

"Objection," Borger interposed. "How can the witness be expected to explain why her husband didn't drink any of the wine that was drunk from his glass—if it even was drunk, and not poured out? Mrs. Prescott wasn't there."

I said, "Ms. Prescott was married to the decedent for five years and was, presumably, familiar with his habits. I think it's a fair question."

The judge shook his head. "I'll sustain the objection."

I shrugged, smiling. I asked Toni, "*Were* you there in the apartment of Alexa Demming on Monday, May 8?"

"No. I wasn't."

"Have you ever been in that apartment?"

"No."

"Had you ever met Alexa Demming, or seen her prior to your husband's death?"

She smiled sourly. "I hadn't."

"But you knew the name."

"Pardon?"

"You knew she had filed a sexual harassment claim against her employer regarding your husband."

The skin tightened around her eyes. "I knew it."

"Your husband told you about it," I said.

"Yes. He told me."

"Didn't it strike you as odd that she would file a claim against him for sexual harassment, then mail him a key to her apartment?" My current thinking was that Brawley had mailed the key to Brooks Prescott, but Brawley and Toni had been friends. He could have given her the key.

"I . . ." Toni bit the word off as Borger climbed to his feet.

"That's argumentative, Your Honor, and assumes a fact not yet in evidence. It's not a proper question."

Judge Cheatham looked at me.

"I'll rephrase the question. Ms. Prescott, your husband told you about a key the defendant sent him, did he not?"

Her eyes moved, her gaze shifting away from me, then back. "No," she said.

"Did he just tell you about it, or did he show it to you?"

Borger was back on his feet. "Objection. The witness has denied that her husband told her anything about a key."

"She hasn't denied that he showed her one," I said. "She hasn't denied knowing about the key her husband had to Alexa's apartment. I'm asking her to clarify the facts for us."

"Objection overruled," the judge said.

"What communication did you have with your husband regarding a key to the defendant's apartment?"

"None," Toni said.

"You have no idea how that key came into his possession."

"No, I don't. I've said I didn't."

"His killer might have put it on his keyring after he was dead, as far as you know."

Borger objected again. This time, Judge Cheatham sustained the objection.

"You never suspected your husband was having an affair with Alexa Demming?" I said.

Her slender shoulders rose and fell. "Not until . . . after."

"After he was dead? If he had moved some of his clothes into her apartment, if he was spending nights in her apartment, surely you'd have noticed something. You never became suspicious? Never followed him to see who he was meeting, where he was spending his time?"

"No."

"Did he ever follow you to see who you were meeting?"

"Me? Of course not. Why would he?"

"Why indeed? Your Honor, may I have a moment?" At his nod, I went to my table, flipped open a folder, and took out an eight-by-ten photograph. I took it straight to the witness stand. "What can you tell us about this picture, Mrs. Prescott?" I held it out so that it rested on the rail in front of her.

"Objection!" Borger pushed to his feet. "Your Honor, this isn't proper courtroom procedure. I haven't seen that photograph. The court hasn't."

Toni Prescott had paled visibly, staring.

"Oh, I'm sorry," I said. "My mistake." I moved the photograph to the bench in front of Judge Cheatham. Borger was on the move, striding forward with purpose. The judge's silver eyebrows rose as Borger reached for the photograph.

Borger's mouth worked, his shoulders bunching beneath his suitcoat. "This is misconduct," he said in controlled tones. "This is contempt of court. This completely irrelevant photograph is an attempt to besmirch the good name . . ."

"It's a photograph of the witness having a candlelight dinner with a man not her husband," I said. "In light of this witness's testimony, I think I'm entitled to ask about it."

"You're entitled to shut your damn mouth!" Borger shouted.

My head went back, and I glanced at the jury box, where everyone seemed to be sitting forward.

The judge's gavel came down. "Confine your remarks to the court," Judge Cheatham snapped. "Mr. Borger, another outburst like that, and I will hold you in contempt."

Borger was breathing like a steam engine. "I'm sorry, Your Honor. It's just that Counsel has not only shown this totally irrelevant photograph to the witness, but she now made a highly inflammatory statement about it in the hearing of the jury. She . . ."

I had shifted position so I could watch the jurors out of the corner of my eye. Now I turned my head in their direction to them a wink.

Borger broke off, his face so red he might have been having a stroke.

"Ms. Starling!" Judge Cheatham said, sounding outraged.

"I'm sorry, Your Honor." I wiped at the corner of the offending eye with my index finger, blinking. "I think Mr. Borger got me in the eye with that last spray of spittle."

Someone in the jury box emitted a bark of nervous laughter, and Judge Cheatham got a sudden, constipated look that suggested he was working to control an outburst of his own. Borger, for the moment, was out of the conversation, evidently choking on his outrage.

I waited for the judge to work out his response, not knowing whether he was going to roar imprecations or bray laughter, but he did neither. In the end, he gave his head a hard shake and said, "Let's try to get to the heart of this. Ms. Starling, why are you showing the witness this photograph?"

Borger recovered his ability to speak enough to squeak, "Not in front of the jury."

"Very well." Cheatham nodded at his court reporter and pushed the button to turn on the white noise in the courtroom, designed to allow us to have a bench conference without the jury hearing what we said. The court reporter moved into place to record our conversation.

"Ms. Starling?" Judge Cheatham said.

"There's been some evidence presented designed to suggest that Dr. Prescott was having an

306

affair with the defendant in this case. Maybe he was, but I can produce evidence just as strong that his wife was having an affair of her own."

"I dispute Ms. Starling's contention that she can prove any such thing," Borger said, his fingers hooked on the edge of the judge's bench. "She's shown us a photograph, but it hasn't been authenticated. We don't know who took it or how it came into Counsel's possession. And what if the witness *was* having an affair? What difference does it make?"

I said, "If she was having an affair, especially with a person as prominent as Virginia's lieutenant governor, her husband might have found out about it. Suppose that he did. Suppose he was making trouble. He might easily have become so inconvenient to his wife that she had to kill him."

"Had to . . . Listen to her, Your Honor: *If. Might have. Suppose, suppose, suppose.* She's on a fishing expedition. There is nothing here but ugly innuendo that holds up innocent people to public censure and ridicule. Counsel has no evidence that this witness was ever in the defendant's apartment, no evidence beyond this unauthenticated photograph that she was ever having an affair, no evidence that implicates the witness in this murder in any way."

"And I never will have such evidence, if the prosecutor is going to go bellowing objections every time I ask a question that doesn't fit with his theory of the case."

"Can you authenticate that photograph?" the judge asked me.

"I might be able to authenticate it by this witness. I can ask her if she's seen it before, if she knows when it was taken, whether it's a fair representation of an occasion when she was seated at a table with the lieutenant governor."

Judge Cheatham looked at the witness, who sat stiffly, her shoulders drawn in and her gaze apparently unfocused as she waited for the outcome of the bench conference. He turned his attention back to me. "Be frank with me. Do you really have a reasonable expectation of tying all this together?"

"I do. I'm not throwing out questions blindly. I have a theory of the case, and, if I'm allowed to ask questions, I think I can introduce evidence to support it."

He studied me. "Ms. Starling, I'm going to allow a question or two about the photograph, but if the witness doesn't authenticate it, you're done with that line of questioning for now."

Borger said, "If the witness does not authenticate the photograph, that should foreclose any questions about this so called affair—not that having dinner with a man is tantamount to having an affair with him."

"You're free to object, but you're going to have to make your objections to specific questions," the judge told him. To me he said, "Don't think you have a lot of leeway here. If your questions don't seem to be going anywhere, I'm going to put a stop to the whole line of inquiry."

"Yes, Your Honor."

"If you have a point to make, you need to come to it quickly."

"I understand." I took the photograph back to the witness box and held it out to Toni Prescott. She took it unwillingly.

Back at the lectern, I said, "Ms. Prescott. The photograph I've handed you appears to show you having dinner with Virginia's lieutenant governor, Nick Cantwell. Do you remember the occasion on which it was taken?"

"No." She cleared her throat. "No, I don't."

"But you have had dinner with the lieutenant governor."

"Objection," Borger said, leaning over his table, his weight on his fists.

"Overruled. Answer the question."

Toni's tongue touched her upper lip. "Yes."

"On more than one occasion?"

"Yes."

"The photograph shows just the two of you sitting at a fairly small table covered with a tablecloth. It was just the two of you, wasn't it?"

"Objection," Borger said. "The witness has failed to authenticate the photograph."

"Sustained."

I tried again. "Have you ever seen this photograph before?"

"Objection. The court has ruled there can be no more questions about this photograph."

The court had ruled no such thing. I said, "Whether or not it's a fair representation of an actual event, the witness still may have seen it."

"I'll allow the question," Judge Cheatham said.

"Have you seen this photograph before?" I repeated.

"No."

"Your husband never showed you this photograph or another one showing you and the lieutenant governor together?" I said.

"Objection," Borger said.

"He did not," Toni said, not giving the judge an opportunity to rule on the objection.

Borger heaved a sigh, rolling his eyes.

"Those are enough questions about the photograph," Judge Cheatham said. "At least until such time as you can produce a witness to authenticate it."

"How did you get your husband to agree to meet you at Alexa's apartment?" I asked Toni.

"Objection," Borger said, holding up a hand to forestall an answer. "Your Honor, that question assumes a fact not in evidence. It is also not proper cross-examination, in that nothing about any meeting involving the defendant and her husband was brought out on direct. On direct she testified about identifying her husband's body, and she identified his clothes. That's all."

"It goes to the bias of the witness, Your Honor," I said.

"Rephrase your question," the judge said.

"Did you arrange to meet your husband at Alexa's apartment?" I asked.

"No, of course not."

"Did you know Peter Brawley?"

"Peter . . ."

"Objection. Relevance. Not proper cross-examination."

"The man you used to pose for when you were a Hooter's girl," I said by way of clarification. "The man who was murdered two-and-a-half weeks ago."

"Ms. Starling," Judge Cheatham snapped. "When an objection has been made, you're to wait for my ruling. Understood?"

"Yes, Your Honor."

He glared at me for several long seconds. "Objection sustained," he said. "You are to ask no more questions about Peter Brawley until some foundation for those questions has been laid." To the jury, he said, "The witness answered neither of the last two questions. A lawyer's questions are not evidence. They have no evidentiary value, and you are to disregard them. Ms. Starling, are you done with your cross-examination?"

"No, Your Honor."

The response earned me another long glare. "How long have you been practicing law?" he asked me.

"Six years," I said. "Almost seven."

"How many jury trials have you had?"

"I think this is number twenty."

"So you know the difference between proper and improper questions."

"Yes, Your Honor."

"From here on, you are to stick to proper questions. Am I understood?"

"You are."

Borger, I noticed, was looking smug.

"Ms. Prescott, where were you on the morning of May 8, the day your husband was killed?"

She looked at Borger, and he gave her a nod. He had asked about other things she had done that day, specifically her identification of her husband's body. It was proper cross-examination.

"I was in Richmond, if that's what you mean," she said.

"Where did you eat lunch that day?"

"I think I ate at home."

"Do you remember what you had for lunch?"

"No, I don't."

"Had you been out that morning?"

"I don't remember. I don't think so."

"No errands to run?"

"Not that I remember."

"You didn't stop by the dry cleaners to drop off clothes or pick some up?"

"Not that I remember," she repeated.

I had copies of five claim checks from the Keen Cleaners, along with a credit card receipt, which was dated the morning of the murder. This time I followed protocol, taking them first to Borger's table. He glanced at them and gave me a puzzled look, which I ignored. I took the receipt and the claim checks to the bench, Toni Prescott watching me without expression. Finally, I took them to the witness stand and handed one of them to her.

"This appears to be a credit card receipt from Keen Cleaners. I believe you testified that was the dry cleaner you and your husband use. Is that right?"

"That's right."

"Does the credit card receipt indicate the date that the items were picked up and payment made?"

"I guess so. Five-oh-eight-seventeen."

"May 8," I said. "Is there a time on the receipt?"

She dropped her gaze to the receipt. "I don't know," she said.

"Doesn't it say ten-eighteen?"

"Is that a time?"

"Possibly less than two hours before your husband met his death," I said. "How much is the receipt for? Can you tell?"

"Sixty-eight eighty."

"And, finally, the signature. It's a bit of a scrawl. Do you recognize it?"

"It's Brooks's."

"Your husband's."

She nodded.

"Yes?" I said.

"Yes."

"The credit card receipt is for sixty-eight dollars and eighty cents. What I'm handing you now are five claim checks. Do you see a dollar amount on any of them?"

She took a moment to shuffle through them. "No."

"Do you see a date?"

"May sixth."

"Two days before your husband's death. Is it the same date on all of them?"

It was.

"What is the first claim check for, the one on top of the stack in your hand?"

"Eight shirts."

"Is that all it says?"

"Well. Two shirts, white," she said.

I went to the clothes rack and lifted off two white shirts. "Next?" I said.

She hesitated as if sensing a trap. "One shirt, blue," she said finally.

I pulled it off the rack. "Next?"

"One shirt, blue striped."

I took a blue-striped dress shirt off the rack, then, as she read them off, four more shirts, a blue-plaid, a yellow, a pink, and a white one. I draped all eight of the shirts over the lectern, then asked her go to the next receipt, which was for one suit, gray, and a dress, pink and white.

"I don't see the dress here," I said, standing with the suit midway between the clothes rack and the lectern. "Let's go on."

As she shuffled the receipt to the back, I laid the suit across the shirts on the lectern. The next receipt allowed me to lay one blazer, blue, on top of the suit. "Again, we'll pass on the skirts and the blouse, lavender," I said. "Let's go on.

We added one pants, black, one pants, blue, and one pants, khaki to the pile. I stood at the lectern with one hand resting on the stack of clothing. "Do you know how much it costs to have all these clothes cleaned when we add a dress, four skirts, and a blouse to the list?" I asked Toni.

"I have no idea."

I had a price list from Keen Cleaners. She admitted to having seen one like it before, and I got it admitted into evidence without objection. I was prepared to call an employee from Keen Cleaners in the presentation of my own case, but this was simpler.

I got a small dry-erase board from my briefcase, and as she read the prices for shirts, jackets, suits, and so on from the price list, I wrote them on the board. I multiplied where appropriate. I added. I calculated the tax and added it to the total.

"Can you tell me how much it cost to have all these items cleaned?" I asked Toni, holding up the dry-erase board and panning slowly.

"Sixty-eight dollars and eighty cents."

"So it appears that your husband picked up these items himself less than two hours before arriving at the defendant's apartment," I said. "Is that right?"

"Objection," Borger said, pushing up only halfway out of his chair. "Argumentative."

"I'll rephrase," I said. At a nod from the judge, I asked, "Do you have any reason to believe that these clothes found in the defendant's apartment are not the clothes that were picked up at the cleaners on the morning of the day Brooks Prescott died?"

She thought about it. "I guess not."

"Are you relieved?" I said. "There's no reason to believe your husband was having an affair."

"I don't understand."

"These clothes found in the apartment are the only real evidence that your husband was staying there. When he went there on May 8, these clothes were in his car. Whoever killed him had every opportunity to take them from his car and hang them in defendant's closet. I don't know what happened to the women's clothes. If you never got them back, I assume the killer just threw them away."

"That's not a question," Borger said, standing. "She's arguing her case."

I smiled. "So I am."

"Ms. Starling," Judge Cheatham rumbled ominously.

I turned toward him. "I withdraw my non-question, Your Honor. I'm done. No further questions."

"Mr. Borger?" the judge said, shifting his gaze.

Borger looked down at his papers, his mouth pushed out in thought as he shifted through a few of them. He looked up. "We may have a few questions on redirect, Your Honor. I see it's near the hour for adjournment . . ."

We looked at the clock. It was four-forty-five. Another few seconds ticked by.

"Very well," Judge Cheatham said. "We'll recess until nine o'clock tomorrow morning."

Chapter 19

The jury filed out, and Alexa left with the deputy sheriff. When I turned to the gallery, Aubrey Biggs and Alexa's parents were there. I didn't see Paul, but James Jordan and Ray Hernandez were sitting together on the back row. Hernandez shot me with his finger, which was either a death threat or they had something for me.

Whatever it was, it had to wait. Aubrey extended his hand across the rail and, when I took it, pulled me in. "I think you've done it," he said. "I think you've raised reasonable doubt."

I gave him a half-smile. "I'm working on it."

"You've got more, then?"

"I hope so." I looked past him to where Jordan and Hernandez were standing in the aisle, letting people flow past them. Mrs. Biggs put a hand on my forearm.

"We're so grateful to you. We really are."

I warmed my smile for her. "Alexa's lucky to have such a supportive family." I shook hands with Mr. Biggs, nodded again at Aubrey, touched Mrs. Biggs on the shoulder. "I'll see you again tomorrow."

I knew lawyers with better bedside manners, but I was doing my best. I turned for my purse and my briefcase. When I turned back, Jordan and Hernandez had left the courtroom, and Paul wasn't there either.

Jordan and Hernandez, at least, were waiting for me by the elevators. "I was afraid you'd run off," I said.

Jordan gave me a half-smile, nodding. "Who wouldn't be?"

"I trust your appearance here means you've got something to report?"

"Why else would police detectives be at the courthouse, if not to report to you?" Hernandez asked.

"Seriously," I said. "Is there any chance you've been working on our little project?"

"A chance," Jordan said, but Hernandez was more forthcoming.

"Names, dates, print-outs from hotel computers . . ."

"Hold it a minute," I said. There were people around us, among them Matt Jones, though I didn't see his partner Emma Michaels. Across the elevator lobby was Jacob Chapman, Nick Cantwell's chief of staff, with his elongated neck that might allow him to pick the leaves off acacia trees with his teeth. There were others I didn't recognize. The elevator door opened, and I pushed at Hernandez and jerked my head at Jordan, ushering them into the elevator, glad no one was moving to join us.

"We even got an affidavit from a hotel clerk," Hernandez said when the doors had closed. "We've got Nick Cantwell and Toni Prescott all tied up for you with a big, red ribbon."

"If you both weren't married and I weren't engaged," I said.

"As enticing as that sounds, we don't want to testify for you," Jordan said, holding out a manila envelope. "We like our jobs. Maybe you can have your pet detective do it. He can verify everything that's in here."

"I thought you were my pet detectives," I said, taking the envelope from him.

"We're tame detectives," Hernandez said. "There's a difference."

"Distinction noted," I said.

We walked out to their SUV, which was parked along the curb in a spot reserved for police. I bent to put the manila envelope in my briefcase as they got in. We exchanged a few more smart-ass remarks—that seems to be what smart asses do—and, as the Ford Explorer pulled away from the curb, Hernandez gave me a series of complicated hand-gestures through the tinted window.

It was a warm day, and I could feel the prickle of sweat on my forehead as I walked along the side of the courthouse. My phone rang, and I shifted my purse to the hand with my briefcase so I could fish it from the pocket of my dress.

I thumbed the screen. "Hey, Paul."

"So where the heck are you?" he said.

"Looking the heck for you."

"I had to go to the men's room. I get back, and the courtroom's empty. You didn't call me."

"I had company. I'll tell you about it on the way home. Burrito not a good choice for lunch?" We'd found another hole-in-the-wall tucked among the buildings of the VCU School of Medicine.

"Maybe not. It was a big burrito."

"Washing it down with a pint of beer might not have helped," I said.

"A pint of beer always helps. Are you at the car? I'm on my way down."

"Halfway there. I'll swing around and pick you up." It was right at five o'clock, but already the big lot north of the courthouse was nearly empty, and my red Beetle sat alone halfway across it.

I ended the call and slipped the phone into my pocket.

"Robin Starling!"

I turned. A tall young man was crossing the street toward me—Jacob Chapman. "You need to take this back," he said, drawing a crumpled document from his pocket. "It isn't right."

The document looked like a subpoena—like one of my subpoenas, in fact.

"Nick Chapman is an important man," Chapman said. "You can't just drag him into court for your own convenience."

"Maybe not. It's something his lawyer and I can argue about tomorrow."

"It isn't right," Chapman repeated, a muscle in his face twitching spasmodically.

"A man's been murdered, and a woman I believe to be innocent stands accused," I said.

"But Nick didn't have anything to do with it."

"He was one side of a love triangle. Brooks Prescott was another side of the same triangle, and now he's dead. Mr. Cantwell's going to have to answer questions, Jacob."

"He has an alibi. He was with me. We were working." Chapman's eyes were blinking, both hands thrust deep into his pockets.

"With you?" I said. "Not Toni Prescott?"

His blinking stopped. "You know about that."

"Just a shot in the dark," I said.

"So you know he didn't have anything to do with Prescott's murder." The whites of his eyes were visible above and below his irises. I didn't like it. It was a relief to see Paul appear at the corner of the courthouse and head toward us.

"It looks like you're the one without an alibi." I gave Chapman a smile as a car horn blared, and Paul stopped on the other side of the street so the car could pass.

Chapman didn't flinch at the sound of the car, just kept staring at me with those too-wide eyes.

Paul crossed the street. "Hey, Robin. Hi, I'm Paul Soldano." He held out his hand, and only then did Chapman turn his head to look at him.

Paul let his hand drop. "You ready?" he said to me.

"I'm ready," I said. "See you, Jacob."

We left him standing at the edge of the parking lot and headed for my car.

"There's a guy who will give you the creeps," Paul said.

"You're telling me." I beeped my car unlocked and walked around it as Paul opened the passenger door. It was only then that I noticed Chapman crossing the lot toward us, moving with quick, jerky steps.

"Paul," I said warningly, and Paul turned just as Chapman's hand came out of his pocket with something in his hand. A gun. Chapman fired, and Paul fell back into the car, hitting his head on the frame hard enough that I heard the impact even over the fading blast of the pistol.

My car was between Chapman and me, which was good, except that Paul was on the side of the car with Chapman, his legs sticking out, his feet pushing at the ground in an apparent effort to keep him from sliding out onto the asphalt.

I slipped my hand into the pocket of my skirt where my cell phone was. "Paul?" I said.

IIe didn't answer.

"Jacob. Don't do anything stupid. This can still be fixed." He was maybe ten yards away, but still coming, advancing behind his extended arm. I glanced down at my phone, touched the phone app, touched the keypad icon.

"Nobody does what they're supposed to," Chapman said. "Nobody can leave well enough alone."

Nobody's been a bad boy, I thought nonsensically. Nine-one-one. I touched the green button and looked up.

"Drop the phone, Ms. Starling," Chapman said.

I let it drop. The phone bounced in its case and landed facedown. "Who can't leave well enough alone?" I asked Chapman. "Peter Brawley?"

Chapman had reached the car. He looked down at Paul, his face working as if he were a lycanthrope whose human face was giving way to something lupine and sinister.

"He's an innocent bystander," I said. "Leave him alone."

Standing beside Paul's legs, he looked over the Beetle's bubble top at me, his eyes unblinking, his facial muscles still twitching beneath his skin. "You're not innocent," he said in a flat, almost mechanical tone. "You're responsible for all of this: you, Brawley, Prescott." He extended his arm over the car's roof, and I tensed, ready to throw myself to the ground against the car.

"What did Prescott do?" I said, feeling desperate. "He was just a man who loved his wife."

A bump sounded inside the car. I didn't look away from Chapman's fixed gaze, and Chapman didn't seem to notice.

"He had evidence," Chapman said. "He was going public."

"Evidence of the affair?"

"Good-bye, Ms. Starling."

I dropped as the pistol went off with a sound as deafening as a crack of thunder, twisting as I went down so that my shoulder hit the side of my car, and then my back was against it. The gun went off again, and I slid down the car to the ground, unable to tell where I'd been hit. Half-deafened by the gunshot, I turned my head against the car, looking for Chapman, not knowing which way to crawl.

"Robin." It was Paul's voice.

"Paul?" He was alive—and conscious. Relief washed through me in a wave.

There was a noise at the back of the car, a hand thumping down on the truck, a foot grinding on loose pebbles. I went onto hands and knees, my head up, ready to spring at Chapman or to scramble away, but it was Paul, lurching toward me with one hand hitting the car with each step.

"You're all right," he told me. Blood soaked the side of his shirt and dripped from his belt. His left leg gave way, and he went down.

"Chapman?" I said, crawling toward him. "What—"

Paul shook his head, and I cradled him against me, one hand pressing as hard as I could against his bloody side. There was a yelp, and I looked up to see a dark-haired woman standing beside her briefcase not far away, her chubby, ringed fingers pressed hard into her powdered face. A man came into view, circling warily.

"You're hurting me. My side." Paul's breathing sounded labored, and his face glistened with a sheen of sweat.

I ignored the complaint. One hand still pressing into Paul's side, I held his head against me with the other. There was another spectator, a young man with a golden beard. All three spectators had their phones out, the dark-haired woman jabbing at the screen with a painted nail, the others evidently taking pictures.

I said to the woman, "We're in the parking lot north of the John Marshall Courthouse. A man's been shot. We need an ambulance."

She turned away from me, her phone pressed to her cheek.

"Is there a man on the other side of the car?" I asked the man with the beard. "He's dangerous."

Paul said something, and I leaned over him. "What?"

He didn't repeat it, just lay with his cheek against my chest. It had sounded like he said, "Not any more," but I couldn't be sure.

"I called nine-one-one," the dark-haired woman said, holding her phone like a shield as she edged hesitantly closer. "That man on the other side of your car—is he . . . ?"

"I don't know," I said. "He was shooting at us."

Her shadow lay over us as she stood poised for flight.

I felt Paul's cheek move against me, and I looked down to see a faint smile.

"Are you nuzzling my breast?" I said. Relief washed through me, though my laugh sounded semi-maniacal. Paul was going to be all right. He was going to be all right.

Chapter 20

The police got there before the ambulance, four marked cars that stopped nose-in to us, one at each of the four points of the compass. Uniformed officers got out, at least some of them with guns in their hands.

"Ma'am, move away from the vehicle." That cop spoke from behind the open door of his vehicle, but others were moving in.

The dark-haired woman, whose head had been swiveling from side to side as the police cars came in, backed away from us, moved outside the perimeter marked by the cars.

"This man's been shot," I called. "He's bleeding."

"What about the other man?"

"I don't know about the other man.

"He's been shot, too," came a man's voice from the other side of the car. After a moment: "He's dead. Oh, God."

I assumed he was looking at Chapman, which, if true, would be a good thing in my book.

An ambulance pulled in behind the police car on my left, and two paramedics got out. A police officer escorted them to us, his hand on the butt of his pistol.

One of the paramedics, a woman, knelt beside us.

"He's been shot," I told her, nodding toward my hand where blood had soaked the fabric of Paul's shirt and was welling between my fingers. "He was conscious until a few seconds ago."

"Still am," Paul murmured sleepily. He opened one eye as the paramedic inserted the point of a pair of scissors into the hole in the shirt and cut outward in four directions. Two dark holes in his flesh were visible under the lighter streaks and smears of blood.

"Are you hit anywhere else?" she asked Paul. Her partner had disappeared around the car, presumably to deal with Jacob Chapman.

"Don't think so." He'd closed his eyes again, though, and his voice was breathy.

"An entrance and exit wound?" I said. "Or two entrance wounds."

"I'd say entrance and exit." She picked up the green packet marked Combat Gauze she'd laid on the ground beside Paul, and she tucked it away. "You're not bleeding heavily enough for a hemostatic agent. That's good." She did put a gauze pad over the wounds. They were so close together that it only took one, though she added another on top of it. "Press here," she told me. "Steady, even pressure."

I put my hand over the gauze as she got out a roll of Coban tape, a self-adhering bandage I recognized because I'd used it before to buddy-wrap a jammed finger from basketball. She wound the Coban around Paul's body twice. She tore it off and started again lower down on the bandage. Paul was a big man: She used up her entire roll.

"It doesn't look like any major organs were hit," I ventured.

"In and out," she said with a short nod.

"A love-handle injury," I said.

Paul opened one eye. "You mean, if I weren't so fat, the bullet would have missed me completely?"

The paramedic gave a short laugh.

"I think of you as chubby," I said. "Big-boned."

"Lots of bones in my love handles," Paul said, and closed his eyes again.

The paramedic had more questions, but Paul seemed to have checked out, and I didn't have any answers. Another ambulance had arrived, and a fire truck. Her partner came back, and the two of them lifted Paul onto a stretcher, raised it, and rolled it to the back of the ambulance they had come in.

"VCU Medical Center?" I asked, getting to my feet. "I'll follow you."

I'd been through this routine before, but the last time I'd been the one taking the ride in the ambulance. That was better than this: I didn't have to worry, didn't have to be responsible for anything. All I had to do was endure.

I squeezed Paul's hand and found it cold. "You hang in there," I said. "It's not manly to die from a flesh wound."

There was a faint return pressure on my hand, but he didn't open his eyes.

Before court the next morning I stopped by the hospital and found Paul sitting up in bed.

"Hey, Robin," he said as I came in.

"You're looking good.". Really, he looked better than good. He looked back to normal. "You scared the wee-wee out of me, you know," I said.

"Literally?" He looked interested.

"No, not literally. It's a figure of speech."

"I don't think I've ever heard it put quite that way," he said.

"I'm too refined to say *pee*."

"Ah. Very delicate of you."

"What I want to know is where that second gun came from," I said. "The gun you shot Chapman with."

"I told you last night. It was in your glove box."

"No, it wasn't."

"I stand corrected," he said.

"Okay. How did it get in my glove box? How long has it been there?"

"Since the trial started. They won't let me carry it into the courthouse, or I'd have had it on me."

"When did you get it?"

"The day after a man with a gun put you in the hospital."

"Back in April, then."

He nodded. "It's a Glock 26."

"Do you have a carry license?"

"I do. I earned it while you were in the hospital."

He hadn't told me.

He said, "You need a bodyguard if you're going to piss the hell out of people for a living."

"Looks like you need one, too."

"I just need to lose weight, evidently. I make too big a target."

I smiled.

"I didn't tell you about my handguns at first because you needed to concentrate on getting better. Then I thought you'd tell me I was overreacting."

"Did you say handguns, plural?"

He moved his head ambiguously.

And he was worried I'd think he was overreacting. "How many handguns?" I said.

"Four."

"Four? Four handguns? You passed overreacting three handguns ago."

"One at your house, one at my apartment, one in each of our cars."

"There's a gun in my house?"

"I should have told you about that one anyway."

"You think?"

"If you need it sometime when I'm not there, it's on your bookshelf, tucked behind your Jane Austens. I've been thinking about getting a smaller gun, too, one I can carry. You worry me, Robin. I'm not going to lose you to some psycho just because I failed to plan ahead. Remember what you said Borger's motto was?"

"There's nothing worth doing that's not worth overdoing," I said.

He put a hand to his wounded side. "I like it. I'm adopting it as my own."

I studied him, thinking that if he hadn't gone hog-wild with the handgun purchases, we'd likely both be dead. "Maybe it's not a bad motto," I said.

"There's something else you haven't asked me. Something that may be more pressing than where I got a gun."

"The gun that saved our lives?" I said. "Hard to think of anything more important than that."

"I said pressing, not important."

I considered, my lower lip caught between my teeth.

"How much did you hear of what Chapman said?" I asked.

"Bingo," Paul said. "I heard it all."

Paul was supposed to get out that morning. Mike, who had no appointments or hearings scheduled until after lunch, was coming by to take him home. I left the hospital and drove to the courthouse, where I parked not ten yards from the space I'd occupied the day before. There was a boxy blue Scion there today—no blood on the asphalt next to it, at least that I could see. I turned toward the courthouse and took a breath, squaring my shoulders.

In the courtroom I greeted Aubrey and his parents. Mrs. Biggs took both my hands. "Are you all right?" she said. "Such a dreadful thing."

"They tell me I'll live." At her sudden look of concern, I said, "I'm sorry. Yes, I'm fine. I wasn't hurt."

Mr. Biggs gripped my shoulder in what I supposed was a manly gesture, giving me a quick nod. Aubrey took my arm and drew me aside.

"The police searched Chapman's apartment," he said. "They found Peter Brawley's laptop and his camera."

"That's good to know."

"Yes. Points the finger at Chapman, at least for Brawley's murder."

If they'd find Brawley's laptop and camera already, maybe they'd be finding other things, too, before they were done. Alexa came in and sat beside me. I gave her hand a pat, and she grimaced in response to my smile.

We were still waiting for the jury—and waiting for Jim Borger, for that matter—when a clerk came through a door behind the bench and approached my table. He leaned over me.

"The judge would like to see you in chambers," he said.

I glanced at Alexa. "I'll be back," I told her. "Hang tough."

"Do I have a choice?"

I got up and followed the clerk.

Judge Cheatham was at his desk, and Borger was there before me, his briefcase on the floor beside his chair.

"Hi, Robin. How are you?" the judge asked me.

I thought it was a good sign that he was calling me by my first name. "One scraped knee, a fiancé in the hospital. Over all, I came off pretty light."

"So," he said. "Where do we go from here?"

I looked from him to Borger. "We go on with the trial," I said. "I'm ready." I was still standing with my briefcase.

"Mr. Borger has a concern he wanted to address in camera," Cheatham said, using the Latin phrase for *in chambers*. "Mr. Borger?" I wondered if they'd been talking about the case before I got there. For Judge Cheatham to have discussed the case with one of us in the absence of the other would have been highly inappropriate, one of those ex parte communications that the law prohibits.

Borger cleared his throat and rolled his shoulders, shrugging into his dignity like a topcoat. "You've subpoenaed Lieutenant Governor Nick Cantwell," he told me.

"You, too? That seems to be what set off his chief of staff," I said mildly.

Neither of them said anything. The judge, I thought, looked uncomfortable.

"It's too bad we don't have a statue of lady justice here at the Marshall courthouse," I said. "Her blindfold and scales would remind us that justice weighs the evidence impartially, regardless of wealth or fame or political power."

Judge Cheatham ignored my high-minded discourse. "What do you hope to prove by Mr. Cantwell's testimony?" he asked me.

"May I?" I gestured at the remaining client chair and, at the judge's nod, sat and crossed my legs. Both men glanced at them, and I sighed internally.

I said, "I hope to prove that Nick Cantwell was having a love affair with Toni Prescott, the wife of the deceased, and that her husband found out about it. Brooks Prescott had evidence of the affair and threatened to go public with it. Either Cantwell killed him, or his chief of staff did."

"You can't prove that," Borger told me. "All that's just talk."

"You may be right," I said, nodding. "Of course, I don't have to prove anything. I just have to raise reasonable doubt."

"Are you willing to share the nature of the evidence you do have?" Cheatham asked.

I looked at Borger, trying to decide whether talking about my evidence now would be giving up too much of a tactical advantage in the courtroom. Finally, I said, "I have evidence of the affair between Cantwell and Mrs. Prescott, quite a lot of it—photographs, hotel registrations all over central Virginia in the name of one or the other of them. Even one affidavit."

"So?" Borger said.

"So, there's every reason to believe Prescott had some of that same evidence."

Judge Cheatham said, "In your mind, the desire to prevent exposure was the motive for the killing?"

"Yes."

"Surely, who you really suspect is this Jacob Chapman, not Cantwell himself," the judge said.

I gave a nod of assent. "We do know Chapman is capable of violence. And, as it turns out, Nick Cantwell may have an alibi."

"If the lieutenant governor has an alibi, why have you brought his name up in this trial?" Borger interjected. "Brought it up repeatedly, I might add."

"I haven't been able to talk to Cantwell," I said. "I don't know for sure whether he has an alibi or not."

Judge Cheatham cleared his throat. "What about this Peter Brawley? How is his murder connected to all this? Or is it?"

"Brawley was a photographer," I said. "If we ever find his camera or his laptop, I think we'll find photographs and other evidence of Cantwell's extramarital affair. It was Brawley who brought Alexa into this mess. The original idea seemed to be to implicate Brooks Prescott in an affair of his own, but Brooks was beyond caring. He was going to bring down the whole house of cards."

"Why do you say he was beyond caring?" Cheatham asked.

"Everybody says he was deep in love with his wife. My guess is he was hurt and resentful, maybe even desperate. Who knows how those feelings played out?"

"Not you," Borger said. "That's all speculation."

"Sure," I agreed.

"How did Brawley come to have these photographs?" Cheatham said. "And how did Chapman know he had them?"

I shook my head. "All I can offer you is more speculation."

"I'd like to hear it."

I glanced from him to Borger, then shrugged. "Brawley might have been trying his hand at a spot of blackmail—or maybe Nick Cantwell was trying to break it off with Toni, she didn't like it, and Brawley was helping her to apply pressure. In any case, the motive for the two murders was the same, to protect Nick Cantwell from exposure."

"How much of this can you prove?" Borger said. "I'm inclined to think not much."

I gave him a smile. I'd admitted it was all speculation. "We'll see," I said.

Judge Cheatham said, "Suppose she can prove it, Mr. Borger, all of it. Would it make any difference in how you want to proceed?"

Borger sat pushing his lips in and out, his nose-breathing loud in the judge's chambers, then his head jerked in what might have been a shrug.

I decided to turn over my hole card. I leaned over my briefcase to extract the manila envelope Jordan and Hernandez had given me and a folder of eight-by-ten photographs I'd gotten off Brawley's phone. I held them in Borger's direction, then Judge Cheatham's, my eyebrows raised questioningly.

Cheatham jerked his head at Borger, and I handed Borger the envelope and folder. He opened the folder first, flipping through the photographs one by one. The last photograph in the folder showed Toni and Nick leaning on a low brick wall, shoulder to shoulder, Toni's head turned toward Nick with an open-mouthed expression of delight. It was really a well-composed photograph, the wall and an overhanging tree framing the subjects, but Borger closed the folder and passed on to the documentation Jordan and Hernandez had collected for me. I'd been through it only that morning. In combination, Cantwell and Toni had rented rooms at Richmond-area hotels on fourteen occasions.

After Borger had gone through it all, he flipped back to the affidavit of a hotel clerk who had identified both Cantwell and Toni Prescott.

"This is all you have?" he asked, looking up.

"So far."

"Proving an affair is a long way from proving Cantwell or his chief of staff committed murder."

"I've got motive," I said. "And now I've got Cantwell's chief of staff killed in the course of attempting to murder the attorney who was about to bring all this out in open court."

"Meaning you," Borger said.

I gave him my most dazzling smile—actually, the smile I imagined to be dazzling, though Borger did seem more soured than dazzled. He and Judge Cheatham exchanged a long glance.

"I'll dismiss the charges against Alexa Demming," Borger said.

"Both murders?" Judge Cheatham asked.

"Yes. Both the murder of Dr. Prescott and Peter Brawley."

This was the moment for a good defense attorney to keep her mouth shut—so I said, "Cantwell certainly has powerful people willing to cover up for him."

Borger turned on me. "Don't think for a minute you're in the clear on this. We know you took evidence from the scene of Brawley's murder."

"You didn't find any of it in Jacob Chapman's possession?" I asked. "Camera, iPad, keyring . . ."

Borger shot Cheatham a glance.

I said, "At my trial for accessory to murder, you're going to have to prove I was assisting the man who later tried to kill me. For my part, I'll be arguing that the man who killed Brawley and took his laptop is a more likely candidate for absconding with the rest of the evidence."

"How do you know about the laptop?" Borger said.

"You're going to have to prove beyond a reasonable doubt that I took whatever items of Brawley's that remain missing—me, and not the man who killed him, not Stephanie Pritchard, and not some third party."

Again, the judge and the prosecutor exchanged a glance.

"I'll dismiss the charges against Ms. Starling," Borger said.

I opened my mouth to complain about important matters being decided in back room negotiations rather than in open court, but this time I closed it again without saying anything. When you've won it all, it's time to stop talking.

Chapter 21

I'd like to jump ahead to my wedding, but there's one more incident to relate before I get there. When I left the courthouse, a dark-haired woman wearing sunglasses stepped toward me.

I recognized her and stepped back defensively, which caused her to step back herself.

"I'm not going to hit you again," she said.

"Good to know." The woman was Anita Cantwell.

"I have one question for you, if you're willing to tell me."

"Okay."

She took a breath, her palms pressed to the front of her thighs. "Is it true?" she said. "That's what I want to know. Is it true, any of it?"

I started to ask her, Was what true? But that would be toying with her. "Yes," I said. "It's all true."

She released her pent-up breath in a long sigh. "How long has it been going on?" she asked.

"Six or seven months, maybe longer. I don't know when it started."

"I see." She got a distant look, and I thought maybe she was reinterpreting certain past events involving her husband Nick. Her eyes focused again, and she said, "You don't have any reason to like me."

"Maybe not," I acknowledged.

"But I have to ask. Do you do divorce work?"

"I never have."

She nodded and started to turn away, but she stopped. "That's not an answer," she said.

"No. Not if you don't want it to be."

"So you'll represent me?"

I smiled. "I've already started."

She looked puzzled.

"I have a briefcase full of evidence," I said, hoisting it slightly. "All of it may not be admissible in a court of law, but, if not, there's always the court of public opinion. I'd be surprised if we couldn't negotiate one heck of a settlement."

Her answering smile was fierce.

What with the murder trial, Paul getting shot, and the next seven days of frenzied preparation, my impending wedding became the source of more stress than I'd felt since the day I first walked into a courtroom. On the day of the wedding, my dress was at the church when I got there, but I had the sense of a dozen things that I'd forgotten, a dozen things undone that hovered just outside my ability to recall them.

"You look sick," Brooke observed. We were in the church parlor with its pale wood paneling, its floor-to-ceiling gold drapes, and the oil painting of a former pastor over the mantel. Brooke was already in her wedding gown, and Whitney Foster, her maid of honor, was working with her veil. Brooke looked like everything a bride should be: happy, tentative, radiant.

"Come on, Robin," Carly said, holding my dress for me. "One small step for Paul . . ."

"One giant leap for Robin," I said raising a foot to step into the dress.

"Can you turn this way and smile?" the photographer asked. She was an athletic-looking woman with a thick brush of kinky blonde hair held back in a ponytail. I gave her a smile as Carly paused with the dress raised only to my waist.

"These are the sort of pictures Peter Brawley took," I said.

"You're perfectly decent," Carly said, and I put my arms in the sleeves as she raised the dress.

"You still look like you're about to throw up," Brooke said. "You can't be scared of life with Paul. Not only does he love you, he's probably the most accommodating man I ever met, at least when it comes to all things Robin."

"I'm not scared," I told Brooke, which was true as far as it went. I wasn't scared, I was petrified. "It's like getting in a swimming pool in early spring. I know I'll be all right once I get in, but still I hesitate to take the plunge."

The flash on the photographer's camera went off again as Carly buttoned up the back of my dress.

"Well, it's marriage. You can't dip your toe in. You're either in or you're out."

Carly started doing something with my hair, and I glanced at the mirror. I hadn't let her curl it—I was getting married, not going under cover—but she'd swirled it and pinned it in a way that gave me almost an elegant look. I lifted my chin as I admired myself.

"Thank you for doing this," I said to Carly. "You've been great."

"Huh. If you hadn't asked me at least to be one of your bridesmaids, I'd have been pretty grumpy about it, let me tell you." She started positioning my veil.

"Well, thank you."

All too soon, we were dressed, and the photographer had taken all the pictures she wanted to take. We walked down the hall and across a courtyard to the foyer of the sanctuary. My father was there, and the organ was playing.

Carly took her flowers from the wedding planner, and the double doors opened in front of her.

My father held out his arm as Carly, my maid of honor, started down the long aisle of red carpet. I put my arm through his, and Dad patted my hand. I could see Paul at the other end of the long aisle, Mike beside him. I smiled. This was the first time I'd seen Paul in his tuxedo. His shirt, his tux, and his tie were ivory white.

Well, I guess he's entitled, I thought.

Still smiling, I looked at Brooke, and she smiled back at me.

The music changed to the wedding march from Mozart's *The Marriage of Figaro*. That was my cue. I took a breath and started down the aisle to meet my destiny.

ABOUT THE AUTHOR

Michael Monhollon took out a semester in college to write science fiction stories and collect rejection slips. His first book sale, a legal thriller, came at the age of 31 at about the time *The Firm* was coming out in paperback. Its sales fell short of *The Firm*'s, though, and he continues to work for a living. Currently, he is the dean of the Kelley College of Business at Hardin-Simmons University in Abilene, Texas.

www.ingramcontent.com/pod-product-compliance
Lightning Source LLC
Chambersburg PA
CBHW072118250626

47159CB00007B/2492